I0708452

Blind Spot

Also by Maggie Smith

Truth and Other Lies

BLINDSPOT

Maggie Smith

Library of Congress Cataloging-in-Publication Data has been applied for.

Paperback ISBN 9798989677917; eBook ISBN 9798989677924

Cover photography I-stockphoto.com;

Book Cover Design and Interior Formatting by 100Covers

Printed in the United States of America

For Scott

Third time's a charm

*"There are two kinds of people in this world — those who
believe laws are all that separates us from chaos,
and those who create the chaos."*

Interview with Rachel Matthews,
Assistant District Attorney, Milwaukee County
Sunday Journal, September 2020

April 24, 2023, County Courthouse

THE KILLER IS SITTING in this courtroom and it's up to me to prove it.

It isn't every day a murder this sensational happens in Milwaukee. Sure, we've had our share of drive-by shootings, domestic arguments that escalated, home invasions that turned deadly. And yes, there was that lurid trial a while back when the deranged sicko drugged, then ate his victims. That one landed our city in the national spotlight. A once in a lifetime case.

But this one's right up there. Everyone involved is high profile. Which means it warrants the top guns. Which means my boss of nine years, Marcus Huntley, Deputy DA, is sitting first chair. I catch his eye and his expression confirms what I already know. This is the most important case of my career, and if the verdict goes south, any hope for that promotion goes right along with it.

But this isn't only about winning for me. There's a lot more at stake. Consequences I don't dare think about or I'll lose my nerve. Because even though the police are convinced this is an open and shut case, I know better.

I know they've arrested the wrong person.

Because I witnessed the murder. But for reasons I can't reveal, I have to keep quiet. Only two people know the whole story and I've sworn them to secrecy.

I watch the crowd. Examine every person in detail. Who's talking to whom, who's staring at their lap, who's looking around the room. Who's fidgeting, adjusting their tie, or rummaging through their purse. Who looks bored and who looks agitated. But even though I'm an expert in spotting a tell, I'm coming up empty.

The electricity in the air ratchets up as the judge enters and the bailiff calls the case. I've been up most of the night, pacing the floor, rehearsing my lines, imagining how today would go. What to say and what not to say. What needs to happen so I can walk out of here satisfied.

Part of me wants to scream. Part of me wants to whimper. Part of me wants to rush out the door and never look back.

But I don't do any of those things. Instead I steel my nerves and set aside the theatrics. A bead of sweat slithers down my spine as I stand to address the judge.

In an orange jumpsuit. And handcuffs.

"Rachel Elizabeth Matthews. you stand accused of first-degree intentional homicide. How do you plead?"

"Not guilty, Your Honor," I reply.

1

Seven weeks earlier

THE TRIAL HAD GONE EVEN better than I'd hoped and I dipped my head in a vain attempt to hide my smile, as the judge banged his gavel and sentenced the defendant to fifteen years. Another win. But more importantly, another wife abuser headed to prison. Another woman free from the violent man who'd vowed to love and protect her. I hoped like hell she and her infant son could reboot their lives.

The past wasn't always easy to outrun. It had a habit of reappearing when you least expected it.

The prisoner spat at me as they hauled him away. "I've got your face tattooed on my brain, you bitch. You haven't heard the last of me."

Threats like that didn't bother me anymore. In my early days as a prosecutor, his words might have kept me up all night, picturing a dark figure breaking into my house, slithering up the back stairs to hurt me, or worse, my daughter Charley. Now, with ten years under my belt, I was immune.

Almost.

The courtroom emptied and I tapped the case files together, tucked them and my laptop away in my wheeled briefcase, and slid my lucky pen into its holder. I'd need to hurry if I wanted to get home, fix supper for Charley, and change clothes before the event tonight. I rode the elevator down to the ground floor, but instead of barreling off as usual, I held the door open for a young woman struggling with a baby stroller, a diaper bag, and a mammoth purse. "They're a handful at that age, aren't they?" I nodded toward the infant, and the mother and I exchanged knowing smiles.

But also a treasure. I thought back to my own baby at that age, all drool and diapers and dimples. Charley had never failed to enchant me, even on the toughest of days. To the world at large, I might be a high-powered district attorney. But the job title I treasured most was mother.

As I exited the limestone-block citadel that housed the court, a rush of cool March wind blew a strand of hair across my eyes, and I hesitated just long enough for a reporter to stick a microphone in my face.

"Congratulations, counselor. Chalk one up for the good guys, right?"

He was fishing for a sound bite, some pithy comment to snare a viewer. All part of the game. I squinted into the lights of the news camera. "Justice is alive and well, Mr. Hyams. Make sure your viewers know that. If you break the law, you'll pay the consequences. Full stop."

***

THE VENERABLE PFISTER HOTEL had stood at the corner of Wisconsin and Jefferson streets in downtown Milwaukee for over a hundred years. I got off the elevator at the seventh floor and made my way to the check-in table to retrieve my name tag. The annual event, sponsored by the Business Journal, honored 40-under-40 leaders and I'd been honored to be a winner last year. Red ribbons were affixed to the lanyards of tonight's recipients, one of them a member of my book club.

I pulled out my phone to switch it to silent mode and noticed a new voice mail left only minutes before. Another dead-air recording, the third one this week. Before I had a chance to mark it for deletion, a delayed message came through. "You ruined my life. Now it's your turn." The voice was raspy, almost metallic.

What the hell? My gaze swept the room. Nothing out of the ordinary. People dressed in fancy clothes milled around the foyer, chatting and sipping wine. No one seemed to be paying any attention to me. I replayed the message, listening for a clue, as a chill crept up my spine. I prosecuted scumbags for a living so threats were part of the job description but this one felt different. More personal. I should watch my step tonight just in case.

I roamed the space, then peeked inside the Grand Ballroom where illuminated crystals on the chandeliers glittered like crown jewels and the tables sported sparkling glass vases filled with snow-white roses. Out one set of windows were downtown office buildings, out the other a sweeping view of Lake Michigan. An elegant setting, though maybe a bit extravagant, given this was a charity event.

The funds raised tonight would benefit Sojourner Family Peace Center, the city's leading provider of services for victims of domestic violence and a cause dear to my heart. As I wandered the Silent Auction tables, I noticed a spa package, complete with seaweed detox, hot-stone massage, and aromatherapy. That might make a nice gift for Rita, my favorite secretary in the office, whose third work anniversary was coming up next month. As I debated how much I could afford to bid, I overheard a conversation nearby.

"There's a mistake here." The forceful voice belonged to a short, muscular man, mid-thirties, dressed in an impeccable white dinner jacket. A diamond stud adorned his left ear and his bald head shone like a cue ball. He was speaking to a young volunteer staffing the high-ticket table. "The instructions clearly state new bids for this casino package have to exceed the previous one by three hundred dollars." He pointed at the sign-up sheet, not even pausing for her response. "This last person only added two." With that, he pulled out a carved silver pen from his pocket and scribbled over the previous entry.

To her credit, the volunteer kept her temper. "I apologize for the oversight, sir, but we can't have you negating other people's bids."

He narrowed his eyes. "So the rules only apply to certain people?"

"No, of course not. I'll keep a closer eye out."

"You do that." He leaned forward, his face practically touching hers, and gave her a sardonic smile. "I wouldn't want to have to report your mistake to the event sponsors."

No doubt satisfied he'd won the round, the man moved to another table where he scrutinized a collectible Brewers shirt. That's when I spotted the red ribbon hanging from his nametag. Well, he might be successful in his chosen field, but he certainly wouldn't win any popularity contests with that inflated ego.

Apparently, I hadn't been the only one eavesdropping because, once the first man moved on, an elderly Black gentleman sidled up to the same table and jotted down a new bid. My curiosity piqued, I discreetly glanced at the sheet. He'd added $1,000 to the last amount, bringing the new total to $3,000, the exact value listed at the top. I couldn't help grinning. Take that, Mr. Blowhard.

"Look at you, all decked out. Great dress." Gracie, a nurse and fellow member of the book club, appeared out of nowhere and gave me a tight hug. I'd dug out the emerald-green beaded gown I'd worn to this same event last year, figuring no one would notice. I'd long ago made peace with the fact that working in public service didn't pay all that well. My household budget didn't leave room for fancy ballgowns.

"You're not so shabby yourself," I said, taking in Gracie's little black dress with its dramatic cape. "What table are you? Please say nine." I'd asked the woman organizing the seating if she could sit our club members together since my idea of purgatory was making small talk with strangers. She'd sounded a bit put out but said she'd try.

Gracie glanced at her tag. "Yup. Table nine." When the overhead lights flashed twice, we made our way to the front and grabbed seats side by side, draping napkins over three other chairs to save them for our friends.

A couple was already seated at the table when we arrived. The woman was reed thin, fragile as a feather, her white-blonde hair tied back in a loose chignon, her skin so translucent I could see a blue vein pulsating at her temple. A diamond ring, easily two carats, adorned her left hand. She was achingly beautiful, the kind of woman a man would fight to keep. The kind of woman he might be willing to die for. I wondered if that type of beauty came at a price.

The man whispering in her ear, no doubt her husband, was her perfect match. His sculpted beard showed off his strong jawline and his dark hair was cut business-short. His only visible imperfection was a one-inch scar above his left eyebrow, but if anything, the anomaly made him even more attractive. He wore a jet-black tuxedo and pleated white shirt, silver cufflinks gleaming at his wrists. The two whispered to each other and when he gently touched her arm, the connection between them seemed so intense, so intimate, I instinctively looked away, feeling like a voyeur peeping through a window at two people making love.

Someone gave a boisterous laugh at a nearby table and the woman startled, her cheeks flaming red as if she'd been caught doing something wrong. It seemed awkward not to speak to them, so I took the opportunity to extend my hand across the table. "Hello. I'm Rachel Matthews. Are you and your husband guests of one of the honorees?"

The woman hesitated, then opened her mouth to speak, only to be cut off by a booming voice belonging to Bald Guy from earlier, who'd snuck up behind her and gently squeezed her shoulders. "Actually, I'm Olivia's husband." He stuck out his hand and shook mine, lingering a bit too long. "Zachary Reid. These two are here because of me." He bent down and put his lips next to his wife's ear. "Right, darling?" Something in his manner reminded me of a guy in law school who hit on every woman in our class. He had that same self-satisfied smirk.

His wife froze in place, changing from the animated woman she'd been only minutes before to a quivering mouse. Maybe her life wasn't so perfect after all. Mrs. Reid glanced at the other man, as though he might rescue her, but he stayed silent, a scowl distorting his face. An undercurrent of unease settled over the group as I searched for a way to finesse my faux pas. Finally, the other man rescued the situation. He leaned across and offered me his hand, breaking the awkward moment. "I'm Ethan Mansfield. Mr. Reid owns Apollo Enterprises and I'm his VP of Sales. We own and operate Burger Boy franchises across the state." His eyes crinkled at the corners when he smiled. "And what do you do, Mrs. Matthews?"

He had the hands of a pianist—long tapered fingers, skin as soft as a woman—so his firm grip caught me off guard. A delicious tingle zinged up my spine. Hooded eyes, full lips, patrician nose. I wondered if women ever said no to this man. His intense gaze caught mine, almost like a challenge, and I gave him one right back.

Gracie broke the silence. "She's with the DA's office. And she's not a Mrs." She let out a small giggle and looked around the table. "In case anyone's interested." She directed this last remark straight at Mansfield.

Oh, dear friend, will you ever stop trying to fix me up? Not only was I not interested in dating, but Ethan Mansfield was hardly a match. A good five years younger and way too good-looking. Not to mention he was obviously in love with Olivia Reid.

"You don't look like a district attorney," Mansfield said, his voice playful.

Why not have a little fun? "Oh? And what *does* a DA look like?"

He seemed taken aback and stumbled a bit over his response. "Well … Maybe that stern-faced older guy from *Law and Order?*" He glanced over at Mrs. Reid. "You do the crime, you do the time, that sort of thing?"

He'd left himself wide open and I went in for the kill. "I'm not old and I'm not a guy, but trust me, if you break the law, you don't want to be in my cross hairs." The minute the words came out of my mouth, I wanted to reel them back in. I'd turned light-hearted banter into a lecture on criminal behavior. When would I learn not to get up on my soapbox in social settings?

Once again, Mansfield came to my rescue. "Thanks for the warning," he joked, giving me a sly smile. "I'll definitely watch my step."

Just then, the other book club members arrived, including the honoree, and I forgot all about the three strangers at the table as my friends and I chatted about that month's book selection. The wait staff served our salads, then an entrée of salmon, roasted potatoes, and sauteed asparagus. It wasn't until dessert arrived that Olivia Reid spoke up. "Any chance I could join your book club? I'm a big reader."

Zach Reid laid his knife and fork symmetrically across his plate, then patted his wife's arm. "I'm sure Ms. Matthews and her friends have been together for a long time, darling. It would be awkward having a stranger insert herself into the group."

Olivia's eyes dulled, but to her credit, she didn't back down. "When we lived in New York, I belonged to a reading group. But since we've moved here, I haven't made many friends. I thought this might be a chance to …" Her voice trailed off.

"You're putting these ladies on the spot. Am I right?" He winked at me as though expecting me to agree with him and Mrs. Reid's gaze dropped to her plate.

What a controlling ass. Actually, I admired this woman's courage in asking for what she wanted, despite her husband's disapproval. It was the very reason Gracie and I had founded the club, recruited like-minded women who'd grown tired of being dismissed by men when they expressed their opinions. I eyed the other members to gauge their reactions, but all I got was blank stares, as though the decision was up to me.

Okay, then. Why not strike a blow for female solidarity and, at the same time, stand up to a bully? I pulled out my business card, copied down my cell number, and handed it to Mrs. Reid. "Give me a call and I'll fill you in on the details. If you're still interested, you're welcome to come to our next get-together and meet the others."

Olivia's face lit up. "That's very kind of you. I'll be in touch." Her fingers trembled slightly as she opened her jewel-encrusted evening bag and slid the card inside. Zach Reid harrumphed under his breath as his wife, her eyes ablaze, silently mouthed "Thank you."

Moments later, the MC for the event tapped his water glass to quiet the room. "And now, before we introduce our honorees, let's announce the winners of our Silent Auction. And a huge thank you to everyone who bid. We exceeded our goal by $20,000." Volunteers scurried around the room, handing the winning bidders the certificates to claim their prizes. I was giddy that I'd won the spa package and Gracie scored a case of wine, which she promised to share next time she hosted the club. When they got to the casino package, Zach Reid sat up straighter and pushed his chair back. Not surprisingly, the MC called his name. The surprise was the amount he'd paid to win. He'd obviously circled back at some point in the dinner and raised his bid to six thousand, twice what the item was worth. Some men are like that. No price is too high to pay if it means you come out on top.

I made eye contact with Mansfield, who raised his eyebrows as if to say *yes, my boss is a jerk*. Olivia frowned, then quickly readjusted her face into a blank stare. As for Zach Reid, he acknowledged his generous donation with a slight bow and an audible snicker.

After a short speech by the organizers, the award winners stood in turn as the MC read aloud their list of accomplishments. Though Reid had bought his first fast-food franchise only two years ago, he already employed several hundred people at dozens of locations throughout the state. He might have the personality of a warthog, but I had to admit he deserved the recognition.

I glanced again at Olivia Reid. The woman's look as her husband stood to acknowledge the applause baffled me. There was admiration there, but also loathing. Maybe a bit of fear.

And not for the first time, I appreciated how lucky I was. True, I might go to bed alone but wasn't that better than living with a man that tried to control your every move? My heart went out to Olivia Reid, a fragile beauty caught in a seemingly impossible trap.

2

WITH BACK-TO-BACK depositions on Friday, I'd barely had time to eat the chicken sandwich I'd stuffed in my briefcase that morning. As I left the office at the end of the day, I booted up my cell, hoping I hadn't missed any urgent messages. Two missed calls, one from my boss Marcus Huntley, the other from my daughter.

First things first. I called Huntley and led with the good news. "They took the plea on the Wallis case."

"Good. Got time to pop over to Murphy's for a quick beer?"

Two things were wrong with that question. First, Huntley made it a point not to fraternize with his staff, much less invite them out for a drink. Second, no conversation with him was ever quick. If he wanted to go over a case, I'd be looking at a good hour plus the fifteen minutes to walk there and back. Glancing at my watch, I saw it was after five. Every first Friday, my father hosted the entire family for dinner. Food appeared on the table promptly at seven and everyone was expected to be in their seats, napkins on their laps. No exceptions. But nobody in the office said no to Huntley if they knew what was good for them. The last ADA who did was working upstate in a three-person office prosecuting insurance scams. "Sure thing. Want to clue me in?"

"It's more of a face-to-face conversation. See you in a bit."

What was this about? My mind clicked through my cases from the last month. There were over a hundred assistant DAs in the office, but only a handful put in as many hours as I did. Most were friendly rivals, except for Shula Kar—divorced, mid-forties, industrious, Harvard Law smart. She treated me like her own private nemesis. Some women were like that. Only room at the top for one driven, ambitious female. Shula noticed every mistake I made and called attention to them when she could.

But I didn't make many. My conviction rate was solid and I worked my tail off. Had I fouled up somewhere along the way and that was why Huntley had asked for this private audience? I headed to the Irish bar a mile down the street. Then I remembered the other notification on my phone and called Charley. "Hi, sweetheart. What's up?"

"I called you like hours ago. I needed a book from the library for my history assignment." The rest was garbled as a kid passed by with a boombox blaring.

"Sorry. What was that?" I put my hand up to my other ear to block the street noise.

"I said, can you swing by the library on your way home and pick me up?"

I'd be cutting it close as it was. "Sorry. Something's come up and I need to go straight to dinner from here. Use my account and call Uber. I'll meet you there."

"But you said—"

I didn't have time for this. "Can you just do what I ask for once?"

Lately, Charlotte argued with me about everything from the mundane (did an apple scarfed on the way to school count as breakfast?) to her classes (why learn French when she lived in America?) to curfew (the other kids stayed out past ten on weekends). I knew my work schedule grated on her. I'd missed a couple of her swim meets last semester and had to cancel our standing date to watch "The Bachelor" on a fairly regular basis. But there wasn't much I could do about it at the moment. As a single mother, my job paid the bills and next year, Charley would head off to college and I'd barely saved enough to pay for the first two semesters.

"But I want to change clothes before I go to Grandpa's."

"Is Spencer with you? Can he run you home?"

She sighed, loud enough to make sure I heard. "Sure thing, Mom. Because I wouldn't want to *inconvenience* you. I'll figure something out."

I willed myself to stay calm. "And remember to feed Ginger and let her out before—" But my daughter had already hung up.

The last thing I needed right now was a petulant teenager. These last few weeks I'd been walking on eggshells around Charley, never sure what would set her off. I knew we should sit down for a heart-to-heart before one of us said something we'd regret. But right now, I had to meet with Huntley and hear what he had to say. I pulled open the etched glass door and stepped into the noisy bar.

***

Murphy's Irish Pub, on Marquette University's grounds, had been a staple in Milwaukee since the early 1980's. I had fond memories of my father bringing me here as a toddler. The owner had fawned over my red hair and green eyes and served me a mint-flavored milkshake with a shamrock-shaped coaster that I still had tucked away with my childhood memorabilia. I'd come here on and off through the years, enough that I still earned a head nod and a wink from the wizened old-timer behind the bar.

The hangout was already crowded, with downtown workers meeting up with friends and singles eyeing a possible pick-up. The exposed brick walls and the lights shaped like beer kegs made me feel right at home as did the Irish folk songs from the overhead speakers. As my eyes adjusted to the dim light, I spotted Huntley sitting near the back at a private booth, a pint of beer parked in front of him and a glass of white wine directly opposite. Dressed in a tailored charcoal suit with a red power tie, his persona signaled authority and ambition. When he'd first joined the prosecutorial ranks, he'd been one of a handful of Black men and women recruited to balance the racial inequity rampant in the department. Now, after twenty years, he'd distinguished himself as a powerhouse prosecutor, someone the newspapers frequently touted as destined for higher political office. I considered him a mentor—smart, fair, straight-forward—and was proud of the work we did together.

I slid into the booth, facing him. "I see you ordered for me."

"I seemed to remember you're not crazy about beer. Did I get it wrong?"

"No, I'm good." I'd have preferred a beer, too, but I'd long ago learned to let small things slide.

"I heard about McDougal. How many abusers does that make that you've put away?"

"It's a bit of a crusade for me."

"And you're good at it. Say, how's your dad doing? I hear he won an acquittal for that lawyer accused of murdering his wife." He grinned. "As fast as we slap the cuffs on them, he gets them off."

"He turns sixty-eight this year but he doesn't show any signs of slowing down." Enough small talk. The anxiety was eating up my insides. "It's not every day the big kahuna asks me to a private meeting. What did you want to see me about?"

In other words, cut to the chase. My bluntness had gotten me in trouble in the past, but Huntley seemed to like that about me. No fake smile up front that hid a knife behind my back. With me, what you saw is what you got.

He cleared his throat, leaned forward, and laced his fingers together. "I'm going to need you to keep this quiet for now."

Not about a case then. Something bigger. When I nodded, he continued. "Deaver's going to run next year."

That surprised me. Donald Deaver, now Deputy Chief, was considered a shoo-in for District Attorney when the current occupant resigned or ran for higher office. "Hyde just got elected two years ago and he's got a solid reputation. Why split the party?"

"He's not looking at the DA's slot. He's going to leapfrog and go straight for mayor. If he wins, he's going to recommend I take over his position."

If Huntley moved up, there'd be an opening at his Deputy DA slot. Tradition dictated the position be filled from within the ranks, which meant all us assistants would be wrangling for the job. Working longer hours, pushing our cases through, running the office help ragged so we could impress the higher-ups. It also meant I'd be reporting to one of my competitors this time next year unless ... My heart sped up and I took a sip of wine. Was *this* the purpose of the meeting today? *Keep your cards close to your vest. Wait for him to make the first move.*

"Congratulations. You'll make a great Chief," I said.

Huntley fixed his eyes on mine. "I'm putting together a short list of candidates to take over my spot. Are you interested?"

Butterflies danced in my chest. He was joking, right? What person in my position would say no to this chance? The truth was I'd do practically anything to land on that list. Sure, I'd won my fair share of cases, but I was only thirty-nine. Historically, I'd be expected to work for another decade before getting a chance like this. "There are three dozen lawyers in the office with more seniority," I said, walking the fine line between sounding interested and leaping up on the table and dancing a jig.

"True enough. And don't get me wrong. You aren't the only one I'm looking at. But you're a strong contender. You're ambitious, you're bright, you don't make mistakes." His shoulders relaxed and he flashed me a brilliant smile, right down to that trademark gap between his front teeth. "I see you staying after hours, taking on extra cases, coming in on weekends. You live and breathe the work like I do and your win ratio reflects that." He eased back against the seat. "Not to mention that when it comes to cross-examination, nobody's better. I've snuck into the gallery a few times to observe lately. You start out gentle, pitch softball questions, lull the defendants into complacency. Then when the time is right, you catch them in a contradiction and go for the jugular. They never see it coming."

The compliment landed and I felt my cheeks warm. Damn my pale Irish skin. It betrayed me at the most awkward moments. "I didn't know it was that obvious."

"Don't worry, it's subtle. Not many people would notice." His voice turned serious. "Plus, there's a fire in your belly. You stand up for the victims, even when they're not around to bear witness. That counts extra in my book." Seconds ticked by. "I've been asked to suggest three people for the spot. I'd like you to be one of them."

Don't look too eager. Ask a question. "I know you directly supervise a group of us as well as prosecute higher profile cases yourself. What else is involved?"

"Occasionally you'll work with outside agencies, like ICE or the FBI, and there's quite a few PR appearances at business luncheons, community forums, and various black-tie affairs. You'd interface with the media more but that shouldn't be a problem—the press loves you. It's also a bigger time commitment and there's some travel outside the state. On the plus side, it comes with a significant bump in pay, fifty percent more than you make now. I'm not sure how important that is to you, but I thought I'd mention it."

No more paying the minimum on credit cards. No more struggling with major expenses like a new roof or a car repair. I could afford to send Charley to any college she wanted, not limit her to state schools, as well as make a sizable dent in my own student loans. Obviously, if money was what motivated me, I'd have joined my father's practice after graduation. The reason I went to work in the DA's office was the opportunity to advocate for victims who'd otherwise be powerless, and in this new position, I'd be able to push for stricter sentences and tougher punitive damages.

And then there was the prestige. I'd be the youngest Deputy DA ever appointed in the county. Who would have predicted a 20-year-old, unwed mother would make it this far, this fast? Huntley was waiting for my answer. My heart shouted yes but my head told me to examine all the ramifications before I agreed.

"I appreciate your confidence in me. When do you need to know?"

"It's early days yet. But once Don declares, things will move quickly. I'm sure you'll want to consult with your father, maybe your brother, but otherwise, let's keep this between the two of us for now and talk again in four weeks. In the meantime, no slip-ups. People will be watching."

I appreciated Huntley noticing my work ethic and my dedication. But this position came with a great deal more responsibility as well as visibility. I'd have even less of a personal life than I did now. I laughed to myself. Who was I kidding? I *had* no personal life.

Who else was on Huntley's list? Shula for sure. She'd been a fast-rising star in the department ever since she won that splashy murder case last year. Maybe Callahan, who'd been around forever and paid his dues. Or Rodriguez, that hot-shot new guy from Chicago.

My early twenties had been a tough time but with my parents' help, I'd turned my life around. And now look. A shot at Deputy DA before age forty. I pictured my father's face tonight when I told him the news. He'd be so proud of me.

I exited the bar and power walked down the street, a grin plastered across my face. I'd forgotten how much I loved this time of year—warm breezes, tulips peeking their heads through the dirt, family cookouts. I nodded at strangers as I passed them, hummed to myself.

When my phone rang, I expected my daughter's voice and answered "hi there" only to be greeted by a high-pitched squealing like an animal in pain, followed again by that eerie mechanical voice. "I'm watching you," it said.

I stopped mid-stride and spun around. No one was lurking in a doorway, no one was following behind me, no one was looking at me funny. This was just someone getting his jollies out of rattling my cage and I wasn't about to let him ruin this moment for me. "Lose this number if you know what's good for you."

All I heard was a click at the other end. No matter. I was Rachel Matthews, future Deputy DA, and I was on top of the world.

3

Making the turn onto Summit Avenue, I pulled up to my childhood home, a stately red-brick mansion with leaded windowpanes and a massive mahogany door. Located one block off Lake Shore Drive, the residence offered a glimpse of the lakefront if you looked through one particular window on the second story and craned your head just so. The structure was better suited to a tenured professor than the struggling young lawyer my father had been when he purchased it, but he was a man who aimed high and he'd gone into debt to buy the elegant fixer-upper. The house was considered a landmark, built near the turn of the century, and the previous home of one beer baron, two mayors, and at least four bank presidents.

I tried not to think about that last phone call which had replayed in my mind all the way here. Tonight was about family. I took a deep breath, relaxed my shoulders, then reapplied my lipstick.

Finally I popped a breath mint in my mouth, parked behind my brother's SUV in the driveway, and climbed the familiar stone steps. The door was ajar, and when I entered the house, I found everyone already seated around the dinner table—my father, my brother Luke and his husband Owen, and Charley. They looked up in unison when I poked my head around.

"There she is," Luke said, followed by my daughter's terse "finally." I apologized for being late, then slid into place at the end of the table. Good old supportive Irina, my father's cook and housekeeper, had obviously held the meal until I arrived. She bustled out of the kitchen, balancing a steaming plate of mashed potatoes, followed by a platter of roast turkey. As usual, the table was set with my mother's heirloom lace tablecloth and good China.

The tradition of First Friday family dinners had started once Luke and I both moved back to Milwaukee. Sometimes I balked at the forced togetherness but secretly, I looked forward to these monthly gatherings and never missed one. I might not be married but I wasn't alone. And Charley enjoyed being the center of attention, fawned over by both her uncle and her grandparents from the day she was born.

As my father said grace, I could swear an Amen echoed in my mother's Irish lilt from the corner of the room. Damn cancer. If only she was still alive to advise about this tense standoff with Charley. She'd been wise when it came to matters of the heart and these last four years had been hard without her to turn to.

Luke launched into an anecdote about his recent trip to California and as he talked, I thought back to when he first joined our family. His father, a widower, was Dad's closest friend and when he died, my parents adopted the orphaned twelve-year-old. At first, I'd resented this interloper who wormed his way into my parents' affection. But now I couldn't imagine life without my wise, funny, and caring older brother.

In fact, I was thankful for everyone gathered around the table. I was incredibly lucky. Lucky to have this supportive family. Lucky to have a job I loved. Lucky to have a daughter who gave me occasional headaches but all in all, was a treasure I probably didn't deserve. I sometimes worried whether I had more than my share. What if one day I woke up and my luck had run out?

When the meal was finished, we all retired to the living room and pawed through board games. As Luke and Charley argued over what to play, I pulled my father aside. "Can I grab you for a few minutes? I've got news." I wanted to share the job offer with Dad first. A part of me was still that little girl who wanted her father's approval.

"Let's go back to the study." We left the others, retreated to the rear of the house, and entered my father's sanctum. A well-worn oak desk, rescued from an old hotel downtown, dominated the far end of the room. Ceiling-high wooden bookcases filled with hardback novels and law tomes lined the walls. This had been my father's private space as long as I could remember. He'd spent most evenings during my childhood here, pouring over reference books, writing briefs longhand, and staying up past midnight reviewing cases. He'd given strict instructions to both myself and my mother not to disturb him here unless it was an emergency. I'd known even at an early age how important his work was to him and when it came time to pick a profession, it was a foregone conclusion I'd follow him into the law.

He settled into his black leather recliner and poured two scotches. For me, the pungent, musty smell of the liquor was like his signature cologne. I sat in the over-stuffed chair which had belonged to my paternal grandmother and told him about my conversation with Huntley.

But his reaction surprised me. "You need to pass on this one, monkey-face. You think you're buried in work now? Wait until you've got two dozen assistants to supervise. You might as well set up a cot in your office because you'll never make it home."

Wait. Where was the praise, the clap on the back, the celebratory hug? He didn't understand. "Once Charley leaves for college, all that's waiting for me is an empty house anyway."

His face clouded over. "Precisely my point. That's what you need to change, not your job. What's it all for if there's no one to share it with?"

Was he really trotting out this same old argument? "I'm fine on my own. Besides, I've got you and Luke."

"Luke's got Owen and I won't be around forever. You need to find someone to be with, and that's not going to happen if you're working eighty hours a week. Honey, your priorities are all screwed up. Your life's unbalanced. All work and no play."

I saw red. "Says the man who worked day and night my entire childhood, who never went to the lake house on weekends without dragging a whole shitload of case files along." Apparently that was fine for him, just not for me.

He didn't answer right away but trotted out his favorite avoidance technique, pulling out his pipe, filling it with tobacco, tamping it down, and lighting it. He'd aged since my mother's death. His hairline had receded, his movements had slowed, and he'd finally broken down and bought a hearing aid. But it was his general ennui that worried me more. I pictured him ten years down the road. How would this man, who prided himself on his quick wit, his encyclopedia-brain, his mastery of the law, deal with the reality of growing old?

He launched into his rebuttal. "Don't base your life decisions on mine. I bought into that whole bread-winner bullshit, thought I had to be a success so I could give my family a comfortable lifestyle. I succeeded but I paid a price. If I had a do-over, I'd decide differently."

Did he really believe that? My father was a blustering bear of a man, six feet four with the body of a defensive tackle. He took on impossible cases, hated incompetence, and never missed a chance to tell you when you made a mistake. But his record of acquittals spoke for itself. Men walked free today because of my father's brilliant legal mind and famous courtroom antics. He might tell himself he did it for the money, but I knew better. He did it for the glory, the praise, the limelight. And because he loved the law. Like father, like daughter. Peas in a pod.

"Where's all this regret coming from?" I gestured around the room. "I'd say you've carved out a pretty nice life for yourself. You're well off financially. You've got a nice family. You're at the top of your profession. What more do you want?"

"But look what it cost. I thought when I reached this age, I'd retire, sell the house, your mother and I would move to the lake, travel, spend time with our grandkids." He stared out the back window, temporarily lost in that dream, then glanced back and sighed. "But your mother's gone, I'm lucky to see you once a month, my only grandchild is almost an adult, and Luke and Owen don't want to have kids. Listen to me, honey. Life's no fun when you're alone."

"I've got Charley."

"Not for long. You should be spending as much time as you can with her, not working longer hours. Before you know it, she'll fall in love, settle down, maybe move out of state. And then you'll be alone like me." He took a sip of whiskey, then leaned forward.

"You know, I think a lot about that night when the three of us sat in this very room and you told your mother and me about the baby. How you were going to raise your child as a single mother, with or without our help. I was so proud of you that night."

One minute, I'd been planning a move to England with the man I loved and the next, he was dead. Then I learned I was pregnant. I couldn't stomach severing my only remaining tie to him and flatly refused to get an abortion. Instead, I'd moved back to Milwaukee and in with my parents. It took six years to make it through college, then three more years of law school. I barely had time for an occasional night out with girlfriends, much less a romantic relationship. And once I'd hired on at the DA's office, the pattern was set. It didn't include a personal life.

My father hadn't given up. "Ever wonder whether you've thrown yourself into work because it gives you an excuse *not* to get involved with anyone? If you close yourself off, you can't get hurt again, right?" His expression softened. "I know you believe Paul was your soulmate but it was eighteen years ago."

Why couldn't he be happy for me? Be proud of how hard I'd worked? "An opportunity like this doesn't come along that often. It's a coup to be considered for this so early in my career."

He leaned forward, took my hands in his and squeezed. "All I'm saying is evaluate your priorities. Don't marry your job. It won't keep you warm at night."

Maybe he had a point. I couldn't remember the last time I'd been warm.

4

A week later I came down to the kitchen in sweats on Saturday morning to find Charley dressed and rinsing out her cereal bowl in the sink.

"Mom, I need the car this morning. Spencer volunteered to run lines with me and this is the only time we can get together." She put her hand up. "And before you lecture me about checking with you first, I looked at the schedule on the fridge. There's nothing on there for today."

The schedule was a new idea I'd floated—a way to coordinate our schedules to avoid arguments—so I was glad she'd used it. I took a mug from the cabinet, popped a pod into the Keurig, and punched the 10-oz. button. "Okay, but could you get back by three? I'd like to run into the office." I grabbed my coffee, added two Stevia packets, and poured in a generous dallop of creamer. "So what's this about running lines? Are you trying out for a play?"

She stopped short and faced me. "Only the senior class musical. *Les Miserables*? Ring any bells? I told you about it last week."

Had she? I vaguely remembered her talking about an audition, but the exact details had slipped my mind. I tried to cover. "You're going out for Fantine, right?"

She hoisted her backpack to her shoulder. "As if. No way I could do that death solo. No, I'm up for Cosette. Cross your fingers. I'll take any help I can get."

My mind wandered to a brief I needed to finish before Monday. "Did you feed Ginger?"

"Like I do *every morning*." She snatched an apple from the fruit bowl.

Our golden retriever was snoozing in the corner. "And you let her out?

Charley doubled down on the snark. "What's with you today?"

Truthfully, I couldn't get those anonymous phone calls out of my mind. I'd been distracted all week and I probably was acting a bit flaky. "Never mind. Be safe. And remember, back by three, please."

She bit into the apple. "Yep, heard you the first time." She grabbed the car keys from the hook near the back door. "And your phone was ringing like crazy while you were in the shower. Someone named Liv wants you to call her back. Her number's on the counter."

Charley bounded out the back door. I grabbed an English muffin from the fridge and popped it in the toaster, then picked up my cell. Who was Liv? Must be one of the new associates calling about a case or someone from the church about the food pantry. I plopped onto a tall stool at the center island and dialed the number.

"Reid residence."

It took me a few seconds to make the connection. Liv must be Olivia Reid, the woman from the banquet. I'd forgotten all about her. "May I speak with Olivia, please?"

"Who may I say is calling?" the voice asked. Jeez, how rich did you have to be to have staff answer your phone?

It took a good three minutes before Olivia answered and when she did, she sounded out of breath. "Rachel. Thank you for returning my call. I wanted to see if you were still open to meeting with me, maybe for lunch? It would be my treat."

The energy in her tone surprised me. At the fundraiser, she'd resembled a wounded bird trapped between two men who both wanted more from her than she had to give. Now she sounded almost giddy, like a toddler asking a new friend for a play date.

I'd offered to brief this woman about the book club over the phone, not share a meal with her. What on earth would we find to talk about? But it would be rude to refuse. Only a lunch date wasn't feasible. I pretty much worked straight through most days, grabbing a bite between court appearances. "Would an early dinner be okay instead?" I glanced at the schedule. "Maybe Thursday of next week?"

"Actually, I meant today. Are you free? I think I overheard you say you lived in Whitefish Bay. I'm headed to Bayshore Mall and I could swing by around noon with take-out, if that works?" Liv's voice carried a note of hope mixed with a touch of loneliness.

Truthfully, I already had my day mapped out. Saturday meant laundry, the kitchen needed a scrubbing, and I'd promised to text over some last-minute receipts to my tax guy. But I couldn't think of a polite way to say no, especially since this woman so clearly needed me to say yes.

I gave her directions and by noon, she'd arrived at my front door, looking like a fresh-faced bohemian in a floor-length gauzy floral skirt, peasant blouse, and espadrilles. She carried a takeout bag from Maggiano's and a wine bottle and lifted both up, a wide, magnetic smile on her face. "Hope you like Italian."

Her carefree mood must have rubbed off on me because I decided in that moment to toss out my agenda and enjoy the day. "Who doesn't like Italian?"

Ginger greeted my guest by barking, then nuzzling her head under Liv's hand, eager for attention. When Liv rubbed her snout, Ginger let out the doggie equivalent of a purr and once the two of us settled around the dining room table with our food, the dog plopped down at Liv's feet.

I filled her in on the book club while we consumed fettuccine with mushrooms and a glass of Prosecco. Soon we moved on to our favorite novels and discovered to our delight we liked many of the same authors. But eventually the subject of books and reading ran its course, and I was left groping for something new to talk about.

"What do you do with your time besides read?" I threw out.

"Well, there's my work, of course."

"Your work? I assumed ..."

Olivia tilted her head to one side and gave me a Mona Lisa smile. "That I sit home all day watching reality TV and arranging flowers?"

I blushed. "I apologize. It was a dumb remark."

Liv's tinkling laugh filled the room. "No worries. I'm used to it. Pretty wife, rich husband, paid staff. Why would I need a career, right? I don't know if that's how your family worked, but I learned early on not to depend on others. If I wanted something, it was up to me."

That wasn't exactly the way I saw it. Yes, children should learn to be self-reliant. But family should be around to support and help. If Liv had no one in her corner growing up, I felt sorry for her.

She continued. "Actually, I'm a sculptor. Wait, I'll show you." She pulled out her cell and scrolled through the pictures. "Here's one I'm working on for a private collector." Her face lit up like a Christmas tree as she turned the screen around for me to see.

The snapshot showed Liv in full hazmat gear complete with goggles and a blowtorch, standing in front of a massive steel and wire monolith in the middle of a cavernous metal shed. I stared at the screen. Talk about not judging a book by its cover. "Where's your studio?"

"Zach built me a workshop behind the garage. Some of my pieces are huge and the process can get noisy." Liv scrolled down, then showed me another shot. "Here's a smaller one I installed last week at a summer home in Connecticut."

Liv obviously loved her work and got a great deal of satisfaction from her career. Another thing the two of us had in common. "I'm no expert, but I really like your stuff."

"That's kind of you to say. Not everyone appreciates art. Some people say it's frivolous."

"I admire creative people, probably because I'm not talented that way. I can't sing, I can't draw. Heck, I can't even decorate a birthday cake. How'd you get started?"

A wistful look crossed Liv's face. "After my parents died, my aunt adopted me. She was a painter, quite a good one, and once she saw I had talent, she arranged for me to attend art school in New York. That's actually how I met Zach. He bought one of the pieces in my first student show. I guess you could say he was my first fan."

"So, he runs the company and you've got your art. What do the two of you like to do together?"

"We go to museums, plays, stuff like that." She twisted her wedding band. "That's enough about me. Let's hear about you. You're a prosecutor, right?" A stray strand of hair fell over Liv's face and she tucked it behind her ear. "What made you decide to become a lawyer?"

My life was awfully dull compared to Liv's. "My father practices criminal law and I used to tag along with him to court during the summer when I was younger. I can't remember ever wanting to be anything else."

Liv stared into the distance. "I'm not sure what I dreamed about as a kid. Probably being independent. Free. Nobody bossing me around." Yet her husband seemed pretty controlling. Had he changed since they'd married? The Reids must have a complicated relationship.

Liv sighed, then directed her gaze back to me. "Is there a significant other in your life?"

I liked Liv, but I didn't really know her yet and frankly, after my discussion with Dad last week, I wasn't in the mood to rehash my love life. "Nothing ever stuck. Most of the men I dated said I worked too much. Add in raising a daughter who wasn't their own … let's just say I came with too much baggage."

Her eyes widened. "I didn't realize you had a child."

"She's not a child anymore. Seventeen going on thirty. Charley. Short for Charlotte. Next year she'll be off to college and I'll be an empty nester." I tried not to think too hard about what life would be like without my daughter around. Best not to go there.

Olivia took another sip of Prosecco. "So you're divorced."

This was getting complicated. "No. Never married." It was bound to come up during a book club discussion at some point so I told her the same story I'd told everyone, including Charley. My parents were the only ones who knew the truth. "A drummer in a rock band passing through my college town one weekend. I'm not proud of it, but I was young and naïve." I shrugged. "I'm ashamed to say I don't even remember his name."

Liv's eyes narrowed. "You sound a bit jaded when it comes to men."

You could say that. Once again, I considered how much to reveal to this woman. But Liv was interesting and intelligent, had a fascinating career, and I enjoyed her company, so I opened up a bit more. Maybe I wanted to appear more worldly, more interesting. "I went through a rough patch in college. Someone I loved died and it took me a long time to get over it. After that, it seemed easier to let that part of my life go. I've got Charley and my work. That's enough for now."

"I'm not just being nosy. Ethan talked about you on the way home from the banquet and said he might ask you to dinner. I'll tell him to back off but tell me if you change your mind. He's a good guy. Someone you can count on if you're ever in trouble." She dabbed the side of her mouth with her napkin. "Here, let me help clear the table." She picked up our wine glasses.

My cell chimed with a new text message, another ADA asking for an e-mail address. "Excuse me. I'll just be a minute," I said as I popped into my home office down the hall, retrieved the information, then rejoined Liv in the kitchen. She'd already washed out the pasta bowls and stood staring at a snapshot on the refrigerator.

"Is this your daughter?" she asked.

"Yes. Homecoming last fall with her boyfriend."

Liv leaned forward and scrutinized the photo. "Her coloring's so different from yours. Blond hair, fair skin. More Nordic."

"She takes after her father," I answered, before realizing how strange that sounded after what I'd said before and quickly added, "what I remember of him, that is." I rinsed off the silverware and the wine glasses and wiped my hands on a dish towel.

Liv gathered her stuff and as she reached for her bag, her sleeve rode up, exposing a purplish bruise on her wrist. "That looks like it hurts," I said.

She quickly pulled down the fabric. "I'm kind of a klutz. I tripped going down the stairs yesterday and Zach grabbed me to break my fall. It's nothing, really. I'd forgotten all about it." I'd encountered enough abuse victims in my work to doubt Liv's story. Yes, Zach might have saved his wife from injury. He might also have twisted her wrist on purpose.

The sound of the garage door caused me to glance at the clock. Good. Charley was home early. As soon as Liv left, I could take off for downtown.

My daughter rushed into the room, jabbering a mile a minute, then stopped when she noticed Olivia. "Oh, sorry. I didn't realize you had company." She parked her backpack on a nearby chair and stuck out her hand. "Hi, I'm Charley."

"Olivia. I'm hoping to join your mom's book club." Liv stared as though memorizing my daughter's face. "You're very pretty."

Charley shuffled her feet. "Thanks, I guess?"

I spoke up. "Olivia's an artist. A sculptor."

"I apologize if I embarrassed you but ..." Liv reached out and touched Charley's cheek. "You've got great bone structure. Have you ever done any modeling?"

"As if," Charley scoffed.

I shot my daughter a look that said *that was rude*, but Olivia took the remark in stride. "If you're open to it, I'd love you to pose for me. Maybe a small figure study. I've got a show coming up and I could use a few more pieces. Would that interest you?"

"I'd LOVE that. Wait until I tell my boyfriend."

I came up from behind and put my hands on Charley's shoulders. "We'll let you know."

"But Mom—"

"I said we'll discuss it. You've got a lot on your plate right now, what with the musical and your studies." Something about Zach rubbed me the wrong way and I wasn't sure how I felt about Charley going to the Reid's home.

Liv backtracked. "It was just an idea. I'll certainly understand if it doesn't work out." She slung her bag over her shoulder. "I should let you two get on with your Saturday. Thanks so much for your hospitality, Rachel. I loved getting to know you better, and I definitely want to join your book club. You're reading *The Power* next, right? Women taking over the world." She smiled. "Wonder what *that* would be like." She jangled her keys and I saw the ring had a unique marble cube attached, like a miniature sculpture. No doubt another one of Liv's creations.

We walked onto the front porch to say our goodbyes, and Liv turned to leave. Then she whirled back around, gave me an unexpected hug, and held me at arm's length. "I so enjoyed today. Can we be friends? I mean, not just acquaintances but real friends?"

What a strange and wonderful thing to say. So straightforward. "I'd like that," I said. "Call me." Liv nodded and strode to her car which she'd parked in front of the house. She tripped over the curb but caught herself, then waved goodbye.

When I re-entered the kitchen, Charley piped up.

"Cool new friend you've got there, Mom. That outfit's to die for and did you see that car? I think it's a Porsche." She poured herself a glass of lemonade. "Do you think she's serious about me posing for her?"

"I'll let you know if she brings it up again."

***

THAT EVENING, AFTER I'D ORGANIZED my tax information and emailed it to my accountant, I clicked off the downstairs lights only to flip them back on when the wall phone in the kitchen rang. That was strange. I couldn't remember the last time anyone had called that number. It had come as part of a bundled package when I signed up for internet service, and we rarely used it.

Probably a robo-call. I picked up the receiver. "Hello. Matthews' residence."

Silence.

"Hello?" I repeated. "Can I help you?"

Someone was there. I could hear breathing. If this was a wrong number, why didn't they hang up? Was this the same person who'd been leaving me voice messages on my cell? "I think you've mis-dialed."

No response. Seconds ticked by.

"I'm still watching you," the voice finally said and then eerie but vaguely familiar music started to play. My pulse kicked into overdrive. Where had I heard that tune before? I listened for a minute, then slammed the receiver back in the cradle, my hands shaking. This wasn't some kid fooling around, some nut making prank phone calls. This was all too real.

I rushed to my home computer, scrolled to YouTube, and pulled up audio clips of movie soundtracks. Finally something clicked in my brain. I typed a keyword into the search engine.

The music that blasted from the speakers turned my blood ice-cold. *Overlay of Evil* by Harry Manfredini with its discordant melody, spooky sound effects, and whispering menace. A pit formed in my stomach as the soundtrack of the granddaddy of all revenge movies, Friday the 13th, enveloped the room.

5

As I DROVE TO work on Monday, I opened my calendar and a packed schedule stared back—three preliminary hearings in the morning and a tricky deposition with a hostile witness later that afternoon. And to top it off, rain was pouring down like a burst water main, resulting in two separate collisions that held me hostage in bumper-to-bumper traffic all the way. When I finally reached downtown, my favorite parking spot was taken so I had to find another one three levels down. I climbed the stairs to the ground floor, opened my umbrella, and splashed across the street, my sneakers squishing with every step. Once inside, I changed into high heels, tucked my wet shoes inside a plastic bag, and rode the elevator to the eighth floor. As I passed the frenetic beehive of the secretarial pool, Rita gave me a broad smile, wiggling her eyebrows. "Looks like someone's got an admirer."

I had no idea what she meant but knew soon enough when I opened my door and found, in the middle of my desk, a massive bouquet of pink and red peonies, my birthday flower. Since my office was no bigger than a broom closet, their strong fragrance was stifling. Had someone decided to send me birthday greetings a month early? Or gotten wind of my possible promotion? Huntley had said to keep his offer under my hat and the only person I'd told was my father. Was this his way of apologizing for his lack of enthusiasm last week? I removed the envelope from the plastic trident and examined the card.

A big red heart, broken in two, with drops of blood floating down. What the hell? I picked up the vase and approached Rita's cubby. "Did you sign for these?"

"Not exactly." Rita sat up straighter. "When I came back from the records room, I saw your door was open and I peeked inside. The flowers were just sitting there. Is something wrong? You're white as a sheet."

First the hang-ups. Then the voice messages. Now this bouquet with its weird drawing. A few oddball incidents I could ignore, but getting access to my office crossed the line. I thrust out the vase. "Find out how these got here and throw the flowers away." With that, I sped down the hall to the staff bathroom, where I splashed cold water on my face and worked to calm down. *Don't overreact. The flowers are nothing more than someone's idea of a sick joke.*

What had that wife-beating jerk McDougal said last week as they'd hauled him away? *Don't think you've heard the last of me.* But sending flowers was hardly his style and he wouldn't know when I was born. Besides, he was behind bars. This had to be someone free to move about. Some sadistic freak trying to throw me off-kilter. Well, I wouldn't give him the satisfaction. I peered at my reflection and wiped mascara smudges from under my eyes.

A toilet flushed and Shula emerged from the stall at the end. Could she be behind this? "Hi, Rachel. Haven't seen you in a while." She washed her hands at the adjoining basin, eyeing me in the mirror. "Are you feeling okay? You're all flushed."

Huntley had told me not to discuss the promotion with anyone in the office. If Shula was on the short list, this could all be part of a plan to rattle me, to get me to make mistakes. I washed and dried my hands, threw the paper towel in the wastebasket, then pushed back a few wisps of hair which had escaped the tight bun at the nape of my neck. "I'm fine," I responded, glad to hear my voice didn't betray me. "And you? I heard the Hawkins case might be headed south. If you need help, my door's always open."

"No, it's under control." Shula's odd smile reminded me of the Cheshire Cat from the Alice novels. "By the way, have you heard the rumors?" When I didn't respond, she added, "Looks like big changes are coming."

She was baiting me but I wasn't going to bite. "I'm not a big fan of office gossip and frankly, I've got my hands full just handling my case load. Speaking of, I need to get back to it. See you later."

I left the washroom, a bead of sweat trickling down my spine. Whoever was playing with me, he'd picked the wrong woman to target. If this went on much longer, I'd file a complaint with the police and get their help to stop this harassment.

After a full day in court, I circled back to the office at five-thirty. Rita had researched the flower delivery and stayed late to explain. A teenage boy in low-slung pants and a torn T-shirt, hair sopping wet, showed up early that morning carrying the gigantic bouquet, saying a man paid him twenty bucks to deliver it to a Ms. Matthews on the eighth floor. The security guard stationed at the building's front entrance made sure nothing dangerous was hidden in the stems, but he hadn't opened the envelope, assuming it was personal. He brought them up and put them in the center of my desk. Nothing struck him as odd; he'd put it down as a romantic gesture. That meant tracing the bouquet was likely a dead end since neither the card nor the envelope had a florist's logo.

***

By the time I wrapped up work at nine that night, the rain had stopped, though a slight mist still hung in the spring air. When I went to change into my sneakers, they were still damp, so I stayed in my heels. Cinching my raincoat around my waist, I scurried to the parking garage, scanning my surroundings in case anyone was following me. I hated being so paranoid but ignoring the threats seemed naïve.

I chose to use the stairs instead of the elevator. Less chance of being trapped. I tromped down three floors to discover the light above the exit door was out, casting the area into shadow. A shiver of unease gripped me but then I gave myself a reality check. Bulbs wear out. It happens. There was no need to imagine a bogeyman behind every door. But at the same time, I wasn't about to stumble blindly into a deserted garage bathed in darkness. I turned on my phone's flashlight to light the way. Thank goodness I had my umbrella along. In a pinch, I'd use it as a weapon, buy myself enough time to call for help.

My car stood silhouetted against the back wall. No one was around. The space was spookily silent, the only sound my own stilettos as they clicked on the concrete pavement. Half-way there, I hit the car's key fob to open the driver's side door and the taillights flashed. As an added precaution, I kept my index finger poised above the alarm button.

What was that? A piece of paper was wedged under the wipers. Please let it be a takeout menu. Or a political flyer. I surveyed the area. No sound. No movement. Only dark corners and the noise of brakes grinding from the level above.

I grabbed the note. It was on white card stock, the message written in block letters in blood-red ink.

It's no use running. I'll catch you.

A hard stone wedged in my throat, making it hard to breathe. Was he watching me right now? Had he been waiting patiently in the shadows all night until I left work? *What do you want, you son of a bitch?* I whispered to myself.

I needed to get out of here. The nearest exit was in the opposite direction, back the way I'd come. A long walk across a deserted garage, with plenty of chances for someone hiding behind a car to rush out and attack me. I was safer here. I glanced in the back seat to make sure no one was hiding there, ready to pounce as soon as I got inside.

A motor roared behind me and a dark sedan came into view from the floor below. The car was at the far end of the garage, headed my way. Lungs on fire, I yanked open the car door and, in my hurry, dropped the note on the pavement where it skidded away. Damn. I bent down, ready to chase after it.

Stop. Think.

If my harasser was in the approaching car or lurking somewhere nearby, what better opportunity to assault me than when I was crawling on all fours trying to retrieve a lousy piece of paper.

Instead, I flung myself into the driver's seat, hit the button to lock the doors, and watched in the rearview mirror as the oncoming car inched closer.

Closer.

The blazing headlights blinded me. I couldn't see who was behind the wheel. The driver passed my car and parked in an empty spot around the corner, only a few yards away. He turned off the engine, then the lights.

I waited, frozen in place, pulse pounding in my ears. Why hadn't I taken this more seriously? Why hadn't I reached out for help? Why was I so stubborn sometimes, insisting on doing everything myself?

Seconds elapsed. No one got out. It was like some old-time Western. High Noon in downtown Milwaukee. I pulled my cell from the pocket of my raincoat, fingers dialing before I had a chance to think.

"9-1-1. What's the nature of your emergency?"

My throat seized. *I received a bouquet of flowers. I got a voice mail. There's a note on my windshield.* It all sounded so nebulous.

"I'm in McArthur Square garage," I began, then swiveled to look at the parked sedan.

An elderly woman with steel-gray hair opened the passenger door, swung one leg out, and hoisted herself out of the car, using her arms as support. The driver of the vehicle, a short, skinny man about the same age, came around and took the woman's elbow and they hobbled together toward the elevator bank, chatting and laughing into the night air.

"Ma'am, are you still there? Are you okay?" said a voice on the phone.

"Yes. Sorry. Wrong number." I disconnected the call as my pulse dropped back to normal. I was safe. For now. Whoever had left the note had come and gone. But I wouldn't make the same mistake twice. Those flowers weren't misdelivered. The note on my windshield wasn't a mistake. Whoever was behind this knew where I worked. What car I drove. Maybe even where I lived.

It was about time I stopped being so goddamn blasé and faced facts. I had a stalker and it was about time I did something about it.

6

WHEN I REALIZED I wasn't in immediate danger, I retrieved the
note, hoping either it or the heart drawing might provide clues to
the stalker's identity. Maybe a similar pattern the police could spot.
And since my best guess was this guy was someone I'd prosecuted,
the following morning I pulled my case files from the last three
months. The stack was two feet tall and I examined them one by
one, paying special attention to the men who'd been charged with
violent crimes against women. But after several hours, I gave up.
None of these men could have put that note on my car. All of them
were still behind bars.

Next I considered my co-workers. Not just the lawyers, but
the paralegals, the secretaries, and the courthouse staff. Was there
someone I worked with who carried a grudge against me, or
conversely, was jealous and wanted to get me in trouble with the
higher-ups? Was this tied to the promotion? But no one sprang

to mind. There was one ADA who'd asked me out when I first got hired, but he'd married one of the county pathologists. And then there was Shula. She'd love to throw me off my game. But something about the whole set-up screamed *male.*

I even double-checked with my father and Luke to see if they'd sent me the flowers and the florist had somehow mixed up the card. Neither of them had any idea what I was talking about.

Then I remembered the dating site. A year ago, after an hour of Gracie's needling, I'd put up a profile and thirty men had popped up. Most resembled either a scared rabbit or a serial killer, but I'd gone on a first date with three different guys, only to turn them all down for a second. That accountant from Hales Corners didn't take it too well. In fact, he'd persisted to the point where I'd had to get unnecessarily mean. But it had been so long ago, I couldn't even remember his name. No, this had to be connected to work. I'd have to dig deeper.

I was tense and jumpy all day, flinching when another associate bumped into me in the hall and startling when Rita stuck her head in unexpectedly that afternoon. When Charley phoned to ask if she could have her friend Stella for a sleepover that weekend, I bit her head off. Finally, after plowing through four thick files on a new child abuse case, I left work early, tucking the remaining information in my briefcase to read that night. Taking time out to look for my stalker had put me behind, and I'd concentrate better at home, away from the constant interruptions. Besides, if I was honest, I felt safer there. Ever since the flower delivery, I'd been on edge, wondering if someone in the elevator or standing next to me in the cafeteria line could be the mystery guy. At least in my home environment, I felt in control.

I pulled into the garage, then walked to the curb to collect the recycling bin. Mrs. Abbott, the older woman who lived across the street, was pulling weeds in her yard, and the two of us exchanged waves. As I wheeled the green bin back to the house, I saw a padded envelope taped to my front screen and my breath caught in my throat. Now what?

I rushed up the steps and read the scrawled note on the package. *I've got my eye on you.*

Damn it. How long since he'd been here? I scanned the street, but other than Mrs. Abbott and a couple of kids shooting hoops a few doors down, the block appeared deserted.

I ran over to my neighbor. "Did you see anyone around my house today? There's a package taped to my front door." My voice sounded like a high-pitched guitar riff.

She shook her head. "No, but I was inside most of the day watching my shows. Maybe Fed-Ex dropped it off?"

Does she think I'm a moron? That's the first thing I checked but there was no receipt, no street address, no postage stamp. I retraced my steps and entered my house through the garage. We kept this door locked but this time I threw the dead bolt as well, then listened for sounds inside.

Silence. "Charley? Are you home?"

No answer. But she'd be back from school any minute.

Heart pounding, I pulled out green plastic gloves from under the kitchen sink and eased open the front door. Taking pains not to contaminate the surface, I slowly peeled off the manila envelope, brought it to the kitchen, and sliced it open. Inside was a USB memory stick in bubble wrap. I knew I should probably take this straight to the police but I needed to know what I was up against. I laid the device in the palm of my hand and walked to my home office.

I paused. What better way to mess with my head than to plant a virus to corrupt my files or spyware to access my emails? I pulled out an old laptop from the shelf instead and plugged it into a power cord. Luckily it still worked. I stuck in the memory device. There was only one folder. *For Rachel.* What fresh hell was this? My fingers trembled as I double-clicked it open.

The video was a mix of moving and still photos, and again, the theme music from *Friday the 13th* was playing in the background. According to the time stamps, the shots were taken over the last two weeks and mainly focused on the front of the house. Some showed me leaving for work. Others were from early in the morning as I filled the bird feeders or as Charley let the dog out. One had me walking to the street to retrieve the mail. Another seemed to be footage from a drone hovering over our back yard. There was even a segment focused on my bedroom window as though the person filming it had been standing on our porch.

The music abruptly shut off and a sign filled the screen, a single word written in red marker spoken by that same synthesized voice.

"*SLUT.*"

I couldn't move. Goosebumps prickled on my forearms. All I could hear was that one word echoing over and over. Who hated me this much? What had I done to them?

"Mom? Where are you?"

Ugh. Charley was home. I didn't want her to see the video so I eased the lid of the laptop shut, making a sound no louder than a blink as fear gnawed at my gut.

She came into the room. "Why's the back door bolted? I had to paw through my purse to find the front door key. What's going on?"

There was no holding back now. These incidents were accelerating and I had to warn her. "Once you've changed, come back down. We need to talk." I tucked my hands out of sight so she wouldn't see them shaking.

"O-k-a-y." She stretched out the word, as though unsure what was going on but afraid to ask. She bounded upstairs and reappeared five minutes later, having changed into her standard outfit of ripped jeans and slouchy top. She hopped on a kitchen stool.

Here I was, scared out of my skin, but Charley was oblivious. She began to jabber. "I made the finals for Cosette. It's between me and Simone and the final audition's tomorrow. So can I borrow the car after dinner? Jessica said we could rehearse together at her house. She's up for Fantine."

I didn't want to frighten her, but there was no way she was going off on her own He could be watching us right now. "How about I drive you over and come back in a few hours to pick you up?" The minute the words were out of my mouth, I knew Charley would never buy it.

"What am I, twelve? I can drive myself. Besides, Spencer's going with me and hanging around until I'm done."

"That's what we need to talk about." I faced her. "These last few days I've gotten some strange phone calls and notes and today, there was a package taped to the front door." I stared hard at her to make sure she was listening. "It had an upsetting video inside. Nothing obscene, but both of us need to take extra precautions for a while. I don't want you going out at night if you can help it and if you have to go out, take Spencer or one of your friends along. Better yet, I'll run you wherever you need to go."

Her eyes widened. She slid off the stool and backed up. "You're scaring me."

"You just need to be vigilant. Look around you. Don't talk to people you don't know. Travel in a group. Invite friends over here if you need to get together. Meanwhile, I'm talking to the police tomorrow about what they can do."

"Is this guy … like, dangerous?"

"I'm not sure." Charley jammed her hands into her armpits and her face blanched. "Let's don't blow this out of proportion. So far, all he's done is make some nasty phone calls and videos. But as for tonight, why don't you see if Jessica can come over here instead?"

She nodded and left, pulling her phone from her jeans to text her friend. An hour later the house was noisy with teenagers, with Spencer and another friend joining the mix. The four of them, with Ginger trailing behind, trooped down to the basement and once they'd settled in, I locked all the doors and windows and turned on every lamp in the house. Then I called Davante Whitaker, a beat cop from the 1st precinct I'd known for years. I reached him on his cell and told him about the tape, asked if there was any way to have an off-duty patrol car sit outside my house tonight as a precaution. He called back minutes later to say he'd come himself, he'd be there within the hour, then insisted I'd need to file a formal complaint. We agreed to meet together the next morning.

When I saw him pull up in his own car and flash his lights, I waved out the window, poured myself a whiskey, and tried to calm down. To distract myself, I booted up my computer and compiled a series of questions I needed to research on my latest case. But it wasn't long before I realized I'd been staring at the same screen for five minutes and couldn't remember a single word I'd read. My mind kept cycling back to that damn videotape.

A phone rang. Not my cell which lay silent on the desk beside me. The call was coming from the kitchen phone again. I lifted the receiver and held my breath.

"I never let you out of my sight."

My neck muscles spasmed. Summoning up my strongest courtroom voice, I shouted, "Leave me alone. I've contacted the police." I listened but when there was no response, I yanked the cord from the wall, stormed out to the garage, and buried the phone under a stack of old clothes marked for Goodwill. *Take that, you bastard,* I thought to myself as I stomped inside.

7

I was through standing passively by while this creep played around with my head. No more. With the tape as evidence, surely the police could figure out who was stalking me. He must have left some digital thumbprint behind.

The first precinct was housed in the same building as my own offices. "Hey there, Jean. Haven't seen you in ages," I offered to the woman behind the bullet-proof glass. "I'm here to see Davante."

"Sure thing, counselor. I'll tell him you're here."

I skirted around reception, swiped my key card, and entered the squad room, a large open space of cubicles, phones ringing, cops coming and going. I helped myself to a cup of coffee from the shared pot, then found Davante's desk and waited.

I drummed the arm rests. The last thing I wanted was to sound like a hysteric. No, I'd simply outline the sequence of events—the phone calls, the flowers, the note, the video—in a calm, relaxed manner and find out what my options were. I shut my eyes and breathed in, out, in, out, willing my heart into a normal rhythm.

"Grabbing a cat nap, counselor?" Davante appeared out of nowhere. "How about we go somewhere more private?" We sidestepped through the bullpen to a nondescript conference room with a standard-issue oak table and two metal folding chairs. "Now what's all this about?" he asked.

"First, thanks for coming last night. I appreciate it." He waved the remark away like staying up all night was no big deal and told me to take my time. I started with the first voice message at the banquet and went on from there. He listened, leaning forward and keeping steady eye contact. When I got to the part about the note on my car, he perked up.

"Did you bring the card? We might be able to lift a fingerprint. At the very least, we can identify the type of paper and ink he used."

In the parking garage, after I'd calmed down and realized I wasn't in immediate danger, I'd retrieved the message from under the car. I reached in my briefcase and pulled out a baggie. "My prints are there, too, I'm afraid. I didn't have any gloves handy."

He nodded, his mouth in a tight line. "We could try to locate the kid, see if he could give us a description of the man who paid him to deliver the flowers. But that's a long shot. He probably paid more attention to the twenty than he did to the guy's face."

"How about the phone calls? Can you trace where they originated from my phone records?"

"He likely used a burner, but it's worth a shot. Any idea who's behind this? Disgruntled ex-boyfriends? That's usually what we see."

"The last relationship I had ended over three years ago and he's the one that walked away because, and I quote, *I was too married to my job.* Since then, only a couple of first dates which didn't go any further. I think that's a dead end, mainly because of this." I laid another baggie with the USB stick on the table. "This is what finally sent me over the edge. I found it taped to my front screen yesterday."

"Wait here." He returned with a laptop, headphones, and a pair of plastic gloves, and watched the video to the end. I kept my eyes on his face and halfway through, his jaw tightened and his left hand balled into a fist. Once the snippet ended, he whipped off the headset. "Have you seen anyone lurking around? Has Charley? Any unfamiliar cars parked on the street?"

"Nothing out of the ordinary."

"You said this was left at the front door. Was it delivered by UPS? Fed Ex?"

"Neither." I pulled out the plain manila envelope and handed it over. "It looks like he simply walked up the steps, rolled off a section of tape, and attached it to the screen. It could have been any time after seven when I left for work and my daughter took off for school."

His gaze met mine. "I'll contact the Whitefish Bay police. Ask them to canvass your neighbors. Maybe someone saw something. But ..." He paused.

I said out loud the words he didn't want to. "I know. He hasn't broken any actual laws. It's not illegal to send someone flowers or to leave a note on someone's windshield. People get prank phone calls every day. It's not even against the law to take photos of a house from the street. Google maps does it. Zillow does it. Hell, every real estate firm in town does it." I let out a sigh. "So even if you track down who's behind this, your hands are tied for now because even though his actions are full-on icky, they aren't anything you can arrest him for." My voice got more stringent. "Plus you can't give me any more protection than you would the average citizen or it looks like I'm getting special treatment because of my job." I waited but he stayed quiet. "That about cover it?"

"I understand why you're upset. Hell, *I'm* upset. You wouldn't believe how many women come in here, complaining someone is following them or sending them anonymous videos in their feed. And now it's happening to someone I know. Someone I care about." He squeezed my hands. "People don't realize how common this is—13 million instances every year and that's just in the United States. One in three women stalked at some point in their life, usually by someone close to them. Serious stuff. The only good news is, so far this guy hasn't made any actual threats. Let's hope he's satisfied with watching you squirm but doesn't have the nerve to take it further."

From his mouth to God's ear. Maybe I'd be one of the lucky ones. "You definitely think it's a guy? The voice is so garbled, I can't tell."

"Statistics show 90% of stalkers of women turn out to be male. So yes, unless we turn up evidence to the contrary, we should assume this is a man."

"I'm pretty jaded when it comes to threats but I have to admit, this one's got to me. Plus, I've got a teenage daughter who doesn't always make good choices."

"Let's start with what we have. I'm opening up a file. Leave this stuff with me and I'll send everything over to the lab and see if they can turn up any prints. They'll also analyze the video for any identifying sounds or visuals and I'll personally go through our databases, see if I can spot another case with the same pattern. Maybe the guy's made a mistake somewhere along the way."

It was better than nothing. Although I doubted our suspect forgot something as basic as wearing gloves. Which meant I was at a standstill until whoever was doing this either slinked away or threatened me more overtly. "Can I ask a favor? Can you keep this between us for now? I'd just as soon not get my boss involved unless this escalates." Because once Huntley knew, he might very well mark me off his list.

Davante shook his head. "You know I can't. You want to tell him personally or do you want me to handle it?"

"No, I'll do it. But can I hold off until after the lab results come back and you've canvassed the neighbors? That way, I might have some answers for him."

"Three days max. Then you let him know. Agreed?" When I nodded, he went on. "And if I were you, I'd take a look at your home security." He pulled out a card and jotted down a name and phone number on the back. "Here's a firm we recommend. Give them a call. It might give you peace of mind."

"I'll do that. And thanks." I stood.

"And Rachel? Be smart. Take precautions. Have someone walk you to your car at night. Have your daughter keep close to home or stay with friends or family if you're away. And let me know about anything, and I mean *anything,* that seems the least bit odd."

I sighed. How ironic that I'd given my life to the law and now when I needed it most, it couldn't protect me.

"I mean it, Rachel. No heroics. Don't downplay this. I've seen cases like this go away on their own, but I've also seen them end very badly."

Davante knew me. He knew I wasn't the type to take a wait and see approach. What if instead of hiding in my house, terrified of every sound, I turned the tables on my stalker? Put myself in a precarious situation to flush this guy out? But I'd need help for that plan. And since the police couldn't do it, I'd have to find it elsewhere.

But for right now, I'd follow Davante's suggestions. Install better home security. Keep tabs on Charley. Hope the lab turned up a lead or one of my neighbors saw something. Pray for the guy to make a mistake. And if he didn't? Well, I was ready to go on the offensive. The only question was how.

***

I was setting the table for an early dinner when Charley got home from school. "Mom, what's with the police cars parked out front? There's a couple of guys going up and down the street knocking on doors. Did that guy try to break in?"

"No, nothing like that. They're asking if anyone's noticed strangers hanging around." I put my hands on her shoulders. "Try not to worry about this. I told you I was contacting the police. And I'm meeting with a security firm on Friday to do an assessment."

The color drained from my daughter's face. "This is getting weird, Mom."

I enveloped my daughter in a hug. "Trust me, okay? I'd never let anything happen to you. Now go change. Dinner's on the table in twenty minutes."

She didn't look all that reassured but retreated to her room and while she was gone, Davante called. The door-to-door canvassing hadn't turned up anything. But since most of my neighbors left early for work and the few residents around during the day stayed mainly indoors, I wasn't all that surprised. But when Davante asked whether I had a weapon in the house, I freaked out. "I've got a gun but I'm not even sure where it is. You think it's that serious?"

"Do you know how to shoot it?" Not really an answer to my question.

"I did some target practice at the range when I first got it but it's been a while. Why?"

"I'd make a return trip one of these days."

I clutched my stomach. Was he implying it was up to me to protect myself and my daughter?

Davante continued. "Do you suspect anyone at the office? In the neighborhood? At church? People aren't always who they seem to be on the surface, you know."

"I make a living going after bad guys, so I've got a keener sense than most when it comes to spotting someone hiding behind a mask."

"Don't be over-confident. Even experts can be fooled when it affects them personally. Doubt everyone. I'll let you know when I hear back from the lab. And if anything unexpected happens, call for help. I mean it. And remember, you need to tell Huntley."

Davante and I went way back. He wouldn't be warning me if he didn't think the threat was real. That night I couldn't get to sleep, hearing unfamiliar sounds in the back yard, the kitchen, on the street outside. I tried to convince myself Ginger would bark if an intruder got inside the house, but it didn't do any good. I finally scrounged around in my walk-in closet and found the gun buried under a stack of blankets. When I double-checked, it still had bullets in the chamber and I tucked it in my nightstand. But I still couldn't relax. Would I actually be able to pull the trigger if someone broke in? At midnight I got up and went downstairs for a glass of warm milk and when I came back, Charley was curled up in my bed.

"Can I sleep with you tonight?" My daughter's voice shook like she'd been replaying scary movies in her head. Her damp hair lay plastered to her scalp.

"Of course, sweetheart," I said, touched she had turned to me for comfort. The truth was I liked having her by my side where I could keep watch over her.

She climbed under the covers and I pulled her close, rubbing her back which was slick with sweat. I hummed an old Irish lullaby, one I'd sung to Charley when she was a baby. Before long, my daughter's muscles went slack and she drifted off, her head still resting on my chest. I closed my eyes and pretended to be asleep, but it took another hour before I drifted off. Even then, my sleep was fitful, filled with nightmares of a faceless figure lurking outside, his gaze glued to our upstairs window.

8

THE NEXT EVENING, WITH Charley safely hanging out at her boyfriend's, I drove to the Reid home in River Hills to pick Liv up for book club. The car's GPS led me down a narrow gravel path with mature pine trees like silent soldiers, standing at attention. There was a strange aesthetic to the landscaping, like it was leading me to the shadowed cloisters of a convent.

As I rounded the second curve, the house abruptly rose up in front of me, a futuristic monolith of concrete and glass, with two distinct wings, an asymmetric roof line, and several walls of floor-to-ceiling windows. A trio of stainless-steel sculptures, each the size of a giant beach ball, lined the front walkway. I wondered if these were Liv's creations.

The housekeeper answered the door and informed me Olivia would be down in a few minutes, then ushered me into a spacious living area where the décor dovetailed perfectly with the home's exterior. Three stark-white leather chairs lined up on one side, a sleek matching couch on the other, all circling a low glass coffee table with an arrangement of ivory pillar candles and a scattering of high-end fashion magazines. Persian rugs were strategically placed on the bleached-maple floors. The large oil painting above the fireplace, by a Brazilian artist who'd recently had an exhibition at the Milwaukee Art Museum, must have cost more than my yearly salary. In one corner a baby grand piano sported a half dozen family photos in sleek silver frames. This austere living space was so different from my own house. What had Olivia thought of my mishmash, lived-in furniture, worn wall-to-wall carpet, and used books stacked alongside mementos of Charley's childhood at our luncheon last Saturday? I must have seemed like the poor country mouse.

Zach Reid appeared in the archway. "Hello, Rachel. You look stunning," he purred.

I rose to my full 5'8", closed the space between us, and thanked him with a gracious smile. He might have Liv under his thumb, but I wasn't the least bit intimidated by this man's swagger. "I thought I'd drive Liv to book club since it's her first time. Help her ease into the group."

"That's thoughtful of you." He moved closer and I stood my ground, so now only inches separated us. "You know, ever since we met at that awards dinner, I've searched my brain for who you remind me of and it finally came to me. You're the spitting image of a woman I dated before I met Liv." His eyes bored into mine. "Except for one thing."

I'd faced off against men like Reid in the courtroom plenty of times. Wife abusers and rapists sometimes hired lawyers every bit as misogynistic as they were. "Oh?" I said, bracing myself for what I thought was coming. Sure enough, he glanced down at my breasts, then back up.

"You're much … *taller.*" We both knew what he was implying and I searched for a clever comeback but then decided he wasn't worth the effort. Let him think he'd won the verbal match.

"Do you think Liv will be much longer? We really need to be going." I glanced at my watch.

Zach grinned. "You're not afraid of me, are you, Rachel?"

This guy's ego could fill a stadium. "I've been a prosecutor for nine years, Zach. I eat men like you for breakfast." Hopefully, he'd take the hint and leave me alone.

Just then, Olivia appeared at the top of the stairs and my face-off with her husband died a quiet death. I stepped around him and approached Liv, who was ravishing as always.

"Ready to go?" I said.

"Absolutely. I'm looking forward to it." She went over to Zach, kissed his cheek, and told him not to wait up, she might be back late.

"Don't overdo the drinking, love. You know how you get."

"Oh, stop raining on my parade, you party-pooper. Rachel's the designated driver. Right?" She turned to me, a radiant smile lighting up her features.

Zach clenched his jaw. "I just don't want anything happening to my girl. You two drive safely."

As we got into the car, I brought it up. "Is he always that protective of you?"

Olivia didn't answer right away. "He does like to keep an eye on me. It can be stifling but I try to remember it's because he loves me."

Or because he wants to control you. But really, who was I to judge? When it came to romance, I was the last person to give out advice.

Olivia's hands fluttered around her hair. "But I appreciate your concern." She rested her head against the side window and stared at the passing cars. I didn't blame Liv for not opening up more—our friendship was new and she probably didn't quite trust me yet. But I'd keep my eyes open, see if she needed my help. Because when it came to Liv and Zach's relationship, I was sure more was going on between them than what they showed in public.

After a while, I tuned the radio to a classical music station. Strains of Mozart filled the space and helped cover the silence.

***

THE LADIES IN THE BOOK club were their usual lively selves. Since I was driving, I limited myself to one glass of wine, but Olivia downed several, getting more talkative and vivacious as the evening wore on. It was like she'd been let out of a cage. She told stories of the three years she'd lived in Greenwich Village in her early twenties, scraping by as a waitress to save enough money for art lessons. I kept my mouth shut, even though I knew Liv's aunt had paid for her education. Let Liv tell whatever story she wanted.

She was still bubbling with excitement as the two of us drove home. "What a great bunch of women. I can't remember the last time I had so much fun."

"You fit right in. Everyone loved you."

"I guess it's no secret I've been pretty lonely since we moved here. But now I've met you and you've introduced me to this wonderful bunch of friends. I'm lucky you came along."

I listened with half an ear because I was focused on a dark SUV behind us in the same lane. When I merged onto the freeway, I glanced again in the rear view mirror and sure enough, the driver took the I-43 entrance as well, keeping enough distance between our two cars so I couldn't see him clearly. I tuned into what Liv was saying in time to hear the phrase *Charley posing for me.*

I flashed to Zach's leer earlier that evening. I didn't want my daughter anywhere near that chauvinist pig. "No," I snapped, more forcibly than I'd intended.

Liv went on. "Charley seemed really excited about—"

Was she purposely ignoring me? "I'm not comfortable with her posing for you. Finals are coming up and she needs to concentrate on her classes." I stared straight ahead, knowing I sounded unreasonable but at the same time, determined to keep my daughter away from Zach Reid. I could handle the man's advances, push back on his suggestive remarks, but Charley was inexperienced when it came to predators like him.

"It wouldn't be all that much time, really." Liv smiled and when I didn't respond, she added, "We could get together on a couple of Saturday mornings and then I could work the rest of the time from photos."

"You're not listening to me. It's a no."

Liv reeled back. "Did I do something wrong?" All the color had drained from her face.

"I'm sorry for yelling. It has nothing to do with you." Maybe Liv wasn't the only one who needed a friend. "It's just this last week … someone's been harassing me, leaving cryptic messages and my nerves are shot."

Liv gasped. "I sensed you seemed rattled but I thought it was work. This guy—do you have any idea who it is?"

"Not a clue." I gripped the steering wheel. "So you can understand why I don't want Charley going off to a stranger's house alone."

"I'm not exactly a stranger, but of course, I get it. A stalker's nothing to fool around with. I had something like that happen to me once. This pervert wouldn't leave me alone, called me at all hours of the day and night, filled my message box up with lewd innuendos."

"What did you do?"

"I married him." Liv laughed, then put her hand on my knee, and added "Seriously. I asked a friend trained in martial arts to track him down. I didn't ask for details, but the guy never bothered me again." But in her case, Liv knew the identity of her stalker. I wasn't that lucky.

"Have you told anyone else about this?" Liv asked.

"I met with the police, but the guy hasn't done anything illegal, just phone calls and notes and a video. They opened a file and questioned the neighbors, then warned me to take precautions."

"But this guy could be a real psycho. You should carry pepper spray in your purse. Or keep some kind of weapon like a baseball bat with you in case he tries to run you off the road."

"Don't worry, I've got it under control. There's a top-notch security firm coming to my place tomorrow afternoon to beef up the alarm system, install cameras, whatever I need to keep Charley and me safe. After that, we'll see."

I'd temporarily lost sight of the black SUV, but now I spotted it four cars back. The driver moved into the exit lane. Something in my body language must have alerted Liv what was going on because she swiveled around and stared out the back window. "Is someone following us?" Her voice quivered.

"I thought so for a minute but no, we're fine."

"Don't go all ballistic on me but do you own a gun?"

I nodded. "I got one a while back but I haven't shot it in over a year."

"But you know where it is, right? And you keep it loaded?" Liv had turned deadly serious. "I keep mine in my underwear drawer. I know it's silly, but it makes me feel safer, particularly when Zach's out of town. Make sure yours is nearby. Better safe than sorry."

"I moved mine to the nightstand last week. That won't be much help if I'm downstairs but at least it's there at night."

Liv leaned back against the headrest. After a few minutes of silence, she turned in her seat and faced me. "This is crazy. When did it get to be open season on women?" Her face flushed. "When I was a kid, I never worried about someone snatching me off the street or attacking me in the park or breaking into my house while I was sleeping. There seem to be psychopaths everywhere," she yelled.

Now I regretted telling Liv about my stalker. "Trust me. The guy's picked the wrong person to bully. I'm going to find him and shut him down."

Just saying it made me feel better. I'd had enough of feeling like a victim. A target. It was time for me to take control of the situation, just like those women in the book. I had to seize back my power. And I should do it now before the threats escalated.

9

I BARELY SLEPT THAT night so when Rita told me the next morning she needed to leave early to drive her son to soccer practice, I probably over-reacted. "I thought you and your ex had worked out a schedule."

"Don got called out of town unexpectedly but it's okay. Jean's covering for me."

It *wasn't* okay. I needed to take off at three to meet the security folks and I didn't trust Jean to manage my incoming calls. One more item on my bulging to-do list. "Don't make a habit of it, okay? Don will take advantage of you if you let him."

"Got it," Rita said. "Say, are you feeling okay? Your eyes are all bloodshot. Did you have a rough night?"

You could say that. I'd spent hours staring at the ceiling, racking my brain for defendants who'd either threatened me during the initial pre-trial phase or cursed me once they were convicted. Now that I'd decided to go after my stalker myself and flush him out, I was eager to get started but also a bit overwhelmed.

I handed Rita the list I'd compiled. "Pull these records for me, will you?"

Rita scanned the page. "The older ones have already been sent down to records."

"Then put in the request before you leave. It's important. And screen my calls. I need time to work on my opening arguments in the Jansen case," I directed.

Once Rita was safely out of earshot, I called Davante. "How soon before you hear from the lab?" I'd pinned my hopes on them identifying a print and pulling up someone in the system. Putting an end to this nightmare.

"I got the results thirty minutes ago, but it's bad news. No fingerprints or hairs on either the envelope, the note, or the flash drive."

"A dead end." It had been a long shot but I hoped we'd get lucky.

"I'll drive by your house in the squad car periodically this next week. Let him know we're keeping an eye out. And Rachel? Keep me in the loop. This isn't over. This guy contacts you again, particularly if there's an overt threat, call me right away. And tell Huntley. He needs to know."

Yeah, he does. But that could wait until next week. As for calling Davante, why bother? So he could offer a kind word? Remind me to lock my doors? Tell me to carry mace in my purse and not wander alone in the park? I needed my stalker tracked down and exposed. All this well-meaning advice was useless. I needed action and I needed it now.

I startled when Rita knocked. "I know you said not to disturb you but Judge Lightfoot's clerk is on the phone. You were due to file a continuance first thing today and they haven't received it."

Because I forgot. "Put him through." I switched to my best prosecutor-in-charge voice and covered. "Greg. You're right. I had one detail I wanted to double-check before I sent over the paperwork, but it's done now. I'll call dispatch. You'll have it within the hour. Sorry about the delay."

If Huntley got wind I'd missed a deadline and pissed off a judge, he'd come down on me hard. I rifled through my files, found the brief which had been ready since yesterday and scribbled my signature at the bottom, furious that this stalker, whoever he was and whatever he wanted, had caused me to take my eye off the ball and put my career at risk.

***

Rita took off at two-thirty and I locked up my office, forwarded my calls, and rushed home to find the representatives from the alarm company already parked out front. When I let them in—a middle-aged woman and a skinny guy who had to duck to enter—I noticed a familiar scent in the entryway. Gardenia? Vanilla? I shoved the fact to the back of my mind and outlined what I needed.

When I'd made the appointment, I didn't mention my stalker, only that there'd been a burglary in the neighborhood. I gave them a brief tour of the house, then handed them a floor plan. As they trooped through, I noticed Ginger hadn't come out to greet us. That was odd. She usually barked up a storm if a stranger came into the house. She must have gone out the doggie door to the back before we came inside. Probably sleeping under a tree. Some guard dog.

The alarm people took their time. They jotted down measurements, tested the locks on all the doors and windows, and snapped dozens of photos. Meanwhile, I checked the yard for the dog but came up empty. Ditto the basement. Where could she be? It wasn't like a full-size golden retriever could simply disappear.

When the security people finished up, they circled back to me. "Your system's crap," the tall guy blurted out.

The woman, Delores according to her nametag, glared at him. "Sam can be a bit blunt, but he's right. Your perimeter isn't well lit and your door locks wouldn't stand a chance against a half-way competent intruder. Here, we'll show you."

The three of us walked to the sun porch and without a word, Sam stepped onto the patio and Delores locked the sliding glass door behind him. He then pulled out a screwdriver from his bag and in less than a minute, popped the latch and entered the house. My pulse spiked. We'd lived in this house for seven years and I'd assumed we were perfectly safe. What kind of parent was I?

"I'm speechless." I leaned against the wall. "My teenage daughter's alone in the house until I get home from work so I need to do something right away. You're the experts. What do you recommend?"

Delores handed over a brochure. "Here's our pricing schedule, showing everything from the basic security package to our top-of-the-line system," she said. "Look it over and see what works for your budget."

Budget? My insides twisted. This wasn't about money. This was my daughter's safety we were talking about. How could you put a price tag on that? Then my rational brain kicked in. Taxes were due, the dishwasher was on its last legs, and there was no telling when, or if, that dangled promotion would materialize. I sat at the counter and paged through the brochure until I found a plan I could afford. It wasn't the most expensive package, but it offered good, solid protection including several outdoor cameras and state-of-the-art locks. The alarm company had had a cancellation for the next day, and I grabbed it.

The minute the security people left, I redoubled my search for Ginger and then thought back to that scent in the foyer. Had someone broken in before I got home and let her out? Or, good lord, taken her? No, not my dog. I pulled out Davante's card but before I could dial, I heard Charley and Spencer burst through the back door, accompanied by a barking golden retriever, leash bouncing behind her on the tiles. When Charley unhooked her, Ginger trotted over for a welcoming pat.

I knelt and ruffled her fur. "You gave me quite a scare, girl."

"She was at the end of the block, tangled in Mr. Adam's bushes. It's weird, she's never gotten out before. Maybe there's a hole in the fence," Charley offered.

"I'm just glad everyone's safe." But we weren't. Not yet. Our dog hadn't escaped. She'd been let out on purpose. Someone had broken into our house, even if I couldn't prove it. One more subtle twist of the knife. This was the last straw.

Later, after Charley had gone to bed, I safeguarded the house as best I could—wedged a broom handle under the patio door and shoved an old chest against the front entrance. When I'd satisfied myself we were okay for one night, I went to brush my teeth and came to a dead stop. An icy dread flooded my body. The toothpaste was on the wrong side of the sink and my comb wasn't resting next to my brush but tucked into the plastic bin with my lipsticks and eyeliner.

That scent at the front door. Now I knew what it was—Dior J'Adore, the fragrance I wore on special occasions. The last time I'd used it was that awards banquet.

The distinctive pear-shaped bottle which generally sat on the counter had disappeared.

That could only mean one thing. The stalker had been in my bedroom today before I got home. Pawed through my things. Stolen my perfume. Let the dog out. He was toying with me. This was all part of some sadistic game.

I scanned the street from my bedroom window. Streetlamps formed speckled pools of light. No sounds. A peaceful neighborhood with friendly, law-abiding citizens. I'd always felt safe here. Now my eyes noticed every shadow, every sudden movement and I found myself wondering who might be lurking around the next corner.

Waiting.

Watching.

Wanting. But what?

10

THERE WAS NO DOUBT IN MY mind that my stalker hadn't disappeared but I did feel safer now that the security system had been installed. We had CCTV's mounted on the back porch and at the front door, motion sensors throughout the house, and an alarm that let out a piercing scream if I triggered it. The purchase had maxed out one of my credit cards but at least my daughter and I were safe in our home.

First thing Monday I went to see Huntley in his office. "You need to know about a situation I'm dealing with." I outlined the details of my stalker, emphasizing that I was handling it and it hadn't affected my work.

"I assume you've reported this to the police," he said.

"They opened a file." Fat help it was but I'd followed procedure.

"Okay. Keep me in the loop." He picked up his briefcase. "I'm due in court. Walk with me." When we reached the elevators, he turned. "Obviously I don't take kindly to a member of my team being threatened, but it comes with the territory, I'm afraid. You sound like you've got the situation under control but let me know if that changes and you need a leave of absence." He put his hand on my shoulder. "And I appreciate you coming to me. I like to keep tabs on my staff, particularly the ones I've got my eye on. Knowing you, I'm confident you won't let this personal matter interfere with your job duties."

I wasn't quite sure how to take that. On the one hand, it was gratifying to know he trusted my ability to handle my stalker on my own. Taken another way, he'd document today's conversation and put it in my file so if anything went wrong, he could cover his ass. And, by the way, if I made any slip-ups, he'd take me off the short list for the promotion and move on. In other words, every man for himself. I was shocked he wasn't more concerned but at least I knew where I stood.

Of course I didn't share any of my thoughts with him, just smiled and thanked him for his time. I had a pile of cases that needed my attention so I went back to work. I spent the morning questioning potential jurors for an upcoming rape case. At the noon recess, I ducked into a nearby coffee shop, placed my order, and stared out the window. I had to stop acting like a rabbit on the run—that had been fine in the short term but it was no way to live. It was time to stop letting my stalker call the shots. I needed to regain control, go after him for a change, maybe even set a trap. But where to start?

"Rachel Matthews? Is that you?" A man with dark-brown hair skimming his ears stood by my booth as a waitress dodged around him. Dressed in khaki pants and a tailored white shirt but no tie, he had a brown leather bomber jacket casually tossed over his shoulder.

I froze. My stalker wouldn't just appear out of nowhere and approach me in a crowded diner, would he? No, of course not. Besides, the person harassing me had to be someone I'd met. And I would swear I'd never seen this man before in my life.

"I'm sorry, but do I know you?" I said.

He gave me a disarming smile. "It's Max Wisniewski." He hesitated, then added, "You know—Elvis? From high school?"

It couldn't be. The loner with the Buddy Holly glasses who smoked cigarettes behind the gym? The guitarist who stole the talent show with "Jailhouse Rock"? The bad boy who, rumor had it, seduced one of the student teachers? The two of us had worked closely together senior year, me as editor of the school newspaper, him as staff photographer. Not only had he grown a good four inches since then, but he'd switched to contacts and his body had the chiseled look of a regular gym rat. His strong jaw, his bent nose, and his intense brown eyes gave him a certain rugged gravitas.

"Wow. Elvis. You've … changed," I managed.

"Says the still striking redhead who broke the heart of every guy at Shorewood High. Imagine running into you like this. What's it been, twenty years?"

"More like twenty-two," I said. A lifetime, in fact. "How are you?"

"Can't complain. And you? I never pictured you staying here in Milwaukee. You seemed destined for bigger things."

Most of my friends in high school had heard the story. How I'd dropped out of college and moved back home, pregnant and unmarried. Maybe Max was too polite to mention my checkered past. "I did live in Illinois for a while, but I moved back years ago. Listen, have a seat. I just ordered."

"Thanks." He slid into the booth across from me, resting his hands on the tabletop. Neatly clipped fingernails. Calloused hands. No ring.

The truth was I'd been a bit in love with Max Wisniewski when I was seventeen, though even then, young as I was, I knew he wasn't right for me. But that whiff of rebellion, that sense of danger, had intrigued me. Made me wonder *what if* more than once.

"I had a bite earlier but I have a few minutes before my next appointment so I thought I'd grab some coffee," he said.

The waitress brought my iced tea and took Max's order. He stretched his arms across the back of the booth. "So, tell me, Rachel Matthews, how'd your life turn out?" He glanced at my bulging briefcase and my tailored navy-blue blazer. "Looks like you've joined the corporate world." The grin he gave me could have melted an ice cube. And had he always had that dimple?

"I'm an assistant DA here in Milwaukee with the Sensitive Crimes division—rape, domestic abuse, sex trafficking." I unrolled my napkin and put it on my lap. "And I've got a daughter, Charley. She'll graduate high school next year."

He let out a low whistle. "Time flies, doesn't it? And Charley's father? What's he do?"

I deflected. "He's not in the picture anymore. I'm a single mom." I sipped my tea.

"Having a teenager must keep you on your toes. But hey, district attorney, that's a big deal. But then everyone knew you'd be successful, no matter what you did. You were driven."

For as long as I could remember, people had said that about me. But I hadn't realized it went back all the way to high school. Funny that's what Max remembered about me. "Do you live around here?"

"My wife and I moved back three years ago. I went straight from high school into the service, two tours of duty, then graduated from college and worked as an undercover cop in New York for eight years."

Max had been that rare teenager who didn't seem to care what anybody thought of him. He played guitar and wrote songs, thus the nickname Elvis, and took his grandmother to mass on Sundays. I could picture him infiltrating an inner-city gang and having enough swagger to pull it off.

"I'm surprised I haven't run into you before. I work with a lot of policemen."

"Oh, I'm not a cop anymore." He broke eye contact and gazed around the restaurant. There was a longer story beneath his words, one he obviously didn't want to share with me.

The waitress materialized from nowhere, slid my chicken sandwich on the table, and plunked Max's coffee down so quickly some sloshed over the lip. He didn't miss a beat, just grabbed a napkin from the dispenser and mopped up the mess, waving away the girl's apology.

"Most policemen I know get so hooked on the adrenaline rush, they can't walk away."

"It can be addicting all right." He offered a fleeting smile. "My last assignment I got shot up pretty badly so I decided to find a different line of work."

"A move back home *and* a career change. You've been busy, too." I took several bites of my potato salad. "What are you doing now?"

He rummaged through his jacket. "Private investigator. Mainly corporate fraud, some identity theft, some spying on cheating spouses. It's not as glamorous as police work but nobody's shooting at me." He smiled, finally found a card, and slid it across the table. *Max Wisniewski and Associates, Confidential Investigations.*

Was the universe pulling my leg? I needed help finding my stalker and now an experienced PI just appeared out of nowhere? But I kept my thoughts to myself for now and the two of us spent time telling stories of classmates from high school. It was the first time in weeks I'd laughed. But when the waitress brought the check, I saw I only had five minutes before I was due back in court.

"Sorry, I lost track of time. I've got to scoot. Can you deal with the check?" I laid a twenty on the table.

He pushed it away. "This one's on me. Go on. We can't have you getting into trouble."

I didn't have time to argue. Besides, I'd made a decision as Max and I talked. I'd start by asking my brother about him, then contact a few people who used him on cases. Because who better to track down my stalker? Elvis, or rather Max Wisniewski, might just have come back into my life at exactly the right time.

11

Liv had begged me several times to attend the casino party Zach had won at the auction. She said she hated company functions, felt awkward as the wife of the "boss", and could use a friend nearby. But I worried I'd be giving my stalker the perfect opportunity to make a move. I texted Liv to beg off, but she changed her story, this time indicating she'd discovered a secret about Zach involving possible embezzlement and desperately needed my advice.

Alarm bells sounded in my head. If Liv had discovered evidence of Zach doing something illegal, and he found out she knew, I wasn't sure how he'd react. Would he threaten her? Hurt her? Since Charley had plans to go to a movie with Spencer, I agreed to come, but I only planned to stay long enough to see what she had to say.

The Potawatomi complex was one of the largest tribally-owned facilities in the country, spread out over several downtown city blocks, encompassing not only five gaming tiers but a 19-story hotel, numerous top-drawer restaurants, spacious meeting rooms, and a series of inter-locking parking structures, full of dark corners for a stalker to hide. I paid extra for valet parking and once inside, I kept to well-lit areas, but even though I followed the signs, I got lost within minutes. Every floor was identical—slot machines, roulette wheels, crowded walkways, the constant buzz of overheard conversations. I wandered for fifteen minutes, only to wind up back where I'd started. The massive concrete building had poor cell reception so my messages to Liv went straight to voice mail. I finally broke down and asked for directions and it turned out I wasn't even on the right floor. After another five minutes and two wrong turns, I spotted a sign with "Burger Boy Celebration" and an arrow pointing down a long hallway. Ethan Mansfield greeted me at the entrance, giving me a wide smile.

"Hi, counselor. Liv asked me to shepherd you around until she got free. This way." He led me into an open room decorated with balloons, streamers, and other festive decorations. Easily a hundred people milled about. A rock band had set up in one corner but Liv was nowhere to be seen.

"I think we got off on the wrong foot at the awards dinner," Ethan said. "How about we start over?"

"As I remember it, I'm the one who put *you* on the spot. So yes, clean slate." I surveyed the crowd. "I've eaten the hamburgers but otherwise, I know nothing about Apollo. All these people work at the restaurants?"

"They're mainly from corporate headquarters plus a few board members. Whoops. I almost forgot." He pulled a plastic lanyard from his pocket and slipped it around my neck. "Food and booze on the house." We walked past several gambling tables, where employees were betting fake chips, and toward an elaborate buffet. I helped myself to a couple of pastel macaroons and a cheesecake petit four, along with a flute of champagne. Ethan hovered, making small talk. Maybe what Liv said was true—maybe he was interested in me. But no. Every time I glanced over, I caught him scanning the room, as though looking for someone.

The guy was hard to read. He seemed too worldly to be satisfied playing second fiddle at a hamburger franchise. What was he really doing here in Milwaukee? Did he have feelings for Liv he was trying to hide, unaware how his every comment, his every move gave him away?

I finally spotted Zach and Olivia standing side-by-side across the room with three older men in business suits, probably the board members Ethan had mentioned. Liv was stunning as usual in a black-and-white knit dress with a peplum waist. Her hair was pulled back and knotted, accentuating her fragile neck, and instead of her usual understated makeup, tonight her lips flamed bright red. Outwardly she might look cool and collected but I sensed unease beneath the façade. Her nails dug into her palms as she looked around. Something obviously had her spooked.

I turned my back to the crowd and continued to talk with Ethan, waiting for a chance to get Liv alone. All of a sudden, a hand brushed aside my hair and a male voice whispered in my ear. "I can't wait to get you alone."

I whirled and bumped straight into Zach Reid, who was lurking so close I felt his breath down my back. I pulled away and as I did, my glass jostled and my champagne splashed, soaking my skirt.

"What the hell?" My voice echoed around the room. The crowd silenced like a gun had discharged.

Zach held up his hands, feigning innocence. "Sorry, sorry. I thought you were someone else." He summoned a nearby waiter, took the serving cloth off the guy's arm, and began to pat at the front of my outfit.

I shoved his hands away. "Get off me." I gave him an icy stare, flabbergasted he had the nerve to accost me in public. "If I'm not mistaken, your *wife* is looking for you." I inclined my head toward Liv, who glared at us from across the room.

Zach gave a mock salute and stumbled away and Ethan steered me toward the buffet table. "Don't engage. He gets ugly when he's had too much to drink."

I hated uncouth men, hated it almost as much when others made excuses for them. "Why does Liv put up with him? She's a successful artist. She could support herself." I hadn't meant to share that thought, but who cared? It was true.

A nervous twitch near Ethan's eye caught my attention. "You don't understand lovely Liv. She likes money. Has ever since she was a kid. And her art doesn't bring in nearly enough to support her lifestyle."

How far back did these two go? "You knew her growing up?"

Ethan gave me a quizzical look. "I thought you knew. She's my sister."

That threw me sideways. Liv and Ethan were siblings? I thought back to the fundraiser—the two of them, heads close, laughing at a joke only they understood. I'd imagined they were lovers. Now it made sense. "I had no idea. I'm … stunned." Puzzle pieces fell into place. Liv trying to fix me up with Ethan. Their closeness. Ethan working for Zach.

"Well, technically she's my cousin. Her mother and mine were twins. After her parents died, my mom and dad adopted her and her older brother. So I think of her as my sister. And I've had a long time to observe what makes Liv tick."

"So why do you think she married Zach? I mean, do they actually love each other or …?"

The muscles in his jaw clenched. "She was infatuated at first—Zach can be quite charming when he puts his mind to it—but that wore off pretty quickly. A better question is why she stays with him. As far as I can tell, it's a marriage of convenience. She likes his money, he likes having a gorgeous, accomplished wife on his arm who tolerates his dalliances." He dropped his head. "It seems to work for them." But it was obvious he was hiding something.

I wasn't convinced the marriage was as mutually satisfying as Ethan implied. To me, it seemed like the balance of power between the two tilted strongly to Zach's side. "I could never live like that."

"You'd be amazed what some people will do for …"

I thought he was going to say *love* but instead he said "security", a note of sadness in his voice. His jaw clenched. "Liv could never tolerate being poor."

I waited for him to say more but when he stayed silent, I lobbed a question. "Her family struggled financially while she was growing up?"

"Not really. Both our mothers came from money and Olivia got a sizable inheritance when she turned eighteen. But she ran through it once she moved to New York. Clothes. Jewelry. Vacations. Nice apartment near Central Park."

I remembered my conversation with Liv that day at my house. How she's said she'd been raised to look after herself. Did that jive with the woman Ethan was describing? Deep down, was Liv just a scared little girl who craved security and thought money would provide it?

"When Zach came along, it was obvious he'd be a success and that was enough for Liv. They'd only dated six months when he proposed."

"She told me Zach bought one of her first paintings."

"Did she?" He gave me a sidelong look. "I suppose it was something like that."

"How long have they been together?"

Ethan downed the remainder of his drink in one gulp. "Too long." He stayed silent for a good minute, then turned back. "Sorry, that was flippant. This October, it'll be ten years."

"She must be a saint." I'd never put up with a douchebag like Zach, no matter how much money he had.

"It hasn't always been smooth sailing," Ethan replied. "There was a time a year or so ago when I thought she'd had enough. She told me she'd met with a divorce attorney. But I guess they made up. Like I said, Zach can be charming when he wants to be."

I probed. "Is that why you're working at Apollo, to watch out for her?"

"Liv knows I'll do whatever it takes to protect her." Ethan spoke so low, I could barely hear him over the crowd. "I always have."

Zach clinked his glass. "Attention, everyone, I've got an important announcement." The hubbub continued until someone let out a piercing whistle and finally the crowd quieted. "We planned this fancy soiree as a thanks to all of you for the long hours you've put in and your dedication to our growth. And today I got news which will put a capper on the evening. Apollo has won the Burger Boy franchise for the entire state of Illinois, including the prime Chicago market. So congratulations to us. We're now the largest franchisor in the country."

On cue, three wait staff popped open bottles of Champagne and rock music blasted through the overhead speakers. The board members took turns shaking Zach's hand while pandemonium broke out in the room, the staff hooting and hollering, a few even breaking into dance moves. Smiles were everywhere.

Except for Liv. I snuck a look at my friend and spotted rage behind that frozen façade. Then her expression morphed and she dutifully raised her glass along with the rest and flashed a grin at the crowd. Why wouldn't someone who loved money as much as Ethan implied be ecstatic at this announcement?

I turned to Ethan. "You're not surprised."

"I had a gut feeling we'd land it. This means my job's secure for the next couple of years. My counterparts at our rivals won't be so lucky."

"It's that cut-throat?"

"The Chicago market alone is worth millions. And this puts us in line to expand throughout the Midwest so yes, it's a big deal." I felt sure Ethan had played a significant role in Apollo winning the contract. And here I'd thought the DA's office was competitive.

Liv left the VIP circle and, with the precision of a drone, made a beeline to Ethan and myself. When she reached us, she turned to her cousin. "Mind if I steal Rachel away for a bit?"

"I'll mingle. See you later, Rachel."

I raised my glass and beamed at Liv. "Congratulations on the new contract."

She twirled her finger around the rim of her champagne glass. "Doesn't affect me that much. Zach's the one who controls the company." She eyed the crowd. "Anyway, lots of happy faces today. Zach does know how to work a room." Her eyes narrowed and I followed her stare to see her husband chatting with a striking redhead in a clingy wrap dress. Zach's arm encircled the woman's waist as he lifted his glass and clinked it with hers. Then he whispered in her ear, and the woman threw back her head and laughed. This must be who he'd mistaken me for earlier. Or pretended to, so he could have a bit of sadistic fun at my expense.

"Let's talk in private." Liv pulled me out of the room and into the hall. "Please don't mention this to Ethan, but I'm worried Zach's gambling again. He got involved with some scary men back in New York, but he told me he had the problem under control. Only this week I overheard two of the investors talking about irregularities in the books. Something about missing deposits. It has to be Zach. He's got access to all the bank accounts and all the purchasing transactions."

It didn't make sense. "Why would he steal from himself? Do you have any other evidence?"

"When we first got here tonight, Zach met in private with three guys from the casino. I saw their name tags."

"They could have been discussing details for the party."

"But they were acting like old friends. Slapping him on the back, all smiles, and buying him drinks. What if he's been coming here when he told me he was working late? That's what happened before. If he's run up gambling debts, that would explain siphoning money from the company. If he took it from our personal accounts, I'd know."

"What are you going to do?" I asked.

"I can't let him rack up huge IOU's again. It almost bankrupted us before. Once the fever hits him, he doesn't know when to stop. But I'm afraid if I ask him about it, he'll …"

Zach seemed like a man capable of violence if he was threatened. Liv could be in serious danger if she confronted him. "I know a lawyer who can advise you. But right now, it seems like all you've got are suspicions."

"You think I'm putting two and two together and coming up with five." She crossed her arms. "You might be right. I do jump to conclusions where Zach's concerned. It's probably nothing."

Or it might be a very big something. This marriage was like a tinderbox, ready to explode. Liv should tread carefully. "Promise me you won't confront him on your own." If, as I suspected, Zach was abusing his wife, accusing him could be dangerous.

Liv agreed and we rejoined the party, mingling with the other guests. Before long, Zach left the room, followed by the redhead a few minutes later. Either Liv was too preoccupied and didn't see them leave or she did and was pretending not to care. Twenty minutes later, the redhead returned, then quickly left. Within minutes, I saw Zach, his tie loose around his neck. He made a beeline for Olivia and took hold of her arm. "Alistair is dying to talk to you about your latest creation, darling. You know what a fan he is." Liv flinched at his touch, but immediately followed her husband to a corner where a board member stood by himself, gulping down Champagne like it was water.

"She should leave him," I whispered aloud before I had a chance to think, then realized Ethan had snuck up behind me and overheard.

"Easier said than done. All that money out the window." He raised his eyebrows. "And someone ready to take her place."

I'd seen enough high-flying corporate types slapped with sexual harassment cases to recognize a lawsuit in the making. "Entangling himself with an employee could land your company in big trouble."

"Heather's a temp, not staff, but regardless, Zach's the majority owner along with a few wealthy shareholders. None of them are likely to oust a CEO who's already made them boatloads of money and just landed a territory everyone in the franchise has been salivating over."

A petite, sandy-haired girl appeared at Ethan's elbow, balancing a tray. "Can I interest either of you in a cheese ball?"

I declined, feeling the need to get going. Charley would be home soon and I didn't like leaving her alone in the house, even with the new security system in place.

I turned to Ethan. "I need to scoot." I made a move to go but he caught my arm.

"Let me walk you out. These hallways can be confusing." That was thoughtful of him and truthfully, I was grateful. Why give my stalker a chance to catch me alone? After ten minutes of weaving down hallways, we arrived back at the front. "It was nice seeing you again," Ethan said, clearing his throat. "I'm wondering if … would you like to have dinner with me sometime?"

His invitation didn't surprise me. He'd been attentive all evening long, and I'd sensed his eyes on me. "Right now I'm really busy at work. Can I take a rain check?" It wasn't only my stalker. I didn't know how involved I wanted to get with Liv's life and Ethan seemed like an integral part of it.

"I hope you do." The valet pulled up with my car. "And Rachel? Liv's lucky to have you as a friend but watch out you don't get sucked into her problems."

So he sensed it, too. There was a ticking time bomb at the heart of the Reid's marriage. Something that could reverberate and affect me. Ethan was trying to warn me off.

Once I got clear of the casino complex and my cell reception resumed, I found a series of texts from Charley. A single message— *where r u?*—repeated every five minutes for the last half hour. My heart hammering, I punched my daughter's avatar and she answered on the first ring.

"Where have you been? I've been texting you like forever. You need to come home right now!" Her voice sounded like she'd been crying.

"What's wrong? Are you hurt? Slow down. Tell me what's going on."

"I'm okay but … there's … Just hurry, Mom. I need you."

12

WHEN I PULLED INTO the driveway, Charley tore out of the house, followed by Ginger barking her head off. My daughter's face was ugly with tears and within seconds, I saw why. Highlighted by the Camry's high beams, the word *WHORE* was smeared in lipstick-red paint across the garage door in block letters, two feet tall.

I'd had enough. Until now, this jerk had been content to hide in the shadows. Anonymous phone calls and filming my comings and goings from a distance obviously upset me, but it came with the territory. But this? Defacing my property, scaring my daughter out of her wits, broadcasting this nasty accusation for anyone to see? No way. I wanted to scream out every obscenity in the book but Charley was watching.

Wait. The new security system included a CCTV mounted at the front door. The camera would have caught this asshole in the act. Once I took the footage to the police and they ran it through facial recognition software, they might be able to identify who was behind this. Plus this was an actual crime—defacing private property. Now the authorities would have to get involved. But when I looked up, a swath of coarse brown burlap was covering the lens.

Jesus. When was I going to catch a break? "Go inside," I told Charley. Then I punched the garage door opener and within seconds, the graffiti disappeared, replaced by a view of the garage interior, including camping gear, gardening hoses, two bicycles, and a rusty snowblower. Well, better that than the expletive. I left the car parked in the driveway, went inside, and pulled my daughter into a hug.

Charley couldn't stop shaking. This hate screed had tipped her over the edge. "I didn't see it when Spencer dropped me off but then ..." Words caught in her throat when she tried to talk. "I got to the sidewalk, and I saw the paint and then when I got closer, and I read it ..." She hiccupped five times in a row, a sure sign she was way past upset and on her way to terrified. It seemed an overreaction but who was I to judge? Everyone handles fear in their own way.

I curse. She hiccups. "You're safe. I'm here now."

"But everybody in the neighborhood can see it. We have to *do* something."

"We will. But for now, it's hidden. I'll call the police and let them figure it out."

Charley sprang back like she'd been scorched. "No, you can't do that. It'll be all over the school by tomorrow." She gripped my arm. "Promise me you won't call anybody. I'll die if you do."

It took me a minute to realize she believed this vandalism had something to do with her, which made no sense. It was clearly the work of the stalker.

Or was it?

The two of us sat together on the couch and I stroked my daughter's hair as Ginger watched us from the corner, head buried in her paws. "Is there something going on I need to know about?"

Charley shook her head but continued to tremble. "I'll take care of it."

She was my daughter all right.

My parents hadn't been ones to jump in and solve my problems. When a bully tripped me on the playground, my father didn't demand he be expelled; he taught me judo. When I'd skipped my shift at Culver's to go to the beach, and my manager fired me, my parents didn't interfere. I'd learned early on that my behavior had consequences and that no one would swoop in and rescue me if I messed up. And I'd raised my daughter the same way.

I lifted her chin. "C'mon, out with it. We don't keep secrets from each other, right?" Except for that huge one I'd been keeping from her all these years. But that was a problem for a later date.

It took a good minute but finally she burst out with "there's this clique at school—The Slut Squad—and they say hateful things and whisper behind people's backs."

"They've targeted you because of Spencer?"

"What? No. Spencer and I haven't … We fool around a little but that's all."

"Then why—"

"Drop it, Mom. I said I'd handle it."

I took her hand in my own. "Honey, I know it's hard to believe but I was a teenager once and I know all about mean girls. But it's one thing to gossip in the school cafeteria; it's a different story entirely when people come to our house and vandalize our property. Have you heard of them doing anything this malicious before?"

Charley sniffed. "They spray painted Andrea's car and dumped garbage on Houston's front lawn." She reached inside the pocket of her jeans, pulled out a tissue, and blew her nose. "One of them dates Clay, this football player. I could totally see him doing this." She tucked her legs beneath her. "Mom, it has to be them. I mean, who else could it be?" In a flash, her expression changed. "Ohmigod, you think it's that creep? Like he was right in our front yard?"

"I don't know. But I'm going to find out," I said, my voice cracking. "Now go wash your face and come back down for ice cream."

We sat on the couch and spooned mint chocolate chip into our mouths while we watched the latest episode of "Dead To Me", then worked as a tag team to slap a coat of primer over the lettering. I'd hire professionals to do the final coat but for now, the worst of the graffiti was gone.

But that didn't solve the bigger problem. There was something going on at school that involved Charley, something I didn't fully understand. I might not know how to shut down a stalker but no pack of mean girls was going to get away with spreading gossip about my little girl, not if I had anything to say about it.

***

IT WAS ONE THING TO leave notes and make harassing phone calls, but if the graffiti on the garage door hadn't been the kids at school but my stalker, I'd reached my breaking point. I called two lawyer friends in the private sector who had used Max Wisniewski on assignments and they both gave him a thumbs up, as did a slew of clients on his webpage. And as a triple-check, I cornered my brother at the family barbeque at his house the next night and asked him.

"I used him a year back and he did a great job," he said, then added, "Is a defense attorney calling him as a witness? Because you won't trip him up. He's smart." Luke examined me more closely. "Hold on. That's not what's going on here, is it? I know you, sis. Level with me."

"What do you mean?" I sipped my wine and stared across the yard, avoiding his gaze.

"Charley mentioned you installed a bad-ass security system at the house. Are you asking about Max because you want to hire him personally? Is something going on I need to know about?"

There was a good chance I'd need Charley to stay with Luke if things got ugly. But before I told him about my situation, I had him promise not to snitch to Dad. Then I dumped it all in his lap, except for the garage incident since Charley had convinced me that wasn't related. He got more upset the longer I went on, pacing back and forth across the lawn, hands flexing. Luckily, Dad had retreated into the house to take a phone call or he'd be questioning the two of us about what was going on.

"It's been two weeks and you're just now telling me? What were you thinking? This is serious stuff, kiddo."

"Don't treat me like some trembling mouse fighting off the big bad wolf who should have run to my older brother for help at the first sign of trouble." I'd expected better from him. "And I *am* taking it seriously. I had a cop I know run tests but forensics turned up nothing. The Whitefish Bay police canvassed the neighbors, but again, zilch. There's nothing more they can do unless or until this guy breaks the law and I can't go on like this. It's affecting my work, it's got Charley upset, and neither of us can sleep through the night. It's time to flip the tables and hunt *him* for a change."

Luke took hold of my arm. "Wait a minute. I know guys like this. Hell, I *defend* guys like this. They don't play by the rules. If you want to catch him, you might have to break some laws yourself. Have you thought about that, Miss By-The-Book?"

"The guy's got me so spooked I can't walk down the street alone." I raised my voice. "And trust me. I don't do victim very well."

Luke crossed his arms. My stubbornness was as much a part of my personality as my work ethic so he couldn't be all that surprised at my decision. "You want to hire Max to track this guy down?"

"Hire a big, bad man to save me? Ah, that would be a no. I'm going to partner with him. I've had nine years' experience prosecuting scumbags like this. I know how they think, the mistakes they make. Between the two of us, he won't stand a chance."

"I hope you're right. Obviously, I'm here if and when you need me. Only promise me you'll be careful."

"Careful about what?" my dad asked. He'd snuck up behind us and we hadn't noticed.

I thought fast. "I signed up for a couple of dating sites and Luke was just warning me to watch my step."

Dad smiled. "Glad to see you're taking my advice. See, your old Dad isn't so dumb."

I put my arm through his. "You're the smartest man I know. Now how about those burgers? I'm famished." I winked at Luke, glad I'd told him, and also glad he had my back. Hopefully, he'd keep his mouth shut when it came to our father. The last thing I needed was the men in my life stepping in to protect me. I was perfectly capable of taking care of myself.

Wasn't I?

13

WHEN I CAME DOWN to breakfast on Monday, my daughter was at the stove, pouring pancake batter onto the griddle. "Thought I'd cook for a change." A food-spattered apron covered her knit top. "And Mom? I went to call Spence and the phone's gone. What's up with that?" She pointed to the spot where the canary-yellow handset used to hang next to the sink.

I didn't want to give Charley one more thing to obsess about so I lied. "Nobody ever calls that number except telemarketers. I figured why pay extra for it? We've got our cells, right?"

"Good *call*, Mom. Call. Get it?" She laughed at her own pun, then flipped a pancake into the air in a perfect arc. I crossed my fingers she'd put the graffiti incident behind her.

"And just so you know, I'm meeting a painter here at lunchtime," I said. "He'll have the garage door back to normal by the time you get home from school." What I didn't mention was I'd also freed up my afternoon to visit with the principal and learn about this so-called Slut Squad. Because no one was going to bully my daughter and get away with it.

***

CHARLEY BARGED THROUGH THE DOOR that evening, threw her backpack on the floor, and exploded.

"How could you DO that? I said to stay out of it." Her face was blotched and swollen from crying. "Now it's all over the school that my mother is flinging accusations around and I'm, like, a pariah. Someone broke into my locker and poured motor oil all over my stuff. You screwed up my whole life!"

Before I could get a word in edgewise, my daughter roared up the stairs to her room and slammed the door. An aching knot formed in my stomach. What happened to our nice, pleasant breakfast, our bonding over ice cream? Charley's mood swings were giving me whiplash.

Well, I wasn't going to apologize. Because I'd learned from Ms. Lauder, the principal, that my daughter was dealing with some serious shit. Not only had she failed her math mid-term, but she'd instigated a fight in gym class last Thursday with one of the seniors. Ms. Lauder hadn't considered either of the incidents serious enough to contact me, mainly because Charley begged her not to, but she'd traced the trouble back to an incident two weeks ago. During the casting call for the school musical, someone had left an anonymous note for the director, saying she should pick Charlotte Matthews for the part of Cosette because she was a bastard, too.

I climbed the stairs and knocked on her bedroom door. Silence. I knocked again. "We need to talk. I heard what happened in drama class."

She yanked open the door. "What are you talking about?"

"I know what the kids are saying. About you being … " I couldn't bring myself to repeat the word.

"Go ahead, you can say it. Bastard. That's what I am."

"I'm sorry that happened to you." I reached out but she swatted my hand away. "I'm going to have a serious talk with that teacher. I won't tolerate having you—"

Charley flinched. "No! You've done enough. I *forbid* you to go to my school. You'll make everything ten times worse." Tears streamed down her reddened cheeks. "Promise me you'll stay out of it." When I didn't say anything, she shouted again. "Promise."

I held up my hand. "Okay for now. But if these girls keep—"

Charley was through talking. She slammed the door in my face, leaving me all alone in the hallway.

Gossip was like kudzu. It didn't go away on its own but swallowed everything in its path. The teenagers at Charley's school didn't know the truth about what happened with Paul in Chicago. They'd made up their own version of the story based on innuendo and then repeated the gossip because they thought it made them look cool.

And I was the one to blame. I should have told Charley about her father and what happened to him years ago. Instead, I'd hidden the truth and bruised my daughter in places that might never heal. All because I didn't want to admit I was human. That I'd done something wrong. That I'd wanted Paul so much I hadn't cared who got hurt. I'd been careless with other people's lives and now my daughter wasn't speaking to me. I couldn't blame her.

Once Charley calmed down, we'd discuss the situation again. I couldn't outright refute the taunt—it was true in the technical sense of the word—but I could coach my daughter about how to fight back. Because saying Charley was a bastard implied she'd been a mistake. That she hadn't been wanted. And that simply wasn't true.

Because I'd wanted Charley more than anything. I'd pretty much blown up my whole life to keep her. And I'd make that same decision today in a heartbeat.

14

Tuesday morning I showed Max into a conference room near my office, and the two of us took seats on the sofa along the side wall. "Can I get you anything? Coffee? Tea?"

He held up a Starbucks cup. "Already primed, thanks."

Okay, straight to business. That was fine with me. I handed him the timeline I'd printed out with detailed notes of all the stalking incidents. Then I spent the next half hour describing everything I'd done until now, including the recent cases I'd pulled from the files. As I talked, I recalled the faces of these men. Truthfully, none of them seemed likely, but we had to start somewhere.

He didn't interrupt as I rambled on, but occasionally he circled a name or jotted down a note in the margins. Nothing seemed to differentiate those men from the rest but maybe he'd spotted something I'd missed. That's why it was good to have a partner in this.

I liked the fact he was a good listener. Most people weren't. They killed time thinking their own thoughts, patiently waiting until it was their turn to talk.

Once I finished, he stayed quiet for a few seconds, then "You're methodical."

I couldn't tell if that was a compliment or a criticism. "Is that a problem?"

"No, it gives me a clear idea of where we stand. Once we've got the suspect pool narrowed down, I can check their whereabouts against this timeline and see who we can eliminate."

"In the older cases, the men have served their time and been released. The more recent ones are still locked up, but it could be a brother or a son of one of them."

He flipped to the second page, then asked "You said you couldn't tell much about the voice, but from the sound of it they'd used some kind of mechanical device."

I nodded. "It was definitely distorted. I'm wondering if he's disguising his voice because he thinks I'll recognize it."

Max tucked the report into the worn canvas satchel at his feet. "This is a good start. I'll get back to you in a few days."

I didn't want to wait a few days. I wanted to get started right now. "Could you make this a priority? I'm glad to pay a premium if that's what it takes."

"This clown's really got you spooked, hasn't he?" Max smiled and once again, I noticed that dimple. "It's not a question of money. This is a lot of information to plow through and I've got a couple of other cases I'm finishing up." When I didn't say anything, he added. "Try not to worry. I'll start work on it today."

But I wanted this to be a team effort. Maybe if I shared a bit more, let him see how anxious I was. I stood and paced. "You know the hardest part? Why me? Why now? What does this person want?" I stopped mid-stride. "I'm starting to doubt everyone around me. Who's my ally? Who's my enemy? How can I tell one from the other? My stalker could walk right past me in the hall and I'd never suspect."

Max stood and put his hand on my arm. "Those feelings are perfectly normal. But you have to remember, this is a marathon, not a sprint. Keep some of that adrenaline in reserve or you'll never last the distance."

The standard platitudes but still, his words reassured me. "I'm usually better at keeping a lid on my feelings."

"I seem to remember that about you. Tightly wound. It's hard to live that way."

But it keeps you safe. No messy emotions muddy up your life. I'd let down my guard with Paul and look how that had turned out.

"I know you think this has to do with a case you prosecuted, and we'll certainly pursue that line of inquiry," Max continued, "but what about a personal vendetta? Studies show it's much more likely to be someone with an emotional attachment to you, like an ex-boyfriend. Anyone you dated who might still carry a grudge? You have a daughter. What about her father? Any hard feelings there?"

"No, he's not around. And I haven't dated anyone seriously for a long time." I gave a half-hearted shrug. "Actually, I lead a pretty boring life." It was hard to admit this to Max, who still remembered me as the popular girl from high school. "That's why I'm convinced this has to do with my job. If the recent cases don't get us anywhere, we can plow through these older ones."

He took in the new stack and whistled. "That's a bunch. Okay, I'll go through these as well. Now it's time for some straight talk. You need to know what you're getting into." He cocked his head. "This isn't what you want to hear, you and your analytical mind.

But there's a chance this is someone you've never even met. There are men out there who get off on controlling women, especially successful women like you. This could be as simple as you looked at him the wrong way in the grocery aisle. He could view himself as a victim. Someone who's sensitive to slights other people wouldn't notice."

"But—"

He cut me off. "Hear me out. It's impossible to tell what sets these guys off. But once the fuse is lit, nothing stops them. They operate from a different playbook than the rest of us. Laws mean nothing to them. Societal norms are meaningless. We can't approach this logically because that's not how he thinks. And you won't be able to walk away from this fight when it gets ugly. You'll have to stand toe to toe with him and do whatever's necessary. So think long and hard. Are you ready for that?"

This wasn't the world I lived in, where I followed the rules, did what was expected, and everything turned out fine. Max was talking about a world where the law couldn't protect me and my daughter. A world where all bets were off. If my stalker wouldn't stop on his own, I would have to stop him. Whatever it took.

I swallowed hard. With Max's help, I could do this. "I'm in. Let's get started."

15

THAT AFTERNOON, RITA KNOCKED on my open door. "Got a sec?"

She dropped into the guest chair, a worried expression on her face, and my stomach twisted. *Crap*. Rita had the same expression that other secretary Sandy had five years ago when she'd quit, complaining that I and a few of the other DA's treated her like a galley slave and never bothered to say thanks. I'd been hurt by the remarks but vowed to do better. I might live and breathe my job but that didn't mean everyone else had to and I'd made a real effort to treat Rita differently. But I *had* snapped at her a couple of times lately and now I had a sinking feeling that this woman I depended on was going to give two weeks' notice.

"You know how much I enjoy working with you," Rita began. "I know you're not exactly my boss, but it's no secret you're my favorite ADA. It's almost like we're a team—I handle the details, keep you on track, skip lunch if I have to so you don't fall behind. And you know how much I need this job. Don's always behind on child support and what with school expenses and my mortgage …"

I relaxed. I'd read her wrong. She wasn't quitting. She wanted a raise and was going to ask me to put in a good word with the head of the support team. "I don't have anything to do with salary decisions, but I'd be glad to talk to Janice, see if she can …"

But Rita waved the remark away. "No, no, it's nothing like that."

Wrong again. My ability to read people was slipping. "I'm sorry I've been short with you this month. I've had some issues at home, but I shouldn't have taken it out on you. It won't happen again."

Rita picked at a loose cuticle on her right thumb and sat still. If she wasn't here to ask me to intercede with her supervisor, and she wasn't angry about my temper flare-ups, what exactly was the problem? I willed myself not to look at the thick pile of reports I still had to plow through today. I should listen to Rita and stop getting distracted.

"I heard through the office grapevine the Thompson case got reassigned to Shula and I was afraid I'd done something wrong."

I didn't see that one coming. "What? No. Whoever said that doesn't know what they're talking about."

That was *my* case. Opening arguments were scheduled less than two weeks away. Huntley wouldn't turn over a trial that important to Shula without telling me. It would be the equivalent of a slap in the face.

"But I got a request from Shula to send over your pre-motion files."

How dare she go behind my back to Rita? "That can't be right. Someone's got their signals crossed. Don't send anything to Shula yet. Let me straighten this out."

Once Rita left, I called Huntley's secretary who, after some hesitation, shoehorned me into a fifteen-minute slot he had open at four-thirty. "Can I tell him what it's about?"

"Pencil in *chain of command,*" I said through gritted teeth.

***

I LEANED OVER HUNTLEY'S DESK, trying to keep my temper under control. "Let me get this straight. You're pulling me off the Thompson case and handing it to Shula without even telling me? What the …" At the last minute, I bit back the words before they spewed out. What had my mother taught me? Flies like honey better than vinegar, or some such nonsense. "Marc, I've been working on that case for months now. I've interviewed all the key players, prepped their testimony, and interfaced with our forensic experts. It's a slam dunk for a conviction. That guy's been abusing his kids and he's going down for it. Now you want me to let Shula take the credit? What gives?"

Huntley came around the side of his desk and leaned on the corner, his arms crossed. "I talked to the DA in Madison about that new trafficking case I assigned to you. He says he hasn't heard anything back."

Talk about blindsiding. "It's only been a week and I've been in court every day plus prepping for Thompson." *Plus, as you're well aware, someone is stalking me.*

"Now you don't have the Thompson trial to worry about. Hand over the files to Shula."

"What about my other cases?" I had five active files I was juggling. None as complex and time-consuming as Thompson but he wasn't going to make me transfer everything to my rival, was he?

"You can keep working them but give this new case priority. Human trafficking is high profile at the moment, the kind of exposure that makes careers. If we crack open this ring, everyone up and down the chain of command will look good. Pull in whatever resources you need and keep me in the loop." Huntley circled back and eased into his office chair, his stare boring into me. All the power in this situation rested with him and we both knew it. When I didn't move, he added "Was there anything else?"

Inside, my stomach clenched. Outwardly, I had to remain professional. There was a time to fight the battle and a time to shut the hell up. "No, sir. I understand."

I strode back to my office, heels clicking, muttering the expletives I'd swallowed down during the meeting. Shula was one-upping me every chance she got. Not only did I need to watch my back to make sure my stalker didn't sneak up behind me, but now I had to watch my flank to make sure my office nemesis didn't speed right past me and snatch up that promotion.

And why was Huntley so pissed at me? It could be like he said—I hadn't immediately plunged into the trafficking case. But something told me it had to do with my stalker. Ever since we'd talked about my situation, he'd been cool to me. And here I'd considered him an ally. You just never know.

16

THE WEEK WENT BY with no word from either the stalker or from Max. Was it too much to hope for that my harasser had tired of this game and moved on? I was mired in discovery motions on a case where a waitress had been stalked for months before her assailant finally raped her. Every piece of evidence, every lab report, every witness statement reminded me of my own vulnerable position. Why weren't there more safeguards in place to protect women from these predators? At least I had weapons to fight back—financial resources, knowledge of the law, and contacts in the system. What about girls like this, barely nineteen, who'd gone to the police and been told, as I had, there was nothing they could do?

I grew increasingly frustrated about not hearing from Max. I wanted to work in tandem with him and was upset he wasn't keeping me in the loop. By Friday, I lost patience and called him.

When he told me he was actively following up on leads and was in fact questioning a suspect that evening, I asked if I could go along. I couldn't sit around doing nothing. And maybe my being there might rattle the guy.

After work, I drove home, dropped off my briefcase and laptop, and changed into more casual clothes. Max picked me up, and the two of us drove thirty miles south of the city to the outskirts of Racine to question Stanley Perkins, one of the people on my initial list. A former high school physics teacher, he'd been arrested two years before on charges of raping a young nurse and I'd been the lead prosecutor. The case had attracted media attention, and although Perkins had been released after only six months when another man confessed, his wife had left him in the interim, he'd lost his job, and he'd been forced to take the only employment he could find as a fry cook at a local diner.

Max and I entered the family-style restaurant and explained why we'd come, and the manager led us to a small office in the back. Minutes later, a middle-aged man, slight in stature with wire-framed eyeglasses, appeared in the doorway. "The boss says you wanted to see me?" Then he spotted me in the corner. "You again. Haven't you done enough?" He took a step toward me. "Look, lady, give me a break. I'm trying to put my life back together again here. I can't afford any trouble."

Max stepped between us. "We just want to ask you a few questions."

Perkins stood his ground. "That's what the police said back then, too. *We're just asking questions.* Next thing you know I'm handcuffed and on my way to jail. So, excuse my skepticism."

"We're trying to track down a person who's been harassing Ms. Matthews here. Can I ask where you were on Monday, March 13th of this year?"

"Are you a cop?"

Max flipped open his license. "Private investigator." Perkins looked jittery but didn't say anything. "Look, we're not looking to get you into trouble. Help us out and we'll cross you off our list. Otherwise, we'll have to question your neighbors, your co-workers, anyone who can give us information on your schedule last month. What kind of car do you drive?"

Perkins glanced toward the door. "Keep your voice down, will you? I told you, I'm not the one you're looking for," he pleaded. "Sure, Ms. Matthews here helped ruin my life, but she wasn't the only one. My wife testified against me. The principal at the high school fired me. That witness picked me out of a line-up. That reporter made me into the fall guy in his column. Plenty of blame to go around. But that's no way to live. I've moved on."

"You haven't answered my question," Max said.

Perkins gave in. "I drive a red Ford pick-up that's on its last legs. And I work every Monday from lunch hour straight through until closing. Check with the boss if you don't believe me." He stared at me. "I'm sorry someone's harassing you but it isn't me. I honestly haven't given you a second thought since the day I left that courtroom. Now please, I need to get back to work or I'll lose my job."

We left the diner and dissected the interview in the car. "He's not our man," Max said. "He's intelligent enough, but he holds a grudge against a whole slew of people, not you in particular. And he's got an alibi for the night you found the note."

"I agree. We can check him off the list." I was trembling. I hadn't prepared myself for the trouble I'd caused that man. I rested my head against the side window.

"Hey, you all right?" Max asked as we sped north on the freeway, the traffic more congested than usual for a Friday evening. A light rain had started and he turned on the wipers.

Max was as good a sounding board as anyone. He knew about the stalker plus we had history. "I think I'm having an existential crisis," I confessed.

He chuckled. "Aren't we all? What's yours about?"

"That man's got me thinking about how little I know about what happens to the people I prosecute after the trial's over. If they're found guilty, I congratulate myself on protecting society from the bad guys and move on." I turned sideways in my seat, facing him. "But what if I convict them and they're actually innocent? Take Perkins. I helped mess up his life. And he didn't really do anything wrong except be in the wrong place at the wrong time."

"You're being too hard on yourself. You said, 'what if I convict them?' But you don't decide their guilt or innocence. That's for the judge and jury."

I shook my head. "You'd get along great with my dad. He says lawyers are nothing more than hired actors in a play he calls *The Trial* and our only job is to know the law and present the facts that support our case. If we start manipulating evidence or witnesses because we know the *real* truth, the whole production might as well shut down."

Max smiled. "You don't see it like that, I take it."

"It's a pretty convenient way to let myself off the hook," I shot back. "I mean, how many innocent people are sitting behind bars because I spun a better story than the defense?"

How many times had I gotten it wrong? How many lives had I damaged in the course of just 'doing my job'?

"You don't get to be our age without carrying around a lot of guilt over the people you've hurt, whether it's on the job or in your personal life," Max said. "When I was undercover, I met guys who were basically good people, but they'd fallen in with the wrong crowd. Did the fact I gave evidence against them ruin their lives? I suppose so. Do I feel guilty because I got them to trust me? No, because I thought back to that little girl without a father, the kid killed in a drive-by, the senior citizen in a wheelchair because of a home invasion. The real victims."

He had a point. "I like to think I'm one of those good people you talked about. But I must have injured my stalker. I wish I could figure out who it is so I could make amends."

Max put on his turn signal and moved into the outer lane. "It'd be nice if we had a time machine, wouldn't it? We could beam ourselves back and correct all our mistakes."

"What would you change if you could?" I asked.

He took his time answering. What decisions had Max made along the way that he regretted? Finally, he replied. "Honestly? Nothing. I chose the path I'm on with my eyes wide open. It'd be a waste of time to second guess myself now. You?"

"It's complicated." I rolled down the window and stuck my head out to breathe the fresh air, as memories of Paul surfaced. His death had haunted me during my pregnancy and for months after, but between 2 a.m. feedings, final exams, and the weight loss I could ill afford, the wound had scabbed over. I'd focused on the present, planned for the future.

And buried the past.

So why, after eighteen years, had so many memories of Paul begun to resurface? Did I still feel guilty about that time in my life?

If I crawled into a time machine and set it back to 2002, would I still trade shifts with Amy that Thursday? Would I still chat up that stranger in the bookstore and accept his offer of dinner? Would

I still share my love of poetry that first night? Small decisions but they altered the course of my life. There was before Paul.

And there was after.

*****

WHAT COULD BE MORE ROMANTIC than meeting the love of your life in a used bookstore? I worked part-time at the one near campus to earn money to supplement the monthly stipend my parents sent. And I loved the idea of spending hours surrounded by the great minds of literature, each one offering me a glimpse of what life might be like outside my isolated little bubble.

I noticed him right away because who wouldn't? A tall, broad-shouldered man, handsome in a rugged cowboy way, hair the color of wheat, picking up book after book from the Local Authors table, flipping to the back to read the bio, then moving on to the next. I approached him. "Looking for anything in particular?" I asked. I wasn't flirting. It was my job to make book recommendations, to turn browsers into customers. But I have to admit, I liked having the excuse to chat up this rather interesting-looking man.

"A fresh perspective," he replied, flashing me a brilliant smile, a twinkle behind his eyes. "Any suggestions?"

"Literary or plot-centric?" When he said he preferred character-driven stories, I retreated to the fiction shelves, pulled out Robert Pirsig's "Zen and the Art of Motorcycle Maintenance" and Raymond Carver's "What We Talk About When We Talk About Love", two books I knew men his age often bought, and held them out like an offering.

"Ah, yes, good old Raymond. Not for me. But it's been years since I read the other one. Probably time to revisit it and see if being older makes a difference." He tucked Pirsig's book under his arm. "Any chance you've got something by Paul Ostoff? He's a local author I follow."

"Let me look." I walked one aisle over, ran my fingers along the spines until I came to the -O- section. "Here's one. 'Tennis At Half Past'. I haven't run across him before. What kind of stuff does he write?" I flipped to the back like he'd done, saw the author photo, and did a double-take. "Oh." I blushed.

He laughed. "Sorry, I couldn't resist. Puffed up of me, I know, but it still gives me a thrill."

I found my voice. "If I'd written a book, I'd tell everyone—friends, teachers, strangers on the street. Clerks in stores." I gave him my best smile. "So is this your only book?"

"My debut was called 'Reckoning', about my stint in the Air Force. And I'm working on a third but trust me, no one's waiting with bated breath for me to finish it."

I cocked my head and felt my heartbeat quicken. "I'm sure that's not true, Mr. Ostoff."

"Mr. Ostoff makes me sound a hundred years old. Call me Paul, please. And you are?"

He wasn't wearing a wedding ring. Otherwise, I'd never have accepted his dinner invitation. And by the end of the evening, it was too late.

I still had that unfinished manuscript at home. Every once in a while, when loneliness crept in and I couldn't sleep, I'd take it out and read a few pages.

And think about fate and chance encounters and how different my life might have been if I'd never told Amy I'd take her shift.

17

WE GOT BACK TO Milwaukee around six-thirty and Max asked if I'd like to come to his place for dinner so we could discuss our next steps. Charley was spending the night at Jessica's—we'd discussed it only that morning. And it was just as well. We could use some time apart. Our interactions had been strained ever since I'd visited her school.

"Sure your wife will be okay with you springing company on her at the last minute?" I'd wanted to get more involved in the investigation and this was my chance but I didn't want to impose.

"Actually …" Max swiped a hand across his face. "I'm divorced. I should have made that clear the first day, but I wasn't sure how to work it into the conversation."

The news took me aback and I wondered why. Had I liked the fact Max had a wife, that my relationship with him would be purely professional, that any rekindled attraction between us would be off the table? Now all that had changed. "Was this recent?"

"Last year." He didn't elaborate and I sensed it was a sore topic so I didn't press. He drove thirty minutes west of town to the Delafield area, an outer suburb Milwaukee locals referred to as Lake Country. Once we exited the freeway, he drove north several miles, made a couple of turns, and pulled onto a small, secluded parcel of land. "Here we are."

I'd been expecting a modest ranch house but instead Max lived in a rustic redwood A-frame, with peaked roof and massive windows on three sides. The first floor had a main living area, kitchen, and dining nook, with a master bedroom and bath off to the side. Max pointed out two skylights high up in the ceiling and an upstairs loft which served as both a home office and spare bedroom and bath. Old growth forest grew right up to the sprawling back deck which ran the length of the house. A small footprint but it had all a single person needed to live comfortably.

"Fabulous space." I soaked in the laid-back vibe.

"I hired a couple of sub-contractors along the way but I did most of the work myself. The land has been in my family for years but no one ever did anything with it. Make yourself at home. I'll see what I can scrounge from the fridge."

I took off my raincoat and hung it on a hook inside the front door, dropped my purse there as well, and stood in the center of the room. There was something about the airiness and openness of the floor plan that I loved but at the same time, with the lights blazing and the darkness outside, I felt uneasy, exposed. "Doesn't it ever make you nervous knowing anyone can see right into the house?"

He stopped short. "Sorry, I should have realized." He hit a button on a control panel on the kitchen backsplash and within seconds, opaque blinds slid down and covered the windows. "Better?"

"Normally it wouldn't bother me, but …"

"Hey, you've got a stalker. You're allowed," he replied.

I soon discovered that not only was Max handy with a hammer and nails, but he was also quite the cook. In fifteen minutes, he'd whipped up a pasta dish with shrimp, mushrooms, and broccoli in a cream sauce, filled a basket with fresh bread he'd baked himself, and poured two large glasses of chilled white wine. It was the best-tasting meal I'd had in weeks, not to mention how enjoyable I found his company. Max was a natural storyteller. During our high school years, while I'd been cramming for tests on Saturday nights, he'd ridden his motorcycle downtown and hung out with jazz musicians. I relaxed as the meal went on, sitting back, sipping wine. Gone was my constant ruminating about my cases, my career, my stalker. Instead I let the atmosphere wash over me as soft music played in the background and Max's rich baritone filled the space.

But once we'd cleared the plates, Max said we should get back to work. I reluctantly agreed, a bit disappointed to lose the mellow vibe. We carried our wine glasses to the living room, settled side by side on the couch, and talked through the research Max had done to date. "I'm afraid it's bad news. Every person in these files has something that eliminates them. Either they're still locked up or they've moved out of state, or like Perkins, they've got an alibi for the day you got that note. Not to mention they don't fit the profile. My gut tells me the person behind this vendetta is clever. He's teasing you, giving us very little information, taking care not to attract too much attention. There's a cunning here that doesn't jive with any of the guys in these cases."

"I'm obsessed with the *why*. What's he getting out of all this? What does he want? What did I do to make him so vindictive?"

"We might never know that. Like I said before, it could be something buried in your past, an event you think of as insignificant. That's why these cases are so hard to solve."

We went back over the same ground we'd covered before. The progression of events, from the first phone call to the delivery of the video. "The harassment has stopped ever since I hired you. Do you think he's given up?"

"I'd love to say yes, but I'd be lying. I think he's got something bigger planned and he's biding his time, making sure everything's set. He's got your attention, knows you've hired outside help, so now he's switched to a long game. He's being patient. Waiting. Like a cat crouched in front of a mouse hole."

A shiver crawled up my spine. "Frankly, the constant tension's got me pretty frazzled. My boss reprimanded me once already about neglecting my work, took me off a big case and gave it to another attorney. He didn't say it was because of my stalker but …" I paused, then added, "I'm on tenterhooks all the time and both Charley and I are having trouble sleeping."

Max took a sip of wine. "Look, we've gone through your old cases and found zilch. Let's go back to the beginning. Is there someone closer to home who has a beef with you? A jealous co-worker? A friend you had a falling out with? A neighbor you argued with?"

"I barely know my neighbors. As for my co-workers, we're all hyper-competitive but I can't see any of them taking office politics this seriously." Shula sprang to mind, but even though I knew the woman wanted the promotion as much as I did, I couldn't imagine her implementing this elaborate plan just to eliminate an office rival.

I swigged the last mouthful of my wine. *Was* there someone in my life that hated me enough to do this? Someone I interacted with on a daily basis who harbored a grudge against me for a slight I'd done to them and didn't even remember? I shook my head, frustrated at having no more leads to suggest. "What now?"

"There's no point in going through any more case files. Perkins was the last of the bunch and we agree he's not the guy. My gut tells me this isn't anyone connected to your work. Either he's someone random, someone you don't know, who's getting his kicks out of watching a high-profile prosecutor squirm, or …" He trailed off.

My pulse hammered in my ears. "Or what? Go ahead. Say it."

He stared hard at me. "Or he's much more dangerous. He knows you, he enjoys playing with you, and he's not going to stop. He's got a plan and he's executing it with methodical precision. We've only got two choices. Wait until he makes a mistake. Or set a trap for him."

A knot of terror wedged behind my lungs. I'd assumed this stalker was driven, obsessed, maybe mentally ill. But the person Max was describing wasn't only disturbed. He was calculating and clever. He knew exactly what he was doing. Goose bumps popped on my arms.

"And it's possible his hatred of you has been growing for a while. I'm talking five, ten, even twenty years. So I'm going to press a bit here. What happened to you after high school? You went to Northwestern but I seem to remember you dropped out. Something about an older guy?"

I nodded. "Paul Ostoff. He came back to school to get an MFA. He was married."

A tender look crossed Max's face. "He's Charley's father?"

I nodded, eyes welling up.

Max stood and paced the room. "I know you don't want to believe it, but we should consider the possibility that he's the one harassing you."

"He's not," I insisted.

"You can't know that. He could have gotten a divorce and now he wants you back in his life. He might even want joint custody, want to have a relationship with Charley, and he's here in town to—"

I broke in. "He's dead." No sooner were the words out of my mouth than the painful memories flooded in.

We'd been on the phone together, Paul driving back after asking Natalie for a divorce. All of a sudden, he screamed, and that was followed by a series of deafening sounds that lasted several minutes—brakes squealing, glass shattering, horns blaring. I couldn't figure out what was happening. I shouted his name, shouted how much I loved him over and over until finally the phone went dead. I don't know how long I sat there. Stunned. Numb. Zoned out.

Finally, I crossed the room in a daze, switched on the TV, and watched as breaking news scrolled across the bottom of the screen. "Thirty-car pile-up on the Kennedy Expressway. Number of fatalities not yet confirmed. Stay tuned for further details."

My mind must have shut off. I remember stumbling to the shower, where I stripped off my clothes, and stood under the scalding water screeching until my voice gave out. I pounded the tiles so hard, my fists bled, then I curled into a fetal position on the floor of the shower, steam burying me.

At the same moment I'd answered Paul's phone call, the neighbor next door had ordered a pizza. When the delivery boy arrived, he misread the apartment number and rang my doorbell instead. I crawled out of the shower, wrapped myself in a towel and answered, eyes swollen, hair dripping water onto the carpet. He took one look, laid the pizza box in the hallway, and silently held out his arms.

Once I ran out of tears, he left. I never knew his name. I never saw him again.

"Charley's father was killed in a car accident before we knew I was pregnant." I took comfort in the fact my voice was the last one he'd heard. That he'd known he was loved.

Max reared back. "Oh, shit. I'm sorry. I didn't know."

"Of course you didn't." I squeezed my eyes shut. When I spoke again, I avoided his gaze. "The only thing I have left of Paul is my daughter. I raised her, provided for her, tried my best to be both mother and father to her. I put my personal life on hold that day and I never restarted it." I sighed. "I'm not complaining. It was my choice. I'm settled, content, comfortable. But I can't help feeling something's missing. I just don't know what it is."

I was lying. I knew exactly what was missing and everyone, including my father and my friends, knew too. Through the years, I had had a series of low-key, manageable relationships, some with men I might have let myself care about, but there was always a reason not to take that final step. One was separated but not yet divorced, and I kept worrying we'd run into his wife and she'd cause a scene. Another had younger children and I worried how Charley would feel in a blended family. The latest one was extravagant and made me laugh, but he worshipped me too much. I'd gotten used to being single—in fact, enjoyed it most of the time. It was only when I thought about the future and whether I'd grow old alone that I felt a hitch in my throat and wondered about the decisions I'd made.

"I think it's time for a break." Max went to the refrigerator, retrieved another bottle of wine, and poured me a generous glass.

"Hey, I almost forgot. I've got a surprise for you. Be right back." He bounded upstairs to the loft.

I slipped off my shoes, nestled back against the sofa, and tucked my legs beneath me. I ran my hand over the suede cushions, so soft to the touch. It was cozy here, away from the noises of the city. Away from my daily clashes with Charley. Away from the constant worry that the next person I encountered wanted to hurt me. I closed my eyes as an owl hooted in the distance and frogs croaked from a nearby pond.

"Where'd you go, roadrunner?" I opened my eyes to see Max standing over me.

I laughed. "No one's called me that since high school." I'd earned the nickname as the star runner on the track team as well as the fact I did every assignment at full throttle. Come to think of it, I still did. Patience had never been one of my virtues.

Max's eyes caught mine. "Has anyone ever told you you've got a great laugh?"

Not for years. Paul was forever telling me jokes, tickling my feet, playing pranks. It felt nice to laugh again. I noticed Max's hand behind his back. "What have you got there?"

"I found this in an old box in the garage when I was moving stuff around." He plopped down beside me and handed me our yearbook from Shorewood High School, Class of 1996.

I fist-bumped him. "Go, Greyhounds." For the next hour, we paged through our shared history while finishing the second bottle of wine. Debate team. Chess club. One picture showed me handing off the baton to my teammate during the 400-meter relay race.

Max flipped to a page he'd dog-eared. "Remember the senior play? Everyone said you were the next Meryl Streep." I'd played Kate in *The Taming of the Shrew*. I'd forgotten how fun that had been, trading barbs and insults in Shakespearean pentameter.

Suddenly I understood why Charley was so excited about the school production.

"What's your best memory from senior year?" Max asked.

I thought back. "Probably prom night. The dance was fun of course, but then strolling along the beach afterwards, sitting around the bonfire, chowing down breakfast at George Webb's at three in the morning. My dad grounded me for a week but it was worth it. How about you?"

"I didn't go to prom. The girl I wanted to ask already had a date. One of those regrets we talked about earlier." He retreated to the kitchen and came back with a bowl of chocolate-covered pretzels. He bowed at the waist. "May I offer the fair lady dessert?"

As I stared at Max, I couldn't help thinking of myself at eighteen. Before college, before Paul, before Charley. Was that where I'd taken a wrong turn?

A sudden longing flared in me. I wanted so badly to be touched. I wanted to be that girl again, the girl with her whole life ahead of her. As if he'd read my mind, Max picked up a remote from the coffee table, pushed a button, and within seconds, the strains of "Love Me Tender" echoed off the walls. He swayed, mouthing the words, then held out his hand. "Still remember how to dance?"

Should I take a chance? This was probably a mistake. Max worked for me. He was fresh off a divorce. I was comfortable being single. But somehow right here, right now, none of that seemed important. I stood, crossed the room, and walked into his arms.

He smelled of sandalwood and pine, a masculine scent that set my nerves on fire. "Brings back memories, doesn't it? Ah, to be that young and innocent again," he whispered in my ear. He pulled back and stared into my eyes. "It may have taken two decades, but I finally got my dance with you." My body pushed against him and he leaned down, his lips almost touching mine when—

Nausea flooded my throat and the room spun. I squeezed my eyes shut, willing the queasiness to go away but that only made it worse. "Sorry," I blurted and rushed to the bathroom where I vomited into the toilet, sweat rolling down my face. I stayed bent over for minutes, then gulped down fistfuls of water from the tap. Once the walls stopped spinning, I stumbled to the doorway to find Max standing a foot away.

He reached out and gently touched my arm. "Are you okay?"

"Too much wine," I croaked. "I should go home. Are you okay to drive?"

Max shook his head. "I've had too much, too. I'll call you an Uber." He gave me a sheepish look. "Or you could sleep here and I could drive you back tomorrow."

A deep lethargy overwhelmed me. How nice it would be to collapse right where I stood. But I hesitated. "I don't know …"

"I fix a mean breakfast omelet. And tomorrow's Saturday. No work. You can take my bed and I'll crash upstairs." When I didn't answer, he added, "You're tempted, I can tell."

The morning after my first overnight at Paul's, *he'd* made me an omelet. It had seemed like such a grown-up thing to do, make love the night before and wake up and fix the woman you loved an omelet out of leftovers in the kitchen.

Charley was safe at her friend's and I couldn't keep my eyes open. The stress of the last few weeks had caught up with me.

"Any chance you've got an extra toothbrush?"

18

I stripped down to my underwear, crawled between the sheets, and pulled the cottony-soft duvet up to my chin. As I lay on my back, eyelids heavy, the soft glow of the moon shone through the window and the occasional cloud cover threw dancing shadows on the wall. I heard footsteps upstairs, then the sound of the shower, and finally the creak of bedsprings as Max settled in for the night.

Running into Max had been a fluke but I had to admit, he'd entered my life at exactly the right time, a lifeline when I needed one most. But tonight, something had shifted. We weren't just colleagues anymore. I'd opened up to him, shared intimate details of my life. These last few days, I'd found myself thinking of him at odd moments, remembering him in high school, wondering what happened between him and his wife to split them up. Was something really going on between the two of us? Or was I so lonely that any kind gesture from a man magnified in my mind into something more?

I closed my eyes. Between the dangling job promotion, my sadistic stalker, and my rebellious daughter, I had enough complications in my life right now without adding in a romantic entanglement. No matter how nice he smelled. Luckily nothing had gone too far tonight. Probably for the best.

***

THE NEXT MORNING I WOKE to the sound of birdsong outside the window. Too early. Much too early. I pulled the covers over my face and repositioned the pillow. Wait. Why was the pillowcase dark blue, instead of green and white stripes? I threw back the sheets. Why was I in my underwear instead of my pajamas? Then last night's fiasco roared back—the music, the dancing, my dash to the bathroom. God, what had I been thinking? When I sat up, my head throbbed, not to mention the furry animal who'd burrowed under my tongue and died there. I stumbled to the bathroom, washed myself, brushed my teeth, then threw on the scruffy navy-blue robe I found behind the door. Careful not to wake Max, who was snoring up in the loft, I padded to the kitchen and brewed a pot of strong black coffee. Last night's dishes were stacked in the sink, so I rinsed them and loaded them in the dishwasher. Once the coffee was ready, I poured myself a mug, added in cream and sugar, and settled on the couch.

The yearbook was still on the coffee table and I paged through it again, this time pausing at my senior picture. *Most likely to succeed.* Had I done that, succeeded? Or was I merely a frenetic, driven woman, running pell-mell toward an out-of-focus finish line, never stopping to wonder if the reward at the end would make me happy? Was my dad right, that I needed to stop focusing on my professional life and take a good, hard look at my personal life instead?

Someone knocked at the door. Should I wake Max or ignore whoever it was and hope they went away? The person knocked again, more insistently this time. "Max? Max, are you in there? Wake up." It was a female voice.

I cinched the robe tighter and padded over, mug still in my hand. A brunette around my age stood on the front stoop, red in the face. "Who are you? And where's Max?" she demanded, peering around me into the living room.

"I … We …" It was still early. My brain wasn't working on all cylinders yet.

The woman scanned my face, took in my bed head and the fact I was standing there in an oversize robe, no makeup and no shoes, at seven in the morning. "Late night, huh?" Her eyes narrowed. "Where is he?"

Our voices must have woken Max because suddenly he was standing barefoot behind me in ratty sweatpants and a Packer T-shirt. "I'll take it from here, thanks." He pushed past me, stepped outside, and shut the door behind him. My curiosity got the better of me and I peered through the blinds as Max and this woman talked in the driveway.

It didn't take a genius to figure out this was Max's ex-wife Michelle. From what I could overhear, Michelle's father had collapsed and they'd rushed him to St. Luke's the night before. Max was close to his ex-father-in-law, so Michelle thought he'd want to know, and when he hadn't returned her phone calls last night, she'd stopped by to tell him. Max didn't say much, just nodded and tried to hug her. But Michelle pushed him away. I cracked open the window in time to hear her parting comment. "I see you've traded in the skinny blonde for a redhead. God, you're such a player." Her tires squealed as she peeled out of the gravel driveway.

I stepped away from the window and scurried to the bedroom to get dressed, that last remark etched in my brain. I dodged a bullet last night. I could so easily have found Max beside me in bed this morning if alcohol hadn't gotten the better of me. And the last thing I needed right now was to get involved with a man who had first cheated on his wife, then dropped his next girlfriend, and was now making moves on me.

***

I PASSED ON BREAKFAST, SAYING I needed to get home to check on Charley and the two of us stayed quiet during the ride back. Max's hands gripped the steering wheel like a life preserver and I stared out the window, replaying the night before. I'd let down my guard. That was a mistake.

As soon as we reached my house, I sprang from the car and punched in the garage code. Max left the car running and followed. "Michelle didn't take our breakup well."

I wasn't interested in hearing the details. Max and I were colleagues, nothing more. Any fantasy I'd entertained last night was the result of too much wine, too much nostalgia, and too many years of being alone. In the cold light of morning, I felt foolish for being so needy. "We should keep our eyes on the task at hand. Let's touch base again on Monday."

He didn't argue. "I understand. And just for the record, I make it a policy not to get involved with my clients. So I'm fine with keeping this strictly professional."

If that's what he needed to tell himself to salvage his ego, fine. But I knew he'd pulled out all the stops last night to seduce me.

Soft music. High school memories. Two bottles of wine. Dance moves. I'd been at this game awhile. I knew how it worked. Max might be sexy, smart, and available, but I needed to stick with the program. Find my stalker. Shut him down.

The rest was noise.

19

"Charley? Are you back?" When I looked out the window, I spied Ginger sleeping under the big oak in the yard. With my head pounding and my stomach growling, I prayed my daughter was still at Jessica's so I wouldn't have to explain why I never made it home last night.

No such luck. Footsteps echoed from the second floor, followed by my daughter's appearance at the foot of the stairs, decked out in her usual torn jeans, slouchy t-shirt and … "What have you done to your hair?" I cried out.

Overnight, Charley's golden locks had turned pink. Not soft pink like a newborn's skin. Fluorescent Day-Glo pink like a swirl of cotton candy.

"Jessica's is lime green." She spun around. "Do you like it?"

"I most certainly do not. You look like a flamingo." I massaged my temples and didn't even try to hide my exasperation. "Go upstairs and wash it out."

"It's my hair and I can do what I want with it. You're not the boss of me."

Why was she yelling? My head was splitting. "I'm your mother and as long as you're living in my house, I make the rules." What would a college admissions officer think if Charley showed up with pink hair? They wouldn't take her seriously.

My daughter stood three feet away, hands on hips, looking like a petulant two-year-old. "And what about you? Sneaking in at eight in the morning, wearing the same clothes as yesterday. Hot date?"

"I'm not even going to dignify that with an answer." I needed her to be quiet. I also needed to find some aspirin.

"You get to interfere in my life but what you do is off limits?" Charley grabbed a banana from the counter, peeled it halfway, and took a bite. "Well, fuck that."

My hands curled into fists. "Go to your room right now, Charlotte Emily Matthews, and do not come down until you're ready to apologize for using that kind of language with me."

"You can't make me." She glanced at the clock. "Besides, Spencer's picking me up in like ten minutes. We've got rehearsals."

I did my best to stay calm. "You got the part? You didn't tell me."

"You haven't exactly been around. Between traipsing off to the casino last weekend and spending the night with your new friend, I've been pretty much on my own." She tilted her head. "Anyway, the play's in six weeks so it's crunch time." She finished the banana and threw the peel in the garbage can under the sink.

I was still working on my response when Charley went on. "And just so you know, instead of going to university, I'm looking into drama schools." Her phone dinged and she snuck a peak at the text message. "Liv says she's friends with a guy who runs a program in New York and she can—"

My irritation ratcheted up. "When were you talking to Liv?"

"On Saturday when I posed for her. She's doing a bronze of me for her art show."

I grabbed my daughter's arm. "Was Mr. Reid there when this was going on?"

"Mom, ease up. You're hurting me." She yanked away. "Besides, what do you care?"

"Answer my question. Was Zach Reid there? Did you see him?"

"We were in Liv's studio and he wandered in to watch. What's your problem?"

I put the pieces together and my temper flared. "Hold on. You posed for Olivia last Saturday? Wasn't that when you had that study class for the SATs?"

"I don't need to study for an exam if I'm not going to college."

"You *are* going to college. Where did this hair-brained idea of becoming an actor come from? You never mentioned wanting to study drama before. You said you wanted to be a lawyer like your grandfather. Like me." The ice maker rattled a dozen cubes into the bin, and I pressed my hand to my throbbing forehead.

"Maybe I changed my mind. Ever thought of that? I mean, all you do is work, work, work. Maybe I want to enjoy my life, not spend it buried in reports and paperwork. Besides, law school takes three years, and that's after four years in undergrad. I'd be like old by the time I got out. I told Liv how much I love being in the musical, letting out my creative spirit, and she told me to go for it, that being an artist is the best career in the world. You get to hang out with free thinkers, people who aren't afraid to be weird, people who don't believe in all the *rules* society tells them to follow."

My back stiffened. Rules were there for a reason. Society couldn't function without them. If nobody followed the rules, civilization would disintegrate into chaos. And where did Olivia get off, encouraging my daughter to flaunt the norms? Her own life was hardly the stuff of dreams. I would damn well tell my new *friend* to stop sticking her nose into Matthew family business.

Now that my daughter had gotten started, she apparently had a lot more to say. "Or maybe I'll take a year off after high school. Travel overseas, have adventures, experience life." With this last statement, she flung her arms wide, a broad grin on her face. "I mean, if I don't sink my teeth into life now and suck all the juice out of it, when will I ever get this chance again?"

If only Charley would stop jabbering. Where had she gotten all these platitudes? She sounded like an informercial for some kooky new-age cult. Life wasn't about having fun, about going on adventures. Life was about setting goals, working hard, and earning a living so you could support yourself and your family. My mouth tightened into a thin line. "What you're saying is nonsense. What if everyone decided to *go off and find themselves?*"

Charley hopped on a barstool. "Not everyone is brave enough," she said with a flounce of her pink hair.

Meaning what? That *my* life was dull and boring? That in Charley's eyes I had chosen the safe route, settled for an ordinary life rather than being bold and daring? "You think it's brave to throw away your schooling, your future, and travel around the world with no goals? What would you do for cash?"

"I figured I'd use the money in my college fund."

Over my dead body. I hadn't scrimped for years so my daughter could take my hard-earned savings and spend it on some wild, harebrained trip around the world. "That's not going to happen. Those funds are there to pay for your education."

Charley rested her chin on her hands. "Didn't you ever want to say screw the rules, screw what I'm supposed to do, I'm going to follow my heart?"

Yes, I had, and the result was the teenager standing in front of me, spouting nonsense. "Okay, enough. I don't know where you got these crazy ideas, but you're not using your college savings to traipse around like a vagabond. You're not becoming an actor. You're not *following your muse* or whatever they call it nowadays. You're going to take your SAT's and go to university and stop driving over to Zach and Olivia Reid's house. And you're going to go upstairs right this minute and wash your hair."

"I HATE YOU!" Charley screamed. She grabbed her backpack and sprinted out the front door instead, slamming it hard in case I needed one more reminder that my daughter was seriously pissed. A quick peek out the front window showed her climbing into Spencer's car. Well, if she thought this talk was over, she was seriously mistaken.

I pulled out my cell and punched the keys so hard my thumb hurt. When Olivia answered, I let her have it. "How dare you tell Charley not to go to college?"

"What? I never said that."

"She says you offered to introduce her to an acting coach you know in New York and encouraged her to apply to drama schools."

"She said she wasn't sure college was right for her and I told her it was a mistake to live the life other people want for you rather than the one you've chosen for yourself. Was that so wrong?"

I saw red. "And I suppose you're a shining example of that? Tell me, did you choose to marry a man that treats you like shit and flirts with other women in front of you? And since we're on the topic, I told you I didn't want Charley anywhere near Zach and you went behind my back and asked her to pose for you."

Liv's voice stayed calm. "Actually, it was the other way around. She called me, asking if I still wanted her to come over. I assumed you'd changed your mind and okayed it."

"Well, I didn't. And just so we're clear, you're not to see my daughter again without my permission. Got it?"

"I didn't mean anything by it," Liv said, a note of concern in her voice. "It seemed like she needed to confide in someone and I didn't see the harm. We're not competitors, Rachel. We both just want what's best for Charley."

My daughter used to confide in me, not turn to strangers for advice. I missed those days when I'd been Charley's confidante. Now Olivia seemed to have taken on that role. And I didn't like that one bit. In a year, my daughter would graduate, leave home for college, and be out on her own and I would have very little say in how she lived her life. But until then, I still made the rules.

"What's best for her is to stay away from your house and concentrate on her studies. Are we clear?"

"You have my word I won't have her over again. Please, don't let this cause a rift between us. Am I forgiven?"

I took a beat and controlled my temper. Clearly, Charley had been flattered by Liv's invitation and initiated the session and she'd no doubt told Olivia I'd given my okay. But it was clear this growing closeness between Liv and my daughter needed to end, not only because of Zach but more importantly, a stalker had us in his sights. It was my responsibility to keep my daughter safe from any predatory adults out there. It didn't matter whether they were strangers.

Or ones much closer to home.

20

THE NEXT DAY WAS Easter Sunday, and once Charley and I got home from church, I spent the afternoon working through my backlog of cases on the sun porch. My daughter retreated upstairs, ostensibly to do homework but no doubt spending most of the day texting her friends and surfing Tik-Tok. The house was quiet. No scary phone calls. No blaring television. No angry exchanges with my daughter. I'd recovered from my over-indulgence Friday night and gotten some much needed perspective. Now wasn't the time to indulge in romantic fantasies about Max or anyone else, for that matter. I needed to concentrate on getting that promotion and shutting down this stalker.

Three weeks had gone by since he'd sent me that video. Had he given up or was he, like Max said, planning an elaborate and final trap? By the time Monday rolled around, my fingernails were bitten to the quick, a bad habit I usually was able to curb. I drove Charley to school, despite her protests. Then I headed downtown, continually checking to see if anyone was following me. Instead of using the garage across from my office, I parked in an open-air lot a block away to make it harder to sneak up on my car.

I dropped off a filing on my way in, so it was after nine when I got to my office. Rita said Huntley had stopped by earlier and asked to see me as soon as I arrived. Fine with me. I'd written up a lengthy report about where things stood on the trafficking case and forwarded it to both him and the Dane County DA on Sunday so he couldn't bawl me out for shirking that assignment. As for the rest of the cases on my docket, I was caught up and hadn't missed a deadline since our last meeting. My work life was under control. It was my personal life that was a mess.

Huntley motioned for me to sit opposite him, then laid it on the line. "When we spoke at the pub, you wanted some time to think about the Deputy DA slot. Well, time's up. I'm finalizing the list this week and I need to know whether you're in or out."

These last few weeks had been hell, what with searching for my stalker, dealing with Charley's issues, and getting up to speed on the sex trafficking case but the job offer was always at the front of my mind and after carefully weighing the pros and cons, I'd made a decision. I'd never forgive myself if I let this opportunity slip away. I'd worked hard for this promotion and I deserved it. I was tired of living off credit cards, driving an older car, and never taking my daughter on trips. But there was another reason as well. I'd learned firsthand how broken the system was when it came to protecting vulnerable women. As Deputy DA I'd be in a better position to advocate for stricter laws and stiffer sentences. "I've thought through the offer and yes, I definitely want to be considered."

"Glad to hear it. I was worried your personal issues might be distracting you. Someone mentioned a late filing?"

Shula again. "That was a misunderstanding. I took care of it."

"And your stalker? Is that situation also taken care of?"

"It's getting there. No need to worry. Everything's under control." While outwardly reassuring him, inwardly my temper flared. I'd worked my tail off these last ten years, taken on extra assignments, worked weekends and late into the evenings, given all I had to this job. Apparently, that counted for nothing. No, even worse. It set up the expectation I'd keep up the same frantic pace going forward. Any time Huntley felt I was letting my personal life interfere with my work, I'd get a lecture. Or worse.

This promotion meant financial security not only for me, but for Charley, plus more challenging cases, more authority, and more prestige. It was time to bring this stalker situation to a head before this promotion slipped through my fingers. But how could I do that when the person behind this vendetta held all the cards?

***

THE REST OF THE day SPED by. I was due in court early the next day to begin the trial of a suspected pedophile. I'd been fielding calls from the accused's lawyer who wanted to discuss a plea deal but I had irrefutable forensic evidence this was the guy. No way was I letting him skate.

It was a good thing I'd arranged for Luke to pick Charley up after school because it was after eight before I stuffed the last remaining files in my briefcase and shut down my computer. As I headed out, the phone on my desk rang. Who would be calling me after hours? But there might have been a last-minute development in tomorrow's case, so I picked up.

"Fifty thousand dollars and no harm comes to your daughter. You have until Friday," the now-familiar mechanical voice said.

My stomach lurched. I dropped into my chair and glanced at the caller ID. Unidentified number. What had I expected? Rage bubbled up. "Who are you? Why are you doing this?"

"Is that a no?"

"Tell me what I did to you. Let me make amends." I put him on speaker phone, hung up the receiver, and grabbed a pencil and a pad of paper.

There was a deep sigh, then the voice continued. "Stop talking and listen. Fifty thousand dollars by Friday night."

Keep him talking. Gather information. "I'm not sure I can raise that amount by then."

"Stop with the excuses. Figure it out. I'll let you know where." A pause. "And no police. Any sign of them or that PI you hired, and all bets are off."

"And if I refuse?"

"Your precious daughter disappears for a day and when I bring her back, there's an oozing, gaping hole where her right eyeball used to be."

My blood turned to ice as that image seared into my brain. Don't you fucking dare, you creep. I pictured my hands encircling this sadist's throat as he gasped for breath. Only I didn't let go. I squeezed harder. I wanted this sicko to suffer.

"Why me? What did I ever do to you?" I screamed into the phone.

"You ask too many questions. Shut up and follow my instructions. I'll check back on Thursday."

"But what if I can't get—"

He hung up. I immediately dialed Charley's cell and waited as it rang five times. Finally, she picked up. Yes, she was fine. Yes, she'd had dinner—my brother had made pizza, then dropped her off at home. She was finishing a term paper on climate change. Yes, she'd set the alarm. No, she wasn't planning to leave. I hung up, my stomach still tied in knots but relieved to know she was safe.

For now.

Then I thought about what I'd just learned. This whole elaborate scheme had been nothing more than a run-of-the-mill shake-down. Here I'd pictured an obsessed villain after revenge, a criminal mastermind whose life I'd ruined. Instead, this was some ordinary guy desperate for money who'd hatched a scheme to frighten me badly enough that I'd be open to blackmail. Not overly bright, but smart enough to realize my daughter was the key to get to me.

And here I'd gone and hired an investigator, involved the police, put my career at risk, and for what? This wasn't an ex-con. This wasn't someone I dated. This wasn't a psychopath. This was just some guy who needed cash and figured out a clever way to get it.

My shoulders relaxed, my spine unknotted, and my breathing returned to normal. I could outsmart this guy. After ten years of dealing with lowlifes like him, I knew what made them tick. If he got what he wanted—money, not revenge—he'd go away. The solution was simple. Raise fifty thousand dollars, pay him off, and this hellish nightmare would be over.

And I could forget turning to outsiders for help. If I involved Davante, he'd insist on fitting me with a wire, surrounding the perimeter, and setting a trap for this guy. But if the stalker caught on and didn't show, he might very well make good on his threat. And who's to say he didn't have an accomplice? When it came to my daughter's safety, I wasn't going to take any chances.

And if I told Max? He'd try to stop me, tell me to be patient, we'd track him down sooner or later. Or he'd insist on going in my place so he could confront the guy.

No, this was between me and my … not stalker. Blackmailer. I'd play by his rules, follow his instructions to the letter, and if everything fell into place, by Friday I'd have my life back.

21

I ONLY HAD FOUR days, which meant I had to move fast. It was terrible timing but the first thing I did was ask for a continuance on the pedophile case. I knew Huntley would be furious if he found out, not to mention all the other people who'd be inconvenienced. But I had a stellar record and this particular judge liked me so he granted the request.

Next: raise the money. Some women would have jewelry to pawn or an expensive car to flip, but I'd lived frugally for eighteen years, first because I had to, with a newborn and college expenses, and later because I chose to work in public service rather than in a tony law firm. Charley and I had a comfortable lifestyle, but there'd never been extra cash left over for luxuries. How could I quickly raise fifty thousand dollars?

Tuesday morning I stopped at my local bank and requested all the cash in Charley's college fund. How ironic that only a few days ago, I'd insisted to my daughter this money was reserved for her education and now here I was depleting the account. Getting that promotion and its bump in pay had just become a whole lot more crucial.

When the manager politely inquired if there was any other way he could help, I wondered how he'd react if I told him the truth, that a blackmailer had threatened to blind my daughter if I didn't pay him off.

Instead I put on the face I wore when I spoke to a jury—the one that said *you can trust me. I'm telling the truth*—and recited the lie I'd rehearsed the night before. "There's a lake property I've had my eye on and the owner insists on cash. It's eccentric, I know, but in this market, what are you going to do?" I led him further into my lie. "There's two other buyers sniffing around and my broker says if I don't move fast, I'll lose out."

He wished me luck, said to circle back if I needed money for renovations, then counted out the hundreds, one by one—ten thousand dollars. I stuffed the bills in a dark-blue duffel bag I'd dug out of the garage.

Next, I drove downtown to Chase, the bank that held the mortgage on my house, and applied for a home equity loan. Once again, I trotted out the story of the lake property. I knew it was a lot to ask, but could they possibly rush through the application? With my stellar credit history and stable work credentials, the bank officer assured me there'd be no problem. He'd have the money ready by Thursday. Another ten thousand dollars.

That left thirty thousand dollars. I took out cash advances on four of my credit cards, yielding another five thousand. I logged into my Schwab account and liquidated ten thousand dollars from my retirement fund. It would mean a tax hit at year-end but it couldn't be helped. At the end of the day, I added everything up.

I'd tapped every available source of cash I had and was short fifteen thousand dollars.

Think, goddamn it. There's got to be a solution. He threatened Charley.

Luke. He knew about my stalker and he'd be able to loan me that much. Then I remembered how, at that barbeque, he'd mentioned dipping into savings to pay for new wiring on his house. Which left one person to ask, one person who could easily lay his hands on that amount, the last person I wanted to turn to.

But I was out of options.

***

I SHOWED UP UNANNOUNCED LATE that afternoon. "What are you doing here?" my father asked when he answered the door. "What's wrong?"

"Can't your only child drop by for a visit without having some ulterior motive? Maybe I was missing you."

"Stop spouting nonsense." He stepped aside and we faced each other in the foyer. "Is this a dining-room table conversation or a let's-go-back-to-my-study-and-shut-the-door one?"

At least I could blurt out what I needed without having to sugar-coat it. "The study."

Once we were there, he motioned for me to sit, then lowered himself into his favorite easy chair. "Okay, out with it."

I cleared my throat. "I need to borrow fifteen thousand dollars."

His eyes popped. "What for?"

"That's the second part of the request. I can't tell you why. But it's crucial you give me that amount in cash by Friday morning."

"Tell me what you've got yourself tangled up in." He stared long and hard at me, not blinking. His courtroom face.

"I swear I'm not doing anything illegal. Past that, I'm asking you to trust me and not ask for the details." My eyes bored into his. "You know I'd never come to you unless I had nowhere else to turn."

"Does this have anything to do with Charley? Is she in some kind of trouble?"

A part of me wanted to tell him but I knew he'd insist on rushing in and saving the day and I couldn't take that chance. "Charley's fine. Giving me headaches at the moment over college, but we'll get past it." I leaned forward. "I need an answer, Dad. Will you help me?"

"You want to borrow fifteen thousand dollars in cash and you expect me to hand it over, no questions asked."

"Yes." I waited several seconds and when he didn't move or say anything, I added, "When have I ever asked you for money?"

"When you dropped out of college," he growled. "Showed up on our doorstep, broke and pregnant, and expected your mother and me to welcome you back, put you up in an apartment, and support you."

My jaw clenched. We remembered that time very differently. Besides, why throw that up in my face today? It was a lifetime ago. "And you refused, didn't you? Told me the only thing you'd pay for was an abortion."

He had the good sense to look ashamed, that ugly time in our lives never quite buried. It was a good minute before he spoke again. "I regret saying that. But at the time, it seemed like you were throwing your life away."

My mother had been the referee that day. She'd told me to wait in the living room while she and my father barricaded themselves in this same room for over an hour. When they emerged, it was with an offer to have me and the baby live here in this house until

I could afford a place of my own. They'd also pay for my continued schooling as long as I maintained a B average and worked part-time in my dad's office. It had been a life-line at the time. I couldn't imagine what would have happened to me and Charley otherwise.

"I'm not looking for a handout. It would be a loan. Once the promotion goes through, I'll get a bump in pay and every extra penny will go toward making you whole."

He scowled. "I thought you'd decided not to take that job."

I hadn't said that, only promised to consider his advice. What he didn't understand, what he'd never understood, was how much of my identity was tied up in my job. Except for Charley, it was all I had.

"Can we focus here? I know your hourly billing rate. It's not like this loan is going to bankrupt you."

"Tell me what's going on, monkeyface. Maybe I can help, pull some strings, make a call. Luke told me you were dealing with some personal stuff but he wouldn't tell me what. Is this request related to that?"

Good. Luke had kept his mouth shut like I'd asked. Which was huge given how close he and my father were. I'd often envied their intimacy, wished I'd gotten even a fraction of that love. My father had always kept his distance from me and left the caregiving to my mom.

I was anxious to be on my way, whether my father agreed to loan me the cash or not, so I played my trump card. "If Mom were here, she'd give me the money."

My father's face turned stormy. "She coddled you."

"No, she didn't. She loved me and wanted me to be happy."

"You don't smile that much," he shot back.

"Can we analyze my life choices some other time?" I stood. "I'm in a bind and I came here hoping my wealthy father would help me. If that's not going to happen …" My words hung in the air. I'd had enough of explaining my decisions to this man.

"Goddamn it. Don't get so high and mighty. I'll give you the money." He left the room and came back in ten minutes with a small valise. He placed it on his desk and popped open the latches. It was filled with cash, bundled in neat stacks. "There's twenty thousand there. Put the extra in Charley's college fund. Now if you don't mind, I'd like to be alone."

I didn't respond, merely nodded my thanks, picked up the cash, and left the house. I was halfway home when Max called. I'd been ignoring him since Friday night.

This time I picked up.

22

I couldn't tell Max about the blackmail demand but if I kept screening his calls and texts, he'd get suspicious. "So you still haven't heard back from our guy?" he asked.

"Between the police patrolling the neighborhood and you being in the picture, I think he got spooked and moved on."

"That's a nice fantasy you've got there but I'm afraid it doesn't work like that. Are you sure you're not keeping anything from me? Because this isn't someone you should tangle with on your own."

"Because I'm a clueless bimbo who needs a big, brave detective to save me?"

"C'mon, Rachel, you know me better than that. But if you're getting ideas about outsmarting this guy, let me warn you. Whatever move you make, he's gonna be two steps ahead of you. I don't want you to get hurt."

Max didn't have kids. He couldn't understand how being a mother changed your perspective. Made you more than willing to pay cash, lots of it, all you had, to keep them safe. To keep them whole. And I wasn't in any mood to argue about it. To justify myself.

It was my money. My decision.

But the good news was this would be over by Friday. Three more days and I could concentrate on getting that promotion. Focus on my job. Start repairing the rift between myself and Charley. Life could get back to normal.

Only three more days.

***

THE DEFENSE ATTORNEY IN THE Jansen case rose to question the witness. "Will you look at my client and tell the court whether this was the man you saw running away from the scene?"

The witness tugged at his shirt collar and cleared his throat. "Well … my wife said he had on a red windbreaker and then I remembered because it matched his hair."

I glanced at the wall clock. I'd be cutting it close. I needed to sign off on the second mortgage, turn that check into cash, then rush back here, all during the lunch hour. The judge interrupted my thoughts. "Ms. Matthews. Do I hear an objection?" I startled, lost in my to-do list.

Shula, sitting second chair, jumped to her feet. "Objection, your honor. Hearsay."

The judge banged her gavel. "Sustained." She turned to the witness. "We're interested in what *you* saw, sir, not your wife."

I tuned back into my surroundings. On re-direct, I took the man back through his identification of the defendant during the line-up to shore up my earlier slip. It was hard to concentrate, knowing how little time was left before my rendezvous with the stalker, but somehow I managed to make it through to the noon recess.

I grabbed my briefcase and was headed out the door when the clerk touched my shoulder. "The judge would like to see you in chambers," he said.

Crap. If I didn't leave soon, I'd run out of time. "Now?"

"Yes, now. This way."

Judge Daniels had been appointed to the bench ten years ago. Her nickname was The Velvet Fist because, under her calm exterior, she suffered no nonsense when it came to antics in her courtroom. She asked me to take a seat. "What's going on, counselor?"

I modulated my voice, hiding my nerves. "I'm not sure what you mean, judge."

"You're missing obvious objections. You're not asking standard follow-up questions. If I didn't know better, I'd say you're a lawyer who has more important things on her mind than trying this case."

If she only knew. But I couldn't have her calling Huntley. Not with Shula lurking beside me, ready to step in.

I threw back my shoulders. "I apologize. My daughter's been having trouble at school and it came to a head last night. It must have upset me more than I realized. It won't happen again." I prayed the judge, a mother herself, would accept the *mea culpa* and let me out of here.

"I'll see you again at 1:30. Be ready to concentrate on the case. You can go."

I rushed out of her chambers, snatched up my things, and bolted to my car. One foot in front of the other. By this time next week, this would all be over.

***

I RETREATED TO MY BEDROOM Thursday night, sure he'd keep me waiting until the last minute. Finally, at eight o'clock my cell phone pinged.

"Have you got the money?" Once again, I heard traffic noises in the background.

"Fifty thousand dollars. Like you said."

"I knew you'd come through. You didn't tell anyone, right? Because if I spot a tail."

I'd almost confided in Max that evening when he called again. But I knew he wouldn't approve of my paying any ransom. "I didn't tell anyone. But you should know this is all the money I have in the world. You won't be able to come back and ask for more. I'm tapped out."

A mechanical laugh. "That won't be an issue." What did he mean by that? Was something else going on here?

Whoever this was, I hated him. Hated being in this situation. Hated being at the mercy of someone so calculating. Hated the fact he'd wiped me out financially.

"Before I pay you, I want to know what I'm buying."

"I'll disappear like a puff of smoke. You and your daughter will be safe."

"How do I know this isn't a con? That you won't come after us again?"

"I guess my word doesn't count for much, given the situation. So let me ask you. Are you willing to take that risk?" It sounded like I'd pissed him off.

He was right. I wouldn't bargain with Charley's safety. He had all the power.

After a few moments of silence, he spoke again. "That's what I thought. I'll call tomorrow between two and three with final instructions. And Rachel? Keep being smart. No tricks. Remember, I'm watching."

23

THE NEXT MORNING, AS I paced the floor in the kitchen, anxious for this day to be over, my daughter shouted from upstairs. "Mom, have you seen my green heels? I've searched everywhere and I can't find them."

I yelled back. "Check under your bed." I didn't have time for this. If Charley kept her shoes in the shoe tree like I repeatedly told her, they wouldn't be missing.

"I tried there. Can you help me look? I'm gonna be late for school."

The last thing I needed today was playing nursemaid to my teenage daughter whose bedroom, when I entered, resembled the dressing room at Macy's on Black Friday. Jeans and sweaters flung on the bed. An expensive tweed jacket half dangling from a chair. Loose scrunchies and a stray purple boot on the floor. Any other day I would have launched into a lecture, but right now all I could think about was how to get my daughter out of the house.

Charley stood in the middle of the room, arms flailing. "I can't find them."

"Then wear a different pair. C'mon, we need to get going. You've already missed the bus so I'll have to drive you."

"Spencer's picking me up. But I *really* need to find those shoes, or my whole outfit falls apart."

That's when I noticed my daughter had on her emerald velvet jacket and a silky cream blouse I'd never seen before. "Why are you so dressed up? And where did you get that top?" I asked.

"Liv loaned it to me. She said I needed something special for the show tonight. Spencer's taking me out for an early dinner and then we're driving straight over there."

I searched my memory and came up blank. "What show are you talking about?

She sighed as she got down on her hands and knees and rummaged at the back of her closet, emerging with the lost pumps dangling from her fingers. "I've told you a million times. Olivia's gallery opening in the Third Ward. It's tonight and she wants me to meet a couple of her acting friends from Renaissance Theater. You're still coming, right? I told Liv you'd be there and it seemed really important to her."

The event had completely slipped my mind. "I'm going to have to beg off."

"What? But you promised," she whined.

"I know I did. But something's come up on a case I need to deal with."

"Can't it wait until the weekend?"

I didn't want Charley to pick up on my anxiety or she'd ask even more questions. It was just as well my daughter would be at the gallery surrounded by people while I took care of the payoff. "What time is the show?"

"It starts at seven and goes on until ten. The Kresge Gallery on Broadway." She stood in the center of the room, hands on hips, classic confrontation stance. "So you'll be there?"

I wouldn't know the time for the meeting until this afternoon and I didn't have a location but it made sense he'd pick somewhere within driving distance. No matter where it was, I should be able to make an appearance at the opening.

"I'm not sure when I'll get there but yes, I'll come."

"I'm holding you to that." A horn honked outside. "That's Spence," she shouted as she raced down the stairs.

I grabbed a couple of her best dresses and hung them in the closet, pulled the comforter over the bed, and picked up assorted gold bangles off the floor. When I opened the bottom drawer on the nightstand to tuck them inside, I saw a shiny white box with colorful rainbow markings on the outside labelled *Welcome to 23andme*. Wasn't that the company that helped people trace their DNA back generations? The package was addressed to Charley c/o an unfamiliar PO Box at a post office fifteen miles from our house. I pulled out a three-page set of instructions, detailing how to spit in the vial provided and mail it back for analysis.

I tore through the contents, turned the box upside down, and searched inside. The vial was missing. *Shit*. Charley had already sent in the sample. Sure enough, stapled to the instructions was a return receipt from the same post office. She'd mailed the package six days ago.

My heart took off at a gallop as I read the pamphlet. The results took ten days to process. Which meant by Monday, Tuesday at the latest, this company would post the results on their site. If I was lucky, no one from Paul's family was in the database. But if fate worked against me? Charley would turn up grandparents, aunts or uncles, maybe even half-siblings. Once she had that information, it wouldn't take long before she'd track down Paul's name, and Google would provide the rest, including the fact he wasn't some random drummer in a band but a well-known author. And at that point, my daughter would know I was a liar.

When Charley turned four and, like all kids, became a whirling dervish of a questioning machine (Why was the sky blue? Why did she have blond hair? What happens when we die?), she'd asked why she didn't have a daddy like everyone else. It came up again when I set my daughter down at eleven to have 'the talk'. That time I had elaborated a bit, talked about my own poor decision-making and the consequences of unprotected sex. It seemed to placate her because she never asked about her father again.

But this DNA kit meant she must be more upset by that incident at school than she'd let on. Otherwise, why, after all this time, had she decided to track her family history? And if she discovered the facts about Paul, what kind of wedge would that drive between us? I imagined Charley's face when she heard her mother had slept with a married man. It would change the way she thought about me forever.

*****

I WAS ON EDGE ALL day, watching the clock tick down to noon. I scarfed down a quick sandwich from the vending machine on the ground floor, then holed up in my office with the door closed.

Two o'clock came and went. I tried to stay calm, only to spring out of my chair a minute later and pace the room. I wandered to the window and stared at the people on the street, envying their ordinary, everyday lives. I went to the restroom, downed a couple of aspirin. I counted the ceiling tiles. Scrolled through my emails, watched a series of pet videos, then two trailers for upcoming movies. Scanned the news feed on my computer. Pulled out an old crossword puzzle from a bottom drawer and worked on it.

Why didn't he call? It was classic gamesmanship. He got pleasure out of making me squirm. Two-thirty. Would this afternoon never end? What was in store for me that evening? Would I recognize him or would he be a total stranger? If it was someone I knew, how should I react?

He called at the stroke of three and I grabbed a pen and paper to write down his instructions. "Come down Lake Drive to Layton, turn off the main road to Sheridan Park in Cudahy. Pull into Lot 23 and wait for my call. Oh, and bring the money. Eight o'clock." He hung up.

He'd picked a location less than ten miles from the gallery. I could hand over the money, get his assurance he wouldn't bother me again, and still have plenty of time to get to Liv's show. I could hug my daughter, drink some wine, and forget this whole nasty business.

I drove home after work to change, too keyed up to eat dinner. I put on dark jeans, black boots, a black t-shirt and hoodie, then tucked a simple black knit dress, along with dress flats and pearl earrings, into a garment bag.

I'd decided marking the bills was too risky. If this person was an experienced blackmailer, he'd catch on and if I made him angry, no telling what he'd do. At the same time, I didn't trust him to just disappear. I might be boxed into a corner, but I wasn't stupid.

First, I snipped the threads of the bottom lining of my duffel bag until I'd opened up a two-inch space. Next, I tucked a mini-GPS tracking device inside and used double-faced Velcro to hold it in place. Then I hauled my old sewing kit out from the back of my closet and closed the hole with tiny stitches of black thread. Once he'd grabbed the money, I'd follow the signal and find out who was behind this. I had to pray he wouldn't transfer the bills on the spot to a different bag.

Should I bring my gun? I could always leave it in the car at the last minute but wouldn't it be safer if I had a way to defend myself? For the second time today, I opened a drawer and got a shock.

First, I'd found a DNA kit in my daughter's dresser.

Now the gun I'd moved to my nightstand had disappeared.

24

Out of sheer habit, I kept checking to see if I was being followed even though that made no sense since I was meeting the person who'd been tailing me. I took side streets from Whitefish Bay into downtown, then got on Lake Drive. My brain spun, conjuring increasingly bizarre scenarios. What if I got into an accident on the freeway and the police discovered fifty thousand dollars in cash in my car? What if my stalker didn't show up, this rendezvous just another of his sadistic games? What if there was a reality TV crew lying in wait to tape my response? What if, what if … Two miles from the location, I spotted a dark SUV in my rear-view mirror, but it turned down a side street and disappeared. *This will all be over soon. Get a hold of yourself. Focus.*

I slowed near the well-known statue of Patrick Cudahy, located the designated parking lot, pulled into an empty space, and waited.

Beads of sweat trickled between my breasts as minutes ticked by and I began to freak out, drumming my fingers on the steering wheel, debating whether what I'd planned was a smart move or the dumbest decision I'd ever made.

When your enemy's got you trapped in a blind alley, you either surrender to your fear or you face him down. At that moment I hated this man more than I'd ever hated anyone in my life. I wanted to strangle him, make him pay for what he'd put me and my daughter through. It was a good thing my gun hadn't been there when I'd reached for it. I didn't trust myself not to use it.

What if I was walking into a trap? Should I drive away and tell the police what I knew? But if I didn't keep the appointment and he blinded Charley …

I wiped the thought from my mind. That wasn't how tonight was going to play out. I was going to meet him, hand over the money, and he was going to leave us alone. No other scenario was acceptable.

My phone rang precisely at eight. "Walk to the pavilion, take a right, and follow the path to the beach."

I got out of the car. But at the last minute, I reached back in and pulled a can of pepper spray from the glove compartment, tucking it into the pocket of my hoodie. Then I popped open the trunk, removed the flashlight, and hoisted the duffel bag containing all the money I had in the world onto my shoulder.

Showtime.

The wind picked up and whipped strands of hair across my face as I headed down the sidewalk and across the park, keeping my eyes peeled for any witnesses. Downtown street sounds echoed in the distance—the wail of an ambulance, the honk of an impatient horn, a distant hub-bub of voices from a nearby party in someone's backyard.

This close to the lake, the air had turned chilly and I wished I'd dressed warmer. I reached the opening in the bushes and headed down the dirt path. The ground was uneven and the way ahead of me pitch black, so even with my flashlight, I could barely see three feet in front of me. I flinched at every rustle, every twig, the only sign I was making progress the increasing murmur of waves hitting the shore. God, please let this go off without a hitch.

I hadn't seen the exposed tree root so I tripped and fell, cracking the corner of my cell, but luckily, the flashlight wasn't damaged. I scrambled up and trudged on, my leg muscles straining. When I rounded the third switchback, a furry shape with beady, yellow eyes stopped me cold. Just what I needed tonight—some rabid animal attacking me. I shone my torch in that direction and whatever it was scurried into the brush.

God, this path was endless. Out of breath, I felt a stitch in my side, not from the trek so much as my growing sense of unease. When I spotted the last turn up ahead, I crouched and crept forward as silently as I could. Visibility was slight. There was a half-moon but cloud cover intermittently blocked its light. My time was up. Sooner or later I'd have to reveal myself. I peered around the bushes, hoping to get a look at my stalker before he knew I was there.

There was a dark-haired man twenty yards away, his back turned to me, feeding kindling into a raging bonfire. A dark blanket lay on the sand beside him along with a wine bottle and two glasses. Did my stalker think this was a celebration? Or worse, was his plan to rape me? The waves slapped the rocks in a haunting, harrowing rhythm as gulls screamed overhead.

Had it been a mistake not to tell anyone where I was going? Not to at least leave a note? I had spotty cell reception and a small fortune in cash on my shoulder. I was alone with a stalker on a deserted beach. If this was a movie, the audience would be screaming at me to run. But I couldn't. I had to see this through.

I straightened, repositioned the duffel bag, and stepped onto the beach. The wind blew sand in my face and hundreds of tiny pinpricks hit my skin. The man must have heard my movement because he turned.

What the hell?

He was on the shorter side, dressed like a pirate, complete with white ruffled shirt, knee britches, black boots, and a silver-buckled belt, a gilt sword in a sheath at his side. I stifled a laugh—all that was missing was a parrot and an eye patch. But the next second, a shiver ran down my spine. There was something familiar about this man. As the moon moved from behind a cloud, I recognized him.

It was Zach Reid.

A wig of dark curls hid his bald head. As the two of us made eye contact, a confused look crossed his face. Seconds later, his eyes darted away from me to somewhere over my right shoulder and he put out a hand as though warding off a blow.

He shouted but I couldn't make out the words and on instinct, I glanced behind me. We weren't alone. Something or someone was moving in the bushes nearby.

Bam-bam-bam. Three gunshots in rapid succession.

I bit back my scream and glanced back at Zach, as a blood stain blossomed like time-lapse photography on his chest, turning his shirt horror-movie red within seconds. He stood silhouetted against the fire, a look of astonishment etched across his face. Then he sank to his knees and fell face forward, arms outstretched like some overly-theatrical Christ figure.

Blood roared in my ears like a freight train as I threw myself on the ground, slamming my wrist straight into a rock which sent a shooting pain up my left arm. I choked back bile, squeezed my eyes shut, and waited for the next bullet.

The one meant for me.

The lone witness.

25

Minutes ticked by. My wrist throbbed like the devil but I didn't dare move as water sloshed against my cheek and sand gritted my teeth. I replayed the puzzled look on Zach's face, the shots, the blood.

It was quiet. Spooky quiet.

Graveyard quiet.

I raised my head an inch and rested my chin on the sand. Nine yards away a body lay sprawled, arms outstretched, left leg at an angle. Blood had stained the sand black.

My chest tightened as sounds echoed around me—the slap of the waves, the whistle of the wind, an owl in the distance. Then footsteps, moving fast through the brush, growing fainter as the seconds ticked by. The shooter was leaving me behind?

Silence again. Was he toying with me, waiting to see what I'd do? The sadistic bastard.

Slowly, I pulled myself to a sitting position, head spinning. The longer I stayed here in the open, the more danger I was in. The shooter might change his mind at any moment, decide to come back, and kill me.

Kicking my body into gear, I grabbed the duffel bag and bolted up the path. I heard rustling to my left, a snapping noise above me, every sound magnified ten times. Every movement morphed into menace. The killer would spot me if I used my flashlight, so I made do with the feeble beam from my cell. My eyes kept scanning the woods, but I missed the first switchback, running straight into a mass of wild brambles. I lost my footing and scraped my elbow and right cheek. But I forced myself up and got back on the path, snot running down my face. Why had I agreed to meet in this godforsaken spot? Why hadn't I told someone what I was up to? Why was I always so damn stubborn?

I stopped beating myself up and kept moving. Otherwise, I could die out here just like Zach. I dodged around potholes, my ragged breath so loud it drowned out the screeches of the seagulls overhead until finally, tears streaming down my face, I reached street level. I braced my hands on my legs, let out several wracking coughs, and clutched the throbbing stitch in my side.

My phone showed three bars and I dialed 9-1-1 but within a second, disconnected. If the police discovered me alone on a deserted beach with the dead husband of my close friend, a shit-load of money, and no logical reason to be there, they would assume I'd thrown the murder weapon in the lake and concocted some wild story of a sniper. They'd arrest me on the spot.

Someone was approaching from my left. I scurried behind a bush as two teenagers jogged past and once they were out of sight,

I crossed the lawn, dialing back my pace to a moderate walk. Fast enough to look like I had somewhere to go but slow enough not to call attention to myself. Every inch of my body was on fire as I headed across the park.

Suddenly a dark sedan barreled around the corner, horn honking, lights flashing. The driver slammed on the brakes, trapping me in his high beams. "Wait right there," a male voice commanded.

I bolted for the parking lot, but the person threw his car into park, leaped out and chased me, so close I could hear him panting. I hit the key fob and grabbed the door handle but the guy reached from behind and slammed it shut. He pinned my arms to my sides and, even though I kicked backwards and clawed at his hands, I couldn't fight him off. My keys dropped to the asphalt out of reach.

"Let go of me," I screamed, reaching for the can of pepper spray in my hoodie. The guy whirled me around and shoved me hard against the car door.

"Stop yelling. What's going on, Rachel?" the man snapped. "Why are you running?"

My pulse pounded in my ears. Max? What was he doing here? "I … Zach … the beach …" I pointed across the way, my words tumbling over each other.

"Slow down. You're shaking like the devil's on your tail. Come here." He pulled me close. A smell like pine trees filled my nose as I collapsed on his chest and he stroked my back.

He didn't reassure me, didn't tell me everything was fine because he obviously knew from my behavior that it wasn't. Instead, he whispered *shh, shh, I'll help you, you're safe* over and over until I finally stopped trembling.

And once I did, the sobs came and I didn't try to stop them. I cried out all the fear, all the anger, all the worry until slowly my pulse returned to normal.

That's when I heard the sirens.

Wiping my nose with my sleeve, I pulled back. "I have to go. I can't let them find me here." I retrieved my key ring off the asphalt.

"Tell me what's going on."

"Down on the beach," I whispered. "It's Zach. He's dead. Someone shot him."

"Who the hell is Zach?"

"My friend Liv's husband. Look, there's no time to explain. I have to get out of here." Sirens blared through the night air. Coming our way. Coming fast.

Max scanned the parking lot. "Do you trust me?"

Did I have a choice? Right now, he was all I had. I nodded.

"I grew up around here and I know the area. Get in your car and follow me." Max raced back to his vehicle and I trailed in mine as we turned down back alleys, drove over three streets, then down a narrow easement, and finally north toward downtown. As I drove, I questioned this whole set-up. Max seemed to have just pulled up but if so, how had he found me? What if he'd been there all along? What if … shit … What if *he* was the shooter? But that didn't make any sense. My brain was rattled. I should watch my step and avoid making any hasty moves.

When we reached the Allen-Bradley clock tower, Max pulled into the parking lot of a deserted warehouse nearby and waved his hand out the window, signaling me to pull in as well. My hands squeezed the steering wheel and sweat pooled under my fingers. He climbed out of his car and jumped into my passenger's seat.

In a low, steady voice, he said, "Okay. We've bought some time. Start at the beginning."

A tremor of doubt seized me. Could I trust Max? How had he conveniently showed up at the exact same time and place as the rendezvous? "You first. I thought I spotted someone following me. Was that you?"

He stared out the front windshield, then faced me. "You've been acting strange all week, ever since you spent the night at my house. Evading my questions, pretending everything was normal, saying you hadn't heard from your stalker. I knew you were hiding something so yes, I started following you a few days ago. You can't hire me, then go rogue, and expect me not to react."

"He told me not to involve you."

"Who did?"

"Who do you think? The guy who's been stalking me. Zach Reid."

"Wait. You talked to him directly?"

I might as well dump everything in his lap. Zach was dead. He couldn't come after me or my daughter ever again. "He called me on Monday and threatened Charley. Said he wanted $50,000 and if I called the cops or you … well, he made it clear it wouldn't be a smart choice."

"So that's what all the stops were about. You were gathering the money."

He *had* followed me all week and I'd never suspected. "We arranged to meet tonight for the hand-off. But you know all this. You were there when—"

"No, I wasn't. I got stopped by a cop for speeding on I-43. You were long gone by the time he finished with me. I'd only pulled up to the park when I spied you crossing the street."

"That can't be true. How did you know where to find me if you got stopped?" Then it dawned on me and my eyes narrowed. "You put a tracker on my car, didn't you?"

I sprang out, kneeled, and ran my hand over the front grill. When I moved on to the front tire, he got out, rounded the car to the back wheel well, and pulled out a square black box, no bigger than an alkaline battery.

"Satisfied?" he said.

My hands balled into fists. "I'm your client. What happened to *trust?*"

"Right back at you, client. You hired me to protect you. That's what I was doing."

"No, I hired you to find my stalker. I can protect myself."

"You sure about that? Because ten minutes ago you seemed like a woman afraid for her life and badly in need of a friend."

I still wasn't sure I should trust him. Well, I knew one way to find out. "Show me the ticket."

He scowled. "What?"

"You said you got a speeding ticket. Show it to me."

He threw up his hands. "God, you're unbelievable." He went to his car, opened the glove compartment, and returned with a yellow slip of paper which he thrust out for me to examine. Sure enough, it was a citation for going twenty miles over the speed limit, issued at eight p.m. I handed it back.

He leaned against the rear bumper. "Look, this isn't getting us anywhere. Either you trust me or you don't. If you do, fill me in on what happened and we'll figure out what to do next."

He was right. Enough of the third-degree. I needed help and who better than an experienced private investigator who knew the situation and was right here? One who had a history with me, maybe even a mutual attraction I could play on. I told him about Zach's phone instructions and then described step by step what happened at the beach.

"Are you sure Zach's dead? Did you examine the body?"

"Are you joking? All I could think about was *I'm next.* I stayed still for four, maybe five minutes and then I ran out of there as fast as I could."

"There's a chance he was only wounded. You should have called an ambulance."

My voice came out shrill and strained. "What? I was scared out of my mind. No way was I launching into CSI mode. But he wasn't moving and there was so much blood. He was shot three times in the heart. He couldn't have survived."

"Okay, okay, calm down. I'm only asking the same questions the cops are going to."

"I'm not going to the police. Don't you see? That's why the shooter didn't kill me. I'm the fall guy. He intends to frame me for Zach's murder. And if he succeeds, I'll lose everything—my job, my license, my child. Hell, I'll be locked up for life for something I didn't do. So no, I'm definitely *not* letting anyone know I was on that beach."

"We don't need to reach any decisions right now. Let's just get through tonight."

I spun around in a circle, running my hands through my hair. "Crap. I totally forgot. I'm supposed to be at an art opening right now." I glanced at my watch. "If I don't show up, it'll look suspicious."

"Okay, drive to wherever you need to be. I'll listen in on the police scanner, see what I can learn, and we'll meet up tomorrow. And don't kill the messenger but before you go inside, you need to repair your face. And change your clothes. You look like the Unabomber."

Apparently, even when someone's shot right in front of you and you barely escape the scene with your life, a woman should make sure she always looks her best. "Thanks for the fashion advice. And don't worry. I'll make sure to reapply my lipstick," I said as I headed to the gallery.

26

Making sure I kept to the speed limit, I drove to the Third Ward and parked a block over from the gallery in a dark alley. The clock on the dashboard read eight-forty. The entire incident at the beach had taken less than an hour yet my whole life had changed. I spotted three sheriff's cars, lights blazing, headed in the opposite direction toward the south side.

Thank God I'd gotten away in time. Now if I could just get through this evening without falling apart.

I couldn't stop rehashing tonight's events. Zach was obviously my stalker; he was there on the beach at the precise time and place of the meeting. But what was his beef with me? We'd never met before that awards dinner. Why target me? The Reids were wealthy so it couldn't have been for the money. But then I remembered Liv's worry about gambling debts. Maybe Zach needed cash that couldn't be traced. Still, there had to be an easier way of getting it than an elaborate stalking scheme. Plus what about that expression on his face before he was shot, like I was the last person he expected to see? Another puzzle I'd need to solve if I wanted to figure out who was framing me.

One thing at a time. Right now, I needed to show up at the gallery, mingle with the crowd, retrieve my daughter, and make it back home. Tomorrow when I met with Max, we could work backwards through everything that happened tonight and see if we could make sense of it.

I climbed into the back seat and, like some kind of human pretzel, twisted and turned until I got out of my jeans and hoodie and into the knit dress. I covered the scrapes and bruises on my arms and my swollen wrist with a suit jacket I kept in the car for last-minute court appearances. There was a shitload of sand in the floorboards so I slapped the floor mats against the trunk and did my best to sweep the rest out of the car. Then I tackled my zombie-like face, with its smudged mascara and bruised cheek. My lower lip was swollen so, despite what I'd told Max, I left off lipstick, reapplied my eye make-up and de-tangled my hair. Finally I changed into my flats and clipped on my pearl earrings. The transformation was complete. I'd defy anyone to suspect I'd just hot-footed it away from a murder scene.

Which now came roaring back. That moment right before the shots, Zach's face, how he staggered back from the bullet's impact, then plunged onto the sand. Oh, God. A man had died right in front of me and here I was, worrying about makeup. I squeezed my eyes shut, tears leaking out the corners, and tried to block the memory. I didn't have time for this. I had to get going.

I couldn't leave my car here in the alley. If it was vandalized or stolen, how would I explain the small fortune in my trunk? Instead

I drove to the well-lit parking garage around the corner, then fast-walked to Liv's show.

The soiree was in full swing when I arrived and a tall kid in his twenties swooped down on me the moment I stepped through the door. "Champagne, ma'am?" It took all my willpower not to grab three glasses and down them right on the spot, but alcohol wasn't the best choice right now. I needed to keep my wits about me until I made it home.

Liv stood across the room alongside Charley and Spencer. Her white-blond hair hung loose tonight, cascading over her shoulders, and her gold and lace chemise clung to her thin frame like a second skin. My heart went out to her. Even though Zach sometimes treated her poorly, might even have abused her, Liv must have loved him once. His murder would send shock waves through her neat, well-ordered life. I watched as she enjoyed these last few minutes of accolades before everything in her world turned upside down.

I was still a bit shaky as I wobbled through the crowd toward them. "Olivia." I touched her bare arm. "Congratulations. The show looks like a huge success."

"Yikes, Rachel. Your hand is freezing. Are you okay?" When I assured her I felt fine, she pulled me over to meet a married couple standing nearby. I fumbled through idle chit-chat as Liv moved on to speak with other patrons.

A sculpture nearby caught my eye. It was a bronze bust of Charley, a spot-on replica of her deep-set eyes, full lips, and cheekbones a fashion model would envy. No wonder my daughter rebelled when I ordered her not to pose for Liv again. Who wouldn't want to be captured at the prime of their life in a sculpture that would last forever?

"How do you like it, Mom? Pretty rad, huh?" Charley shifted her weight from foot to foot, obviously beyond excited to be part of this event.

"Totally rad," I responded, my heart swelling with love for my daughter. Thank God she was safe. Zach could never make good on his threat. That was all that mattered. I thought of the DNA kit I'd found that morning. Somewhere in the middle of all this mess I'd have to tell her the truth. But that could wait. I just needed to get through tonight. "The sculpture's beautiful." I touched my daughter's cheek. "But then so is the model."

Charley blushed and stared at the floor. "That's all Liv. I mean, she makes me feel special, you know? Being around her."

A pang of envy shot through me. Maybe Liv was right. Maybe I was jealous of the close relationship she had with my daughter. Charley and I had been like that once. I'd give anything to recapture that feeling but I was at a loss as to how. "Well, between the two of you, you've created something lovely. I'm tempted to buy it for your grandfather for Christmas." But when I glanced at the price tag, I saw a red dot next to it, meaning someone had gotten there before me. Not to mention it had sold for two thousand dollars, far more than I could afford to spend.

I hadn't heard Ethan come up behind me so when he reached out and touched my back, I flinched, then quickly recovered. I needed to watch my reactions, calm down and behave as though nothing was wrong. I pasted on a smile. "Olivia must be pleased at the turn-out. I noticed she's sold quite a few pieces."

"She lives for nights like this. She doesn't always get positive strokes at home."

She won't have to worry about that anymore. The reality of the thought slammed into me. Zach was dead. Shot. I'd been there when it happened. It still seemed surreal, like something I'd heard about on some true crime podcast.

From the corner of my eye I saw two deputies from the sheriff's department enter the gallery—an older guy with a walrus mustache and a younger woman whom I recognized. Since the shooting had happened in a county park, the sheriff would have jurisdiction, though I suspected they'd soon pull in city police with their larger and more experienced Homicide Division. They must have already identified the body. But how had they known where to find the victim's wife so quickly? My heart galloped in my chest as I anticipated what was about to happen.

The two officers questioned the girl at the front desk, and she pointed to Olivia standing in the far corner with her back turned. As they made their way through the crowd, whispers broke out and the art patrons moved to one side. I stepped closer to Liv so I could hear what was going on as the owner of the gallery intercepted the two. "Can I help you, officers?"

"We need to speak privately with Olivia Reid. Is there a back office?"

The gallery owner whispered in Liv's ear, then led her and the two deputies through a door. When she came back, she raised her voice slightly and said to no one in particular, "No worries. Mrs. Reid must have forgotten to pay a parking ticket," followed by a slight laugh. "Meanwhile, please continue to enjoy the show. And drink up. There's lots more Champagne." With that, she blended into the crowd and the event went on as though nothing unusual had happened.

Until a high-pitched keening made us all startle. The sound continued for several seconds, followed by sobbing. No one moved but stood, flutes in hand, frozen like mannikins in a shop window. I approached Ethan and pointed to the back. "You should check on Olivia. See what's going on." He nodded but had only gone a few steps when the female deputy emerged and made a beeline for him. They exchanged a few words and then she approached me.

"Ms. Matthews. I'm not sure you remember me, but we worked together on that robbery last year. Mrs. Reid is asking for you. Would you come with me?"

Charley touched my arm, a confused look on her face. "Mom? What's going on?"

"I'm not sure, honey. Let me find out. Stay here." I followed the deputy into a cluttered room where Olivia sat on a couch, face puffy and drained of color, streaks of mascara running down her cheeks. Ethan had knelt in front of her and held her hands, but when I entered the room, she pushed him away, rushed over, and practically fell into my arms.

I playacted confusion. "What's happened?"

"I'm afraid Mrs. Reid's husband has been killed," Pullman explained.

Remember, you know nothing. "Was it a car accident?" I hoped Pullman might elaborate and tell me what theory the police were pursuing.

Unfortunately, she followed protocol. "I can't share any details at the moment."

"I don't understand." Liv clung to my hand. "They say Zach's been shot on the beach. But he left this afternoon for Chicago." She visibly shuddered. "Tell them, Rachel. Tell them there's been a mistake." Her voice was a croak. "It … it can't be him." Liv was no longer the cool, collected woman I knew but a wife, now a widow, trying to make sense of the fractured reality her life had just become.

"Are you sure it's Zach Reid?" I addressed the question to Pullman. "Could there have been a mistake?"

"We found his wallet, his credit cards, a driver's license, and his cell phone. When we called his home, the housekeeper was just locking up for the night. She's the one who told us where we could locate Mrs. Reid."

Olivia went back to Ethan and whispered, "You should call the staff together at headquarters first thing before the rumors start. And the investors. They need to be told, too. Otherwise, they might … they might…" Then, reality hit again, her face contorted, and she buried her head in her hands.

He put his arm around her. "Don't worry, I'll take care of everything. The last thing you need to worry about tonight is the business."

"Mrs. Reid?" Pullman said. When Liv didn't respond, she repeated herself. "Mrs. Reid." Liv lifted her head and faced the deputy. "Someone from homicide will want to interview you about your husband's whereabouts in the last twenty-four hours. Will you be home tomorrow morning?"

Liv's face was wet with tears. "I don't understand." Her eyes were wild and she swung her head back and forth between me and the deputies. "I don't know anything about this."

Predictably, Ethan came to her rescue. "My cousin's not in any state to be questioned. She'll likely need to be medicated tonight. Can't this wait a few days?"

"It's better to get all the details she can remember as soon as possible if we're going to stop the person who did this from coming after anyone else."

What was she implying? Did they suspect Zach wasn't the only person at risk? What was their theory about what had happened? I desperately wanted some insight about what line of inquiry the sheriff was pursuing.

"You mean I'm in danger?" Liv's voice quivered as she glanced at the male deputy. When he didn't say anything, she raised her voice. "Is that what you're saying? Someone might harm me, too?"

"We have no reason to think you're at risk. But you should go home and get some rest. Someone from the department will be in touch tomorrow." Pullman took over, rattled off Liv's home phone and address to confirm, then addressed Ethan. "Would you be available to come to the station and answer a few questions about the deceased? We can have you make a positive ID of the body as well, to make sure there's no mistake." When Ethan nodded, Pullman handed him a card with the address, and she and her partner left.

The two cousins moved to a far corner of the room and whispered together for a few minutes. I overheard the words "stocks" and "financials" but the rest was garbled. Liv shook her head several times, as though she disagreed with what Ethan was saying. Finally, she turned to me.

"Can you spend the night at my place and stay until the police question me? I know it's a lot to ask, but if Ethan goes to the station ..."

The last thing I wanted was to get pulled into this weird family dynamic. But Liv was in such distress, it would look odd if I refused and the last thing I wanted at this point was anyone questioning my behavior. Besides, this way I could be there when the detectives came by tomorrow and get a chance to hear what they'd found at the scene. The more I knew about what leads the authorities were pursuing, the better I'd be at keeping myself out of their crosshairs.

But I also didn't want to be seen as intruding. When I made eye contact with Ethan, he nodded his agreement, so I said yes. "I'll make arrangements for Charley to stay at her uncle's, and then drive over to your place. I should be there within the hour."

So much for making it home and having time to detune. Once again, I'd let myself get sucked into the quagmire surrounding Olivia Reid.

When I had plenty of problems of my own.

27

"Mr. Reid was killed? Who would do that?" At least Charley was so fixated on the murder, she didn't notice the stray sand on my side of the car and on the back seat. But I needed a break. "Can you please stop talking about Zach Reid? He wasn't a nice man so I'm sure he had plenty of enemies."

That silenced her for a minute but then she piped up again. "I think the police are jumping to conclusions. I mean maybe he dropped his wallet and someone else picked it up."

"And then *that* person was shot? You've been watching too much television."

"But it can't be him. When Olivia got to the gallery, she said she'd dropped him off at the train station a few minutes before. If that's true, how did he—"

My nerves were shredded so I had to work to keep my voice steady. I didn't want Charley obsessing over the murder or even worse, thinking I knew more than I'd let on. I reached across and patted her arm. "The police are good at their job, honey. Give them time. They'll figure it out. The important thing now is for us to support Liv however we can." What I really thought was, once the initial shock wore off, Liv would realize she was better off without Zach. Granted, that sounded harsh, but it was true. No more abuse. No more cheating. No more catering to his whims. And Olivia was no doubt the beneficiary of Zach's estate, so there'd be money as well. Which, according to Ethan, was one of the major reasons Liv hadn't followed through on a divorce.

Zach Reid had made my life miserable this last month with his harassing phone calls, his sadistic tape, and his creepy notes plus he'd threatened to maim Charley in a truly gruesome way. Honestly, I wasn't all that sorry he was dead. If that made me a terrible person, so be it. I could live with that.

***

AFTER I DROPPED CHARLEY OFF at Luke's house, I drove to the Reids. When I arrived, Liv led me into the living room, then collapsed on the sofa, a tumbler of whiskey already on the glass table in front of her. Even in this bizarre situation, she remembered to play hostess, pointing to the bar cart in the corner and telling me to help myself. After fixing a scotch, I sat opposite her. Outwardly, Liv seemed to have recovered from her near breakdown at the gallery. In fact, she seemed eerily calm. Probably in shock.

Ethan entered from the back of the house. I'd assumed he'd already left for the sheriff's department, but it made sense he'd waited until I got there to make sure Liv wasn't alone. He sat beside his cousin and dropped a small white pill into her hand. "You should take this. It'll help you sleep."

She dutifully washed down the tablet with the remaining alcohol in her glass, then gave a slight smile, and wiped her eyes. "I keep expecting him to burst through that door and laugh about how stupid the authorities are." After blowing her nose a couple of times, she yawned twice, finally saying she was going to turn in. "Rachel, would you mind coming along so I can talk to you in private?"

She led me upstairs to the master bedroom, which was spacious, with pale-beige walls and an adjoining bathroom with a whirlpool and walk-in shower. Olivia plopped down on the king-sized bed and I sat beside her.

Her cheeks were still streaked from her earlier tears. "I don't understand what's going on. Who would kill Zach?"

Men like Zach Reid made enemies as easily as most people made friends but Liv was in no shape to hear that right now. "It's a lot to take in, I know," I offered. "Get some sleep. The police will sort it out." I was trying to reassure myself as well as Liv.

"We didn't have the happiest of marriages." She gave a weak laugh.

"None of that matters now. Come on, let's get you ready for bed."

Goosebumps covered her arms. "There's something I need to tell you." The words came out in a rush, as though she couldn't contain them. "I'm afraid … what if Ethan's somehow involved in all this? What if he's the one that killed Zach?"

She wasn't thinking straight. "I can see him telling you to get a divorce, but he wouldn't commit murder."

"He didn't get to the gallery until right before you did, even though he promised to be there when it opened. Maybe—"

Could Ethan be the shooter? Had he been following Zach, looking for a chance to help Liv out of an untenable situation? Even if her husband hadn't abused Liv physically, Ethan knew how unhappy she'd been. And it would explain why I hadn't been killed. Ethan wouldn't hurt me, even if it was risky to leave a witness behind. I needed to keep my eye on him, see if he acted strange, see if his story had holes in it. The fact he was late to the gallery meant he had opportunity. "Did you ask him where he'd been?"

"I'm afraid to. What if he murdered Zach to protect me?" Liv grabbed my hand and squeezed. "What should I tell the police?"

"Tell them the truth. If they want to question Ethan about his whereabouts, they will. You don't need to draw attention to the fact, though. That's their job."

She was still crying a little even though she was doing her best to hide it from me. "I can't lose Ethan. I need him, I mean, not only because of Apollo, but he's my rock. I depend on him." Liv yawned again and her eyelids drooped.

"Looks like that pill's working. Get some sleep. And stop worrying. I'll stay with you until after the police leave tomorrow morning." I waited while Liv changed into her nightgown and then tucked her into bed as though she were a child. I flipped off the lights and eased the door shut.

As I headed downstairs, I passed a door to another bedroom down the hall and peeked inside. This space was obviously Zach's, with its dark walnut flooring, ebony night tables, and leopard-patterned spread. A Robert Ludlum thriller lay face down on the arm of the recliner. So the couple maintained separate bedrooms. It didn't surprise me.

I rejoined Ethan in the living room. "I'm heading over to the sheriff's office," he said. "I imagine I'll be there a while, so I'll crash at my condo downtown. You two should be fine here tonight but

I'll keep my cell on if you need me. And let Liv know I called a nine o'clock meeting at headquarters to brief the staff." Ethan, ever the rock. I saw why Liv depended on him. "Where's your phone? I'll type in my number."

I handed it to him. "That pill's taken effect. I expect she'll sleep through the night." For my part, I wasn't ready to turn in quite yet. I wanted time alone to write down everything I remembered about the shooting. I'd been so terrified I didn't trust my memory.

"Will you do me a favor?" Ethan asked. "When the detectives show up tomorrow, don't let Liv talk too much. There's no need to give them intimate details of her marriage that don't have anything to do with Zach's death."

I frowned. "I understand your need to protect her, but she should share as much information as she can so the authorities get a clear picture of Zach. Who he interacted with. Who his possible enemies were. Who stands to benefit from his death."

An odd look crossed his face. "Besides Olivia, you mean."

"The police will look at her, of course, but she's got a solid alibi so I wouldn't worry."

"Let's hope you're right." Ethan stood. "I should go. Let me show you to your room."

He pushed past me down the hall, and I trailed him to a mother-in-law suite at the back part of the house, complete with kitchen, bedroom, and bath. "This is cozy," I said.

"It's where I stay when Liv needs me to sleep over. At one time, she talked about Jasper coming here for a long visit, but nothing came of it."

"Her brother? Liv seems reluctant to talk about him. What's his story?"

"I'm not entirely sure. He never lived with our family full-time like Liv did. He was older, sixteen when their parents died, and he moved in with a buddy of his so he could graduate from the same high school. I heard he moved to Iowa after that and the rest of us scattered, too, so we just kind of lost touch. Liv hears from him occasionally, usually at holidays, but that's about it. I guess he's got his own life." He shrugged. "His address is around here somewhere. I should probably write to him and let him know about Zach."

I flopped my bag on the bed, anxious to have some privacy, but Ethan didn't seem in a hurry to leave. "I'll lock up and set the alarm. You shouldn't need it but the code is 0315. Like Caesar. You know, the Ides of March." He reached into the drawer of the nightstand and pulled out a small handgun. "And if anyone threatens you, and I mean *anyone*, don't hesitate to use this."

"You think whoever killed Zach may come after Liv, too?"

"Let's just say I'd breathe easier knowing you can defend yourself. The last thing I want is anything happening to you." His eyes swept the room. "Either one of you." He tucked the gun back in the drawer. "I'd better be going. Lock the door behind me." With that, he left.

I didn't think there was any danger, but I did as he asked. Then I moved to the desk in the corner, rummaged around in my bag until I found some blank paper, and wrote down step-by-step everything I remembered from the last day, from when I first left the house until the moment Ethan led me to this room. I jotted timelines next to each bullet point. No matter which way I lined up the events, nothing made sense.

How naïve I'd been, thinking that once I'd paid off my stalker, I'd be free. Now I was like a rat in a maze, every turn leading to another dead end. No answers, only more questions. My problems weren't solved. In fact, they'd gotten a whole lot worse.

28

Zach's lying face up on the ground, three bullet holes in his chest and I'm holding a gun. No, not a gun. My gun. Blood bubbles at the corner of his mouth and he's saying something I can't make out, but I know it's the key to everything. I lean in, and then he grabs my wrist, pulls me toward him. He opens his mouth and—

I bolted upright from the dream, my skin slick with sweat, sheets wrapped around my legs like a straitjacket. Buzzing. My cell. I glanced at the screen. Max.

"Hey, there," I whispered, my breath still ragged.

"How are you holding up?" he asked.

"You woke me from a nightmare. Zach was dying and he was trying to tell me something." My thrumming heartbeat had slowly returned to normal.

"I promise it will all look better in the morning. How's Charley?"

"She's spending the night at my brother's place. I'm at the Reid's house."

"Wait, what? Why? What's going on?" Why did he sound angry? So much had happened since we'd talked and I didn't feel like rehashing it right now.

"It's a long story. The police came to the gallery and Liv didn't want to be alone … anyway, the detectives are coming tomorrow morning to question her, and she wants me there. But I still want to meet up with you. Will one o'clock work?"

"No, I'm … never mind, I'll make some calls and cancel my other appointment. Call me when you're ready to leave," he said. "And Rachel? Watch your step with the police. You're a friend of the victim's wife. Nothing more. Don't let Liv's situation distract you. Understood?"

We made plans to meet at the kite stand near McKinley Marina the next day. Talking to Max calmed me down but my whole body ached, both from the frantic run from the beach but also from holding so much fear inside for hours. I popped a couple of Advil before lying back down and this time, I drifted into a dreamless sleep.

Until three in the morning, when Liv screamed out my name. When I unlocked the door, she fell trembling into my arms, her face splotchy and wet. "Someone's trying to break in. It's Zach's killer, I know it is. They're after me, too," she cried, her words running together. Liv's nerves were stretched thin. She was close to her breaking point and I was afraid for her.

I tried to calm her down, but she kept raving. Finally, I grabbed her head with both hands and got in her face, my voice stern and forceful. "Be quiet. Settle down and tell me what happened."

She nodded and her breathing slowed, although the trembling continued. "The wind was so loud." She covered her ears. "Then the windows started to rattle and when I looked outside, I saw a man hiding in the shadows. He had on a ski mask and there was a huge knife in his hand." She shook my shoulders. "You have to believe me. Someone was out there, I swear."

"Of course I believe you. Let me call the police. They can be here in no time." I grabbed my bag, searching for my cell.

"They'll think I'm being hysterical."

"Who cares what they think?" I scoffed. "It's their job to protect us. You stay with me. We'll be safe until they get here." I locked the door, wedged the desk chair beneath the knob for good measure, then dialed 9-1-1 and explained. In less than fifteen minutes, a squad car pulled into the driveway. Two officers circled the house and walked through the grounds before finally ringing the doorbell. I threw on a robe and joined Liv in the living room, where we turned off the alarm system, then explained what Liv had seen.

"We didn't find any signs of a prowler but he could have taken off when he saw us," the older man said. "Just to be safe, we'll circle back a few times tonight. Make sure he knows we're watching. Once we leave, re-set the alarm and double-check that all the doors and windows are locked." We nodded, and he added, "Have a safe night, ladies," tipping his hat.

After they'd left, Liv pleaded with me. "Will you sleep with me upstairs? It's just for tonight, I promise. Please, Rachel."

The request was awkward but understandable. "I'll be up in a minute." Liv floated upstairs, and I returned to the guest suite to retrieve my phone and my toiletries. And then I opened the drawer of the nightstand and took out the gun, tucking it into the pocket of the robe. Ethan had been right to worry. The killer was still out there. The question was whether he'd been coming after Liv.

Or me. The witness he'd left behind.

29

Two POLICE DETECTIVES KNOCKED on the Reid's door the next morning at nine o'clock. By the time they arrived, Liv and I had eaten breakfast and downed several cups of coffee. Liv's eyelids were no longer swollen and her face had gotten back some color. In fact, she seemed more relaxed and at ease than I had seen her in a while. She'd dressed in lounge pants and a soft pink T-shirt, her hair pulled back in a ponytail, making her look closer to seventeen than thirty.

As I had predicted, the county sheriff had pulled in Milwaukee PD's Homicide Division to handle the investigation. Bob Farina, the lead detective, was someone I knew from my early days as a prosecutor. A veteran police officer, he still spoke with the distinctive twang of his Texas childhood. His rumpled clothes hung from his skinny frame and his hair had receded since I'd seen him last. His partner was a young woman a foot shorter with smooth caramel skin and dark eyes. Bob introduced her as Kalisha

Washington, and the two of them settled into the side chairs while Liv and I sat side-by-side on the white sectional couch. At first, the detectives seemed thrown by me being there, but Liv explained I was her best friend and they acquiesced. After all, this wasn't official testimony, just a fact-gathering interview.

"Let's start with an easy one, okay, Mrs. Reid?" Farina said. "You showed up at the gallery around six and didn't leave the premises until the officers arrived. Right?"

Liv nodded. It was a standard opening. Record everyone's movements during the relevant time frame. Apparently, a jogger reported hearing shots in the park at precisely 8:12 by his Fit-Bit so Liv had an iron-clad alibi. Over fifty people had seen her at the time her husband had been killed.

The next questions centered on Zach. "It'd be a big help to know your husband's activities yesterday. When did you last see him and what'd he tell you about his plans for the night?" Farina asked.

Liv crossed and recrossed her legs before answering. "He said he was going to spend the weekend in Chicago and be back Sunday afternoon. I dropped him at the train station at 5:30."

"Why Chicago?"

Liv twisted a lock of hair around her finger and I saw she'd removed her wedding ring. "I can tell you what he told me, though I realize now he must have been lying. Our company had just won the Burger Boy franchise for Illinois, and Zach said he was going to meet with executives from the home office to go over details of the contract. I'm afraid I didn't pay much attention to what he said—I was too preoccupied with my gallery opening. Who was coming, how the pieces were being displayed, details like that."

Washington chimed in. "But your husband never got on that train. As far as we can tell, he never even bought a ticket."

Liv looked perplexed. "All I know is what he told me, that he'd be gone all weekend. I specifically remember because I was angry.

The gallery show was important to me and I'd asked him to put it on his calendar weeks ago so he wouldn't forget."

Washington again. "Did he seem worried about anything this last week? Any financial issues with the new contract? Or problems with an employee?"

"Nothing that I know of." At that point, Liv seemed to zone out. She straightened the fashion magazines on the glass table, then took a sip of coffee. Finally she added, "You should probably talk to my cousin Ethan. Ethan Mansfield. He'd know more about that kind of thing. He's not here now but I expect him soon."

"Does he live here with you and your husband?"

Liv tittered. "Of course not. He's got his own place downtown. But sometimes he stays over in our guest suite."

Farina popped up. "He's vice-president of the company, right?"

A note of defiance crept into Liv's voice. "It's not nepotism, if that's what you're implying. Yes, he's family, but he's also a very savvy businessperson. My husband offered him stock shares equal to ten percent of the company to entice him to come to work for us. Zach valued his expertise."

That took me by surprise. Ethan didn't just work for Apollo. He had a stake in the company, which meant he benefitted financially from Zach's death.

"Did your husband have any enemies you know about? People who might want him out of the way?" Washington asked.

Liv's reply came in seconds. "There's no one."

Her answer troubled me. I was sure she was hiding something. My eyes flickered to her, hoping she'd tell them about our discussion at the casino party but when she didn't, I interrupted. "What about his gambling habit, Liv? You were worried he might be involved with some unsavory people. If he ran up some debts that he couldn't pay ..." The police needed to know about any enemies Zach might have and of course, I had a vested interest in them looking anywhere but at me. Not to mention they were also better positioned to get information about loan sharks or criminal elements than either myself or Max.

Olivia's face clouded over. Was she upset I'd shared something she'd told me in confidence? She turned to Farina. "But if he's dead, they can't get their money, so that wouldn't make sense, right?"

"Why don't you leave that to us to decide?" Washington said. "What can you tell us about those debts, Mrs. Reid?"

"Only that Zach had a gambling addiction when we lived in New York. It's one of the reasons we moved—the crowd he ran with took regular jaunts to Atlantic City and he signed some hefty IOU's. But that was all behind us."

Washington persisted. "Then why bring it up with Ms. Matthews here?"

Liv hesitated, as though deciding how to frame her response and her voice had an edge of exasperation. "Our CFO had noticed some irregularities in the books, cash allocations he couldn't match up to purchases. He told Ethan about it and he also told me. I was afraid Zach might be siphoning funds from the company so I wouldn't notice. And at the casino party, I noticed him talking with some big-wigs from there, so naturally I was on alert. But when I asked Zach about it later, he said he knew about the discrepancies. An employee in accounting had made an error but he'd straightened it out."

"We may ask you to look at some photographs to see if you can identify the men from the casino your husband met with. That won't be a problem, will it?" Washington asked.

"Of course not. Whatever you need," Liv said.

The questioning went on for another half-hour, covering not only the broad outlines of Apollo Enterprises, but also Zach's schedule in the last month, his family background, their marriage, and his hobbies which, to my surprise, included historical re-enactments. Maybe that explained the costume?

"I gotta say, Mrs. Reid, there are some weird goings-on with this case," Farina said. "One's the get-up your husband had on. Pirate stuff—ruffled shirt, black breeches, leather boots, the whole nine yards. Any thoughts on that?"

The bewildered look on Olivia's face was all the answer they needed. "I don't understand—a pirate? Like with an eye patch? That's absurd."

"So he never played dress-up? Got kinky during sex?"

"Certainly not." Her hands fluttered around her face. "And frankly, what you're suggesting is insulting. Back in New York, we were both involved in theater productions—mostly summer stock—but that was years ago. And as I explained before, he participated in re-enactments. But that was Civil War era, not … Pirates of the Caribbean."

Washington leaned forward and lobbed a question out of left-field.

"Did your husband own any guns, Mrs. Reid?"

Liv glanced at me, a question in her eyes and I nodded at her to answer. "Zach had a permit for a handgun. Fast-food's a cash-based business and there were times when he handled large sums of money. He thought he'd be safer if he carried a weapon with him when he traveled alone around the state. And I believe Ethan has a handgun he keeps here." She didn't mention her own gun, the one she'd told me she kept her in her room.

"Do you know where those guns are now?"

"Zach usually kept his in the car. Ethan's might be in the guest bedroom."

"Well, if you're okay with it, how about we go ahead and do a sweep of the house? If you want, we can run down a judge for a search warrant but that'd take time and sooner's way better than later in a case like this. We'll also want to take a look at his computer, phones, files, stuff like that." His tone was casual, like his request was no big deal. A throwaway.

But Liv wasn't that gullible. She turned to me. "Rachel?"

They would likely turn up evidence of Zach's stalking activity, which would circle back to me but it would seem odd if I advised Liv against it. Farina was right. He could easily get a warrant. Plus, I wanted to be here to see what they turned up.

"The sooner they get a clear picture of Zach, the sooner they'll be able to figure out who might want to harm him." I turned to the officers. "Mrs. Reid doesn't have anything to hide. She's as anxious as you are to find out who killed her husband." Liv nodded her agreement.

Farina made a phone call and within minutes, two police cars pulled up, obviously waiting around the corner for the go-ahead. Three officers bustled in, carrying evidence bags, boxes, and carts. They started in Zach's home office, then scoured the garage, then the basement, sorting and labelling computers, electronics, and contents of cabinets. They worked in silence for an hour, until one of them came back into the living room, pulled Farina aside, and handed him a medium-sized cardboard box. The detective lifted out a garden-variety black cell phone with a slight crack in one corner.

"This was buried under some gardening equipment, Mrs. Reid. Ever seen it before?"

"No." Liv looked confused. "Zach and I both have I-phones. Mine's rose-gold and his is … was platinum."

"This isn't a regular phone. It's got a special adaptor for changing your voice. Gamers use them to hide behind an avatar."

My adrenaline spiked. The type of device my stalker would have used to disguise himself during calls. That clinched it. Zach had been my stalker.

"Why would Zach need to disguise his voice?" Liv asked.

"No idea. We'll run a trace on calls to and from this number and see what pops up."

I swallowed back the bile in my throat. There was a good chance Zach's messages to me were on that phone. Now was the perfect time to speak up and share what I knew. But instead I held back. Stayed quiet. I needed to buy myself time.

"Can I ask when my husband's body will be released? I need to plan for …" Liv's voice broke and she dabbed at her eyes.

"It'll only be a few days. The medical examiner's a little backed up, but our liaison officer will call you later today to go over the details," Washington said.

Another officer stood in the doorway holding a grocery shopping bag. "Boss? There's something else you need to see." Again, Farina retreated into the next room and the two of them spoke in low voices for several minutes.

The detective eventually rejoined us in the living room and pulled a small hand-held video camera from the bag. "Does this look familiar, Mrs. Reid?"

Once again, Liv shook her head. "Zach was never big on making a record of his activities. But if he'd wanted to make a video, he'd have used his phone."

"We also found video-editing software on his computer. Ever seen your husband splicing still pictures together into videos, laying down soundtracks? Could be for a training video or some marketing project for the company."

Olivia smiled. "I'm the artist in the family. Zach was all thumbs when it came to anything the least bit creative. And we've got a marketing department that handles the ads we use."

Farina continued. "Sorry to be insensitive but was your husband into watching adult films? Maybe even making them? Something he wouldn't want to store on his regular phone?" He lowered his voice to a whisper. "Any chance he taped you without your knowledge?"

"Of course not." Liv spat out the words and abruptly stood. "I'm sorry, I need to stop for today. I'm feeling light-headed and

I need to lay down." Before anyone could respond, she flew up the stairs.

"Pushed too hard on that last one, I guess," Farina said to me with a shrug. "But hey, it's a legitimate question."

"The woman lost her husband twelve hours ago. Cut her some slack, okay?" I replied.

The two detectives exchanged looks, then stood. "Tell Mrs. Reid we'll be back in touch. And let Mr. Mansfield know we'll be reaching out to talk to him as well."

I walked them to the front door and watched as they drove away, all the time turning over that last exchange in my head. There was no doubt in my mind Olivia would never have permitted Zach to film her. In fact, with separate bedrooms, I doubted whether the couple even had sex on a regular basis.

No, Zach used that film equipment for other purposes. Like producing that video still sitting in a case file at the police station with my name on it. It was only a matter of time before Farina put two and two together and knocked on my door.

30

The fact the police had turned up video-editing software at the Reid's home didn't surprise me. But now the clock was ticking. It wouldn't be long before they'd traced calls from that burner to my phone. I had to get rid of any evidence that put me on that beach and I had to do it today.

As soon as I got home from the Reid house, I gathered up everything I'd worn the night before—hoodie, jeans, tee-shirt, sneakers—wrapped it all in an old sheet, and stuffed it in my trunk. I transferred the money to a different bag and tossed the original duffel onto the pile. Next, I drove to an abandoned dump site north of the city. I scanned the perimeter to make sure I wasn't being observed, then retrieved everything from the trunk, dumped it into a rusty barrel leaning against concrete blocks, doused the lot with kerosene, and tossed in match after match. Within seconds, a wall of flame whooshed and I watched, eyes tearing, as everything turned to ash.

Minutes passed but still I stood—frightened, exhausted, the wind whipping my hair across my face, arms tight around my body. A part of me was disgusted at what I'd become. The sole witness to a murder destroying evidence. A zealous lawyer covering up the truth. An officer of the court lying to the police. But what choice did I have? I'd always believed the law was our last, best defense against a chaotic world. Now I knew sometimes the law can't protect you.

Sometimes you have to protect yourself.

At the first gas station I came to, I filled my tank, vacuumed the car seats and trunk, and drove through the car wash, hopefully flushing any remaining evidence down the drain. If the police did get a search warrant for my vehicle, they shouldn't find any definitive evidence that put me on that beach. For now, I was safe. I turned east toward the marina to keep my appointment with Max.

He stood silhouetted against the backdrop of Lake Michigan, staring at the water, his wavy hair catching the sunlight. I flashed back to last night—how he'd stroked my back, calmed me down, helped me with no questions asked. I shouldn't have blown up about him following me. Where would I be if he hadn't?

He turned when I reached him and squeezed my shoulder. "Holding it together?"

"Not really." My voice trembled in spite of myself. "It feels like I escaped a burning building and sailed straight into a hurricane."

"How did it go with the police?"

"Liv let them search the house, and they hauled away all kinds of files. They found a voice changer so that answers one question. Zach was the one behind this."

We found an isolated park bench. Max stretched his long arms across the back, stuck his legs out in front, and crossed his ankles. Probably sending me a subliminal message not to stress, everything was under control. Which was easy for him to say. He hadn't witnessed a murder, hadn't collapsed face down in the sand, hadn't run for his life up a dark, winding path, waiting for a bullet to end his life. I straightened, took a deep breath, and got my emotions under control.

"Mind if we start back at the beginning?" Max said. "I'm playing catch up here so I apologize ahead of time for asking so many questions." He turned slightly, resting his head on his hand. "Tell me about the Reids. How do you know them again?"

Good. Cold, hard facts. Something to latch onto. "We were seated at the same table at an awards dinner the first week in March." And for the next few minutes, I stepped Max through my first impressions of the couple, how Liv asked to join the book club, then that initial lunch at my house. "She seemed lonely and frankly, I liked her. Bright, funny, full of life. Plus she met my daughter that day and the two of them hit it off, too. Charley even posed as a model once or twice for her until I put a stop to it."

He seemed puzzled. "Because?"

Because my daughter seemed to like Liv better than me. But Max wouldn't understand that. "I didn't like the vibes I got from Zach. I suspected he might be abusing Liv physically and I didn't feel comfortable having Charley around him."

"*Was* he abusing her? There might be a motive there."

"My gut says yes but I don't know for sure."

"So you were friends with her but steered clear of him. Then what reason would Zach have to harass you?"

"I have no idea. I can count on one hand the number of times I was in the same room with him. That first dinner, then once when I picked Liv up for book club, and then a casino party they hosted."

Max leaned forward, hands on his knees. "Think back. Maybe you knew him from before. In college? Or from a previous case?"

"He's not someone I'd forget. Besides, Liv said he was raised in Philly. And before they moved here, they lived in New York."

"If you didn't know each other, maybe he wasn't your stalker after all."

"He showed up at the meeting place. It had to be him."

Max asked me to describe everything that happened again. They were the same facts I'd blurted out the night before but maybe he was testing me, seeing if I'd change my story.

When I finished, he stood. "Mind if we walk? It helps me think." We took the path that encircled the lakefront. It was a good three minutes before he asked, "You said when Zach saw you, he looked peculiar. What did you mean by that?"

I thought back to the seconds before the shot. "If I had to guess, I'd say he'd been expecting someone else and couldn't understand what I was doing there instead. But that doesn't make any sense. He told me when and where to meet."

"It's also weird he was dressed like a pirate. Any idea what that's about?"

"Apparently Zach was involved in theater back in New York. Liv also said he participated in reenactments, like when people dress up as soldiers or Star Wars characters. I suppose it could have been a way to cover up his identity. Or a fetish? But why wear it to meet me?" I couldn't make sense of it.

"His look and his costume. Two questions that need answers. Okay, let's get back to you lying in the sand. When you decided to move, you got up and ran. Why didn't you check on Zach? Or duck behind a bush and phone the police?"

I bristled. "I was scared shitless! And even if I had a signal down there, which I didn't, how would I explain being on an empty beach with a massive amount of cash and a dead body?" Max only wanted to help but honestly, this third degree was wrecking my nerves. "I know it looks bad. But I was afraid for my life. All I could think about was getting the hell out of there." Max squinted as he processed what I'd said. "And then you showed up and you *told* me not to call them," I said.

"Because it was too late. You'd already left the scene of the crime."

Steel bands of pressure squeezed my temples. "I'm screwed, aren't I?"

"What about fingerprints? Hair? Fibers from your clothes?"

"It was a beach. Sand. Wind. Water. My guess is they won't find any evidence I was there from forensics. But just in case, I vacuumed and cleaned out the car, and burned everything I wore." I held up my hand. "And before I get a lecture—nobody saw me."

He shifted uncomfortably. "You hope."

"There's something else." I'd left it for last, knowing how bad it was.

"It's all going to come out eventually. Go ahead."

"Remember I told you I thought someone had broken into my house before I installed that new alarm system? Well, before I left last night, I thought about taking a weapon to protect myself. But when I searched for my gun, I couldn't find it. When I first bought it, I kept it at the back of my closet but a week ago, I moved it to my nightstand. Anyway, it wasn't there. The drawer was empty."

He stopped and faced me. "Are you saying someone broke into your house, stole your gun, and used it to shoot Zach?"

"I know it sounds crazy but it's missing and it had to have disappeared before I installed the alarm. But if Zach was the stalker, then *he's* the one that broke into my house, so he'd be the one who stole the gun, right?"

"When was the last time you shot it?"

"Maybe a year ago?" I stared at my shoes. "I told you it was bad."

He resumed walking and picked up the pace. "What happened at the gallery?"

He took out a small spiral notebook and pen from his pocket and jotted down notes as I talked. I stepped through how I'd been there when the police arrived. How Liv had asked me to spend the night. My discussion with Ethan. Liv's report of a man in the yard with a knife. What the police asked Liv the next morning.

Finally I stopped and faced him. "You have to believe me. I had nothing to do with this murder." I wasn't sure whether to say this next part, but if I couldn't trust Max, who could I trust? "When I got to the park, all I could think about was how much I hated this guy. How I wanted him to suffer. How dare he threaten to blind my daughter? I've never been a vengeful person, but I wanted to unleash the hounds of hell on him. Maybe that's why I thought about bringing my gun." My voice broke. "Maybe at a gut level I *wanted* to kill him."

Max took hold of my arms and forced me to a stop. "But you didn't. Listen to me, Rachel. There's a big difference between thinking about committing murder and actually killing someone. There's a line there and you didn't cross it. Remember that."

He went on. "But you *have* landed yourself in the middle of a murder and at this point, you can't go to the police. You fled the scene instead of staying put and telling the police what you knew. Not to mention I helped you get away, so they could arrest *me* as an accessory. And if they find your gun, and it's the murder weapon, they'll have no choice but to charge you. And you know how it works. Once they have a viable suspect in custody, they stop looking."

My throat closed up, so dry I wasn't sure I could get the words out, even if I knew what to say, which I didn't. "What ...what should I do?"

"Right now, the police can't connect you personally to Zach. You're a friend of his wife, that's all. But once they analyze that videocam, they'll question you. Admit you had a stalker because there's already a police file on that. But act dumbfounded when they tell you the stalker was Zach. Insist you barely knew the man. Right now, they're going to be concentrating on Zach himself, digging into his background, his friends, and his business dealings. Maybe they'll turn up another viable suspect. Meanwhile, you and I will investigate on our own."

Was I up for this? Right now, all I wanted was to crawl into a hot bath, lock the door, and have a stiff drink. I needed time alone to think all this through. Another reason not to confess my involvement to the authorities. I tucked my arms across my chest. "I feel like I'm running around in circles. Nothing fits."

"For now, Zach's all we've got. Let me research what happened in his life before he showed up in Milwaukee. As for you, don't go off on your own again. We need to work together and pool our information. Are we clear?"

I'd left him out of the loop and as a result, I'd implicated him in a murder. He had every right to be upset. "I'm sorry I didn't tell you about the payoff. He was watching. I was afraid he'd hurt Charley and—"

"I get it. You wanted to protect your daughter. Don't worry, I'm on your side."

"Thank you. I can't do this on my own." There was a giant target on my back and Max was my ally, not my enemy. "I'm screwed, aren't I?"

"Don't go there. For now, it's business as usual. Don't let anyone see you're rattled." Max paused. "A murder this theatrical doesn't happen in Milwaukee—wealthy CEO, isolated setting, sympathetic widow. The local media's crawling all over it already and by tomorrow the national press will show up. Since you knew the Reids, you won't be assigned the case but you can still poke around, ask questions, and see what you can find out. Let's touch base on Monday night. Until then, keep a low profile. It might be a good idea if you weren't around tomorrow in case the police drop by to question you. We need to buy more time."

The DNA kit popped into my head. Zach's murder and all the subsequent events had pushed that discovery to the back of my brain, but now it came roaring back front and center.

Charley had forced my hand. It wasn't a choice anymore. I had to tell my daughter the truth about her father. A conversation I'd been dreading for seventeen years. And I needed to do it before Tuesday when the results hit her inbox.

31

THE MINUTE I DISCOVERED that DNA kit in my daughter's room, I knew I only had two choices—come clean and tell her everything or leave it to some impersonal biotech firm in northern California. One way or another, the truth was going to come out.

Clarence Darrow had nothing on me when I got in front of a jury. Fluid phrasing, logical thinking, solid persuasive skills—check, check, and check. But this conversation wasn't one I could finesse. It was too personal and too important. In fact, just thinking about Charley's face once she knew what I'd done had my stomach tied up in knots. Where would I even begin?

***

WHEN I PICKED CHARLEY UP at my brother's house, I floated the idea of us taking off the next day for a hike in the Holy Hill area. We used to spend time together every weekend when Charley was younger, making the rounds of the state parks, but since becoming a teenager, my daughter preferred spending time with Spencer or her girlfriends. But this time I insisted. I needed to get her away from the distraction of computers, social media, and texts, somewhere isolated where she couldn't run out the door or lock herself in her bedroom once she realized what I'd kept hidden from her.

With Ginger sprawled across the back seat, we hopped into the car at eight the next morning. The whole way there, Charley chatted non-stop about Zach's murder. It was apparently the talk of the school and she was a minor celebrity since she'd been in the thick of things, knew the victim and his wife, and had a mother who'd not only spent the night with the widow but been there when the police questioned her. I finally had to beg her to stop. The last thing I needed right now was to dwell on the murder investigation. I needed to stay focused, work out how best to tell Charley about Paul.

Once we reached the woodland preserve, I secured the bag with our picnic lunch to my back, fastened a leash around Ginger's neck, and we took off into the pine trees. For two hours, we hiked through the forest, recalling previous adventures, like the day Charley came across a nest with three eggs in the crook of a tree, setting off a flurry of squawks as the feathered parents dive-bombed her. Eventually we arrived at a sun-drenched clearing and broke for lunch. The words I'd rehearsed tumbled through my brain but now that the time had come, they sounded artificial, almost trite.

I unpacked the food while Charley spread out the checkered tablecloth and filled the portable dog bowl with water. While my daughter scarfed her ham sandwich in record time as well as an apple and two raisin cookies, the three bites I managed to swallow tasted like dirt and sat in my stomach like stones. I pushed my plate aside, nerves on fire, and gazed at Charley.

She'd leaned back on her hands and was gazing at the sky. "Thanks for dragging me here. Nature rocks." She held up her cell and took a selfie, then typed, no doubt posting the snap to TikTok. She glanced at my plate, then back at me. "Are you okay? You're all sweaty."

"I love you. You know that, right?"

She frowned, obviously sensing something was up. "What's going on? Why are you acting funny?"

I couldn't put it off any longer. "There's something we need to talk about."

Charley rolled her eyes. "Can we *please* not argue about college again."

"This is something else. Something I need to tell you," I began, my heartbeat a drum in my chest.

She sat up and wrapped her arms around her legs, worry lines across her forehead. "Are you sick? Is Grandpa?"

"No, nothing like that." I took a deep breath. "I found a DNA kit in your room on Friday when we were looking for your shoes."

"Oh, that." My daughter flicked her hand. "The girls at school …"

"I get it. You want to know more about your father. Maybe even find him. Right?"

She fidgeted. "You told me you didn't remember his name. I thought maybe they could track him down."

I dug my fingernails into my palms. "You need to listen to me carefully, honey." I reached out and took hold of her hand. "I know who your father is." I paused for a few seconds, picking my words with care. "I've always known."

"Wait, what? You said—".

"I know the story I told you. But I made it up." Every word I spoke hung in the air between us like dangling knives.

Charley snatched her hand away and shook her head. "Are you saying you've been lying to me, like all this time? That's so messed up." She frowned, then bolted upright, screaming and crying at the same time. "No, I don't believe you. Why would you keep something like that a secret? You wouldn't."

I stood too, my words coming out in a rush. "I'm so sorry. Please listen. I know you're upset but—"

She broke in, her hands curled into fists. "Okay, then who is he? Who's my father?" She closed the distance between us, yelling into my face, grabbing my arms, and squeezing. "Tell me!"

I inhaled as much air as I could and blurted it out. "Your father's name is Paul Osthoff. He was a writer. I met him when I was in school at Northwestern."

She backed away, confusion distorting her face. Then she started to pace. Back and forth, back and forth, muttering "I don't get it. Why didn't you …?" Her chin trembled and she folded her arms across her chest. "Why hasn't he ever …?" Ginger ran in circles between us, barking and jumping.

This was going all wrong. It was nothing like I'd planned. "Please. Give me a chance to explain. I know I messed up but I was only trying to protect you."

"No," she shouted, wagging her finger. "God, that is *such* a cop-out. Nobody forced you to *lie* to me. You *chose* to." Her hand flew to her mouth. "Wait, does he even *know* about me? Did you keep me a secret from him, too?" Her face flushed bright red, then she doubled over, howled, and clutched her stomach. I moved to comfort her, but she stopped me, a scowl on her face. "Don't you *dare* touch me." Tears streamed down as she yelled, "Was he another of your one-night stands?"

"What? No." I choked out the words. "I never had any one-night stands. I made that up. I was in love with your father."

"Then why didn't you get married?" Charley spewed out. "I could have had two parents like everybody else instead of being a *bastard.*"

Heat crept up my neck. It might as well all come out, like ripping off a band-aid. "He was already married. He had children."

Tears welled in her eyes and she swiped at them. "You really are a piece of work, Mom, you know that? You act like you're this perfect person who follows the rules, never makes a mistake, and always knows what's best. When really, you're a big, fat hypocrite." Every word out of her mouth was a bullet that pierced my heart.

Ginger's bark had reached fever pitch and I grabbed the leash to hold her in place, praying no one was around to overhear. "We can't help who we fall in love with."

"That's a pretty good excuse if you ask me," she spat out. "Maybe that graffiti on the garage door wasn't about me after all."

Her remark slammed into me like a plunge into frigid water. My daughter had never spoken to me with such venom, such loathing. Sure, I had events in my past I wasn't proud of, history I prayed would never come to light. And sooner or later every child realizes their parents are fallible. But for Charley, the realization was coming hard on the heels of so much other information, it was no wonder she lashed out.

"I know I should have told you the truth before now. At first I didn't because … well, you were a child and then when you got older … I'm not proud of how I handled this."

Charley wiped her nose with her sleeve, whispered "God" again, then whirled and ran at top speed into the woods, shouting over her shoulder. "Do *not* follow me. I need to be *alone*."

Ginger yanked at the leash, set to give chase. I kneeled next to the whining dog, then collapsed on the ground, sobbing into her fur. I'd opened Pandora's Box, and all the ugly truth had spewed out.

No, not all of it. I still needed to tell her the hardest part. The worst part. Ginger whimpered and licked my hand as we waited for Charley to return.

***

ONE NIGHT WHEN MY CHILD was only a few months old, she'd started crying at three in the morning and wouldn't stop. I nursed her and changed her diaper, but she wouldn't settle. I tried rocking, humming, and pacing the floor but nothing worked. We were still living with my parents at the time and my mother, awake by then too, suggested we take Charley for a drive. "Something about the rhythm of the road relaxes them," she said. "I don't know why, but it works." Grateful for her guidance, I held my daughter as the three of us drove around the neighborhood and sure enough, within minutes, the baby was fast asleep, her body a dead weight, tiny spit bubbles falling from her mouth. And I, who loved order and structure, learned a lesson that night. Raising a baby meant throwing the rules out the window.

"I'm not cut out for this," I said to my mother the next day. "I have no idea what I'm doing. What happens when she gets sick? How do I keep her safe? What about when she starts school? When she gets her period?"

My mother threw her head back and laughed. "She's four months old, sweetheart. Enjoy who she is now and stop worrying. The rest will come. You'll grow along with her and when she's older, you'll be older too, and you'll know her better and you'll instinctively know what she needs. Trust me."

And, as usual, she'd been right. As Charley grew, our relationship evolved. First I was a caretaker, someone who provided for her basic needs. Then I became a teacher, someone who praised her, encouraged her, challenged her. Finally, I morphed into a best friend who took her shopping, watched movies on Saturday night, and comforted her when a boy first broke her heart.

Which was why this last year had been so hard. Granted, rebelling against your parents was a rite of passage for teenagers. I knew Charley had to test the limits and assert her independence. I'd been a rebel myself at her age. It was all part of becoming an adult. But knowing that intellectually didn't stop the hurt I felt when the two of us argued.

Paul wasn't the love of my life, not really. That was Charley. She was my child, the only child I'd ever have. And today, after all we'd been through together, I'd inflicted a blow so sharp, it felt as though I'd stuck a blade into my daughter's chest. The wound might not be visible to the naked eye but it was there and it was deep. I hoped with every ounce of my being that she'd forgive me.

***

IT WAS A GOOD HALF hour before Charley tromped out of the woods, head down, face still puffy and red. She walked to where I stood and dropped onto the blanket. There was a painful silence that stretched until I thought I would burst. Did she hate me? Forgive me? Had I damaged her in a way I'd never be able to repair? I waited for her to make the first move.

"You said he *was* a writer. He *was* married. He's dead, isn't he?"

The final blow. I nodded. "He died before you were born."

"Did he even know about me?"

"I didn't realize I was pregnant until a week later."

"What happened to him?"

Tears caught at the back of my throat but I swallowed them down. All the grief, the pain came roaring back as I described that day. When I'd finished, the questions began, as rapid fire as a machine gun. *How did you meet? What happened to his family? Where did he grow up? What did he look like? What kind of a writer was he?* On and on it went for one long hour. I answered as honestly and openly as I could but it wasn't easy and I broke down a few times, struggling to distance myself from the memories and only partly succeeding. Finally, I came to the end, emotionally drained but also cleansed. This huge secret that had stood between me and Charley was out in the open. I'd shown her the worst of me, and she hadn't run away.

"Why didn't … you could have had an abortion."

That was a question I hadn't prepared for. "Yes, that was one choice. But I loved your father so much I couldn't lose all I had left of him." I shook my head. "I saw a therapist that first month and she had this saying on her wall: *Grief is love with nowhere to go.* And I realized how lucky I was. I could send the love I had for your father straight to you." That first year was hard and Charley saved me. I could have given in to my sorrow but I had a baby to nurse, to rock, to change, to take for walks and wipe her nose. I didn't have time to sit in a darkened room and cry.

"Did you go to his funeral?"

I squeezed my eyes shut. "I showed up at the cemetery but they made me leave." The memory stung. I'd stood behind a tree but even still, his wife had spotted me and realized who I was. She whispered to a man nearby who approached and said I wasn't welcome.

Charley's lips tightened to a thin line. "We have to go visit him. He needs to meet me." It wasn't a question.

I knew going back there would dredge up painful memories but after the trauma I'd put her through, I was grateful to have something tangible I could offer Charley to help with her pain. But the cemetery was a good four hours away and I had no energy left. Besides, we both needed time to absorb this new reality. "We'll go next weekend. I promise."

That is, if I wasn't behind bars.

32

WHEN I GOT TO work on Monday, Zach's murder was all anyone could talk about. A few of the staff had learned that I was a close friend of Olivia's, so every few minutes, one of the staff poked their head around the corner to pump me for information. I was tempted to post a sign on my door: *Yes, I knew the victim. No, I don't know anything more. Go away.*

Not true, of course. I knew plenty.

It was mid-afternoon when the police came calling. I'd been expecting them but my heart still sped up when I spotted Farina and Washington in my doorway. "Got time for a few questions? If it's not a good time, we can circle back," Farina said.

"No, this works," I answered, as though I had nothing to hide. "Let's grab one of the conference rooms."

"No face time in a year and now twice in one week," Farina said as we walked, a broad grin on his face. Once we'd settled, he lobbed his first question. "How long have you been friends with the Reids?"

"My only interactions with Zach were because of my relationship with Olivia. I met both of them for the first time in March at an awards banquet and Liv joined my book club shortly after that." Short, succinct. Let them fill in the blanks.

He continued. "What'd you think of the marriage? Happy?"

I could hedge and say I had no idea. But since Liv had an alibi, there was nothing to lose by painting a more realistic picture. "Zach was abusive to Liv, certainly psychologically and I suspect physically. I urged her to seek help but for some reason, she refused." I leaned across the desk and directed my next response to Washington. "Plus he had a roving eye. Always flirting around and making innuendos, if you know what I mean."

Farina nodded but Washington followed up. "Were you ever the object of his 'flirting' as you put it?"

That took me aback. It suggested a closer relationship with Zach than I wanted to imply. "Not exactly, no. A comment here and there. But I did observe his behavior at a work function with a temp, a woman named Heather. It didn't seem to be an isolated incident." I skipped over Zach's inappropriate comments to me both at his house and the casino party. That was a rabbit hole I wanted to avoid.

"How did his wife react to this behavior?" Washington asked.

"She looked the other way." I folded my hands in front of me. "Acted like it didn't bother her. Maybe it didn't."

"How would you characterize Olivia Reid?" Washington asked. "When we questioned her at the house, I got the feeling she was hiding something."

"Her husband had just been killed. Plus the night before, she'd spotted a man in the back yard with a knife. So yes, she was definitely rattled that morning, but I don't think she was purposely keeping anything from you."

Farina asked some questions about Apollo Enterprises, whether I had heard anything that might be tied to the murder. They wanted to know more about Heather and what I'd heard about her involvement with Zach. I kept my answers vague, saying they should speak with Ethan if they wanted to know more. Then I repeated what Liv had already told them about possible gambling debts. Let the police pursue that avenue while Max and I worked the case from a more personal angle.

Rita knocked and poked her head in. "You're due in court in a half hour. Should I call and tell them you'll be a few minutes late?"

"Hold on." I shot a questioning look at the detectives.

Farina stood. "We're good for now. Thanks for taking the time."

I showed them to the door. I'd been dreading this conversation but now that it was done, I felt confident I hadn't appeared flustered or ill at ease. On the contrary, I'd been the epitome of a cool and collected legal professional viewing the facts dispassionately and doing my best to steer the police in directions that might help them solve the case. I'd painted an accurate picture of Liv and Zach's marriage, and told the police about Zach's extra-marital dalliance, which for all I knew might provide a suspect in the form of a jealous boyfriend. All in all, I felt good about my performance.

As we left the conference room, Washington caught my eye. "Oh, one more thing. We understand from some witnesses that you arrived late to the gallery opening Friday evening. In fact, you'd only been there a short while before the deputies showed up."

The hairs on the back of my neck stood up. What was she implying? "As I remember it, the show was from seven to ten and

I got there about halfway through. Eight, eight-thirty, somewhere around then."

"Next time we talk, we'll want to go over where you were in the hour before you arrived," Washington said with a slight smile. "You know, for the record."

My heart flip-flopped. Here I'd been so confident when all along, Washington must have sensed the turmoil beneath the surface.

I needed to keep my wits about me, stay one step ahead of the police. Any mistake at this point, however minor, could focus attention on me. Any false move might result in my arrest. And that was something I couldn't let happen.

***

I READ THE MEDICAL EXAMINER's report later that day. Zach had Viagra and a trace amount of cocaine in his system, but otherwise nothing out of the ordinary. He'd been killed instantly, the shots coming from a semi-automatic pistol, probably a Glock or a Sig Sauer, fired from around 40 yards away. All three shots were centered in a tight cluster near his heart, indicating the shooter was either extremely lucky or more likely, a trained marksman. Other than the gunshot wounds, Zach was a healthy 35-year-old male, with a history of hypertension, a tattoo on his left shoulder that read *Olivia*, and a mild case of alopecia which he'd dealt with by shaving his head.

My missing gun was a Glock.

On Wednesday, his will was read and Ethan called to tell me the results. Olivia inherited everything, including Zach's ownership stake in Apollo. Normally that would make her suspect number one except she had that alibi. Not to mention she'd been blindsided by Zach's death.

I spent time during the week putting the money back into the accounts I'd tapped and cancelling the second mortgage, explaining each time how the lake home had gone to another bidder. My father took his cash back with no questions asked.

As far as I could tell from the preliminary police reports, they were pursuing the lead I'd given them on the gambling tie-in, as well as digging into Zach's business associates, his immediate family, and his time in New York. No viable suspects yet and there was pressure from both the higher-ups and the media to charge someone soon.

His body was released and per his instructions, Liv had him cremated. In lieu of a funeral service, she organized a wake at her home for that Friday afternoon. I knew I had to attend, but Charley didn't want to, saying she'd feel out of place. Since the killer might have a personal connection to Liv and Zach, they could very well show up so I invited Max to go with me. Two sets of eyes would double our chances of spotting a clue.

And we desperately needed a clue.

33

MAX AND I RODE to the wake together that Friday. As soon as we stepped over the threshold, Liv rushed up and engulfed me in a tight hug. Once she let go, I made introductions.

"This is my friend Max Wisniewski," I said. "I hope you don't mind me bringing him along." I didn't offer any further explanation and if Liv thought it was odd I'd invited a stranger to the event, she didn't let on. In fact, she barely glanced at Max before pulling me to one side.

"Everyone's looking at me like I'm responsible for the murder," she whispered, her face a death mask. In spite of her efforts to pull herself together, and despite being surrounded by both friends and family, she was still a walking bundle of nerves.

"It's your imagination," I said. "Why would anyone blame you?"

"The police have been here twice this week, asking me questions. It's horrible. They keep swarming all over the house, pawing through our phone records, our tax returns, and our computers. And it's not just here. They've seized company records and questioned half the staff."

"That's their job. They want to find out who killed Zach like we all do."

"I know it sounds awful, but I don't really care." Liv's eyes glinted with tears. "He's gone. Nothing's going to bring him back. What does it matter who shot him?"

I held her at arm's length. "Don't say that. People can't murder someone and get away with it. Now put that out of your mind. Is your family here? I'd love to meet them."

Liv sniffled, then straightened her shoulders. "My aunt and uncle are stuck over in China but my cousins flew in. Come on, I'll introduce you."

I turned to Max, a question in my eyes. "You two go on," he said, squeezing my elbow. We'd planned to split up anyway, so this was the perfect excuse.

Liv steered me to two women in their late twenties who turned out to be Ethan's sisters, then she moved off to mingle. Alana, a short, quiet brunette, was finishing a master's degree in art history at Columbia and Robin, a tall, bubbly blonde, worked in Los Angeles as a set designer.

"Let me get this straight," I said. "You're Liv's cousins, but since your parents adopted her while all of you were still growing up, she's kind of like a sister, too?"

They both laughed. "It's confusing, right?" Robin said. "And don't forget Jasper, Liv's *real* brother. We're like that old TV show."

"I can't imagine having five kids around."

Robin smiled. "Jasper only stayed one summer and then he moved back to his hometown. And of course Alana and I were angels. I can't say the same about Olivia and Ethan."

I raised an eyebrow. "Who was worse?"

"Both," they said at the same time, then Alana elaborated. "Ethan and Liv were the oldest so they were always two steps ahead of us when it came to misbehaving." She turned to Robin. "Remember that time they stayed out all night and hid in the garage under those old tarps? Our parents were frantic. They almost called the police."

"I know Ethan and now I've met you two. Tell me more about Jasper. Is he here?" I surveyed the room. The sisters exchanged glances and Alana took the lead. "None of us have heard from him in years," she said. "Guess every family's got an odd one out, right?"

Robin piped up. "That was his choice. I mean, it's not like we're hiding."

I stayed quiet even though I knew something was off. Ethan had said Liv had heard from Jasper in the last month, that he'd planned to come for a visit. But it didn't seem like she'd shared that information with the rest of her family.

An awkward silence followed and I felt I should move on. Even though chatting with strangers made me antsy, a wake was the perfect venue to learn more details about Zach and I'd barely had a chance to scratch the surface. Anybody and everybody close to him was here today. I glanced around for another group to infiltrate.

But Max picked that moment to sidle up to me. "Sorry to interrupt but I could really use some food. Want to join me?" His eyes darted to the kitchen area.

The space was deserted except for two wait staff refilling hors d'oeuvre trays. "Have you turned up anything?" I asked.

"I met Zach's parents and they're in shock. His mother's pretty shut down but his father is on a rant about how the police are dragging their feet. He's making noises about talking to the press if they don't make an arrest soon. As for the marriage, they liked Olivia when they first met her but then after Zach bought the franchise and they moved here, the two of them stopped visiting as much. His mom didn't come right out and say it, but I got the impression she wanted grandkids and was upset Liv and Zach didn't seem interested in starting a family."

I tilted my head at a couple of men huddled together in a nearby hallway. "Did you spot the two detectives? They're doing the same thing we are, chatting up anyone who looks like a potential suspect."

Max popped a carrot in his mouth. "I eavesdropped on a group of Apollo investors and your instincts were right. They've turned up irregularities in the latest set of financials. Might be something there but the police will be in a better position than we are to uncover it."

"You found out a lot more than I have. Why don't we schmooze a bit more and then make our excuses? I'll meet you in fifteen minutes near the front," I said.

I chatted with a few more people but didn't learn anything useful and finally searched for Liv so I could say goodbye. When she wasn't on the sun porch, in the dining area, or in the living room, I made my way upstairs, where I found her on the edge of her bed, shoulders slumped, head in her hands. When she spotted me standing there, she startled. Mascara tears streamed down her cheeks and the bones of her face resembled a bust of Nefertiti.

"It's too much," she whispered, her voice brittle.

I sat beside her. It seemed strange to see Liv so upset, knowing her marriage hadn't been a happy one. "Nobody expects you to entertain them. Take as much time as you need. Ethan can handle whatever needs doing."

"Yes, he's been my rock. I don't know what I'd do without him." She smoothed down her skirt and reached for a tissue on the nightstand. "Can I ask you something? Who do the police think did this? I mean, not *who* exactly, but *why?*"

"I'm not really in the loop about the investigation. My boss is heading up the team and what with you and I being friends …"

"You mean in case I'm involved?" When I avoided her eyes, she added, "Hey, I watch television. I know the spouse is the first person they suspect."

"No one's saying that. But obviously I can't work the case. I wouldn't be objective."

Not to mention there was every chance the police would be asking me down to the station any day now, questioning me about my own whereabouts Friday night. If only I could tell them what I knew. It would let Liv off the hook and might even give them a clue to finding the killer. But revealing I'd been at the scene would focus attention on me and I wasn't prepared for that. Not until I knew more about Zach Reid and who might want him dead. I had to keep quiet until either the police or Max and I turned up another viable suspect.

Liv stood and paced the room, arms wrapped tightly around her core. "I'm not going to lie. My marriage was a nightmare."

"I sensed that."

"Zach changed once we got married. He wasn't happy and that turned him mean. It wasn't only with me. He was like that with everyone."

This was hardly the time or place but I was desperate to uncover any lead. Besides, it might help if Liv focused on facts rather than dwelling on her loss. "Did Zach alienate someone in particular? Did you sense someone had a grudge against him?"

"The police keep asking me that same question but I can't pinpoint anyone. I mean, murdering him because he treated them badly? That's pretty extreme, isn't it? What kind of person would do that?" Liv stopped walking and dropped back onto the bed.

I put my arm around her. "You'd be surprised how little it can take to make someone snap." Max had said practically the same thing to me about my stalker. "But you're right. It's more likely tied to money. Someone who stands to gain by his death. A rival franchisor, maybe? Or someone inside the company? I know you inherited his shares but who's going to actually run Apollo now?"

Liv thought a bit. "Probably Ethan. He's already familiar with the ins and outs, he knows the board, plus he's family. Are you saying that's why this happened? Someone who benefits from Zach being out of the picture had him killed?"

The obvious answer was yes, and the obvious person was Ethan. Or someone else who thought they could manipulate Liv better than they could Zach. Jasper, her missing brother? Had he disappeared for long periods of time because he'd run afoul of the police? Been in prison?

"The police will be looking at the timing, his murder happening so soon after he won the new contract. Ethan said the deal's worth millions," I said.

I examined her more closely. She was so pale. "How are you holding up? Are you getting enough sleep? Eating okay?"

She avoided my gaze. "I'm not much of a cook."

"Doesn't your housekeeper do the cooking?"

Her neck muscles tensed. "She wasn't hired as a cook. She was hired as a spy. Zach had her watch me and report back to him." She shifted around to face me. "I'd catch her tiptoeing around, lurking behind doorways, making surreptitious phone calls to him. Anyway, I fired her."

Another common characteristic of abusive spouses—the desire to control every aspect of their victim's lives. I didn't blame Liv for getting rid of her. "So is Ethan staying with you?"

"For now. And I'm fine at night when he's here. But when he goes to work, it's bad. Everywhere I look I'm reminded of Zach. I tried working on my sculptures but my creative juices have dried up." She wiped at her eyes. "There's something else. Do you think the same person who killed Zach will come after me? If it's something to do with the company, then—"

"I don't think you're in any danger." I thought back to the intruder in the back yard the night I'd stayed over. I'd put it down to Liv's over-active imagination, but what if I'd been wrong? Maybe this was about money. After all, it was the driving force behind most crimes and with Liv inheriting the company … "It wouldn't hurt to hire someone to watch the house until the police catch whoever did this. And you should update your will."

Liv wasn't listening to me. She seemed preoccupied by a silver statue of an owl about three inches tall, sitting on the side table. She stood, picked up the statue, and turned it in her hands. "I remember when Zach gave this to me. He took me to this ultra-fancy restaurant in Manhattan and handed me a box. Inside was this little guy." She stroked the bird's stone feathers as though it was alive. "He said I was the smartest person he knew and he loved me with all his heart. That between my brains and his ambition, we could do great things. He promised he'd never leave me like my father had." Tears sprang once more to the corners of her eyes. "He was so dear to me in the beginning. I thought it would always be like that." Her voice was so low, I could barely hear her.

"People change," I whispered.

She let out a long sigh. "Yes. People change." She tucked a loose curl behind her ear. "Well, I've got a house full of guests. I should get back to them."

"Are you sure you're up for it?"

"Zach may not have been the man I married but I owe him that." She paused, leaning against the doorframe. "Rachel, promise me the police know what they're doing."

I reassured her and we rejoined the crowd downstairs. Liv drifted off to talk to some employees in the sunroom and I veered in the opposite direction, winding up next to the grand piano and its display of framed pictures—Liv at her high school graduation, posed portraits from Liv and Zach's wedding, and a digital picture frame with a rotating album of family snapshots. Collages of Zach stood on easels around the room. In one, he was a toddler, standing beside a red Schwinn bike. In another, he stood at home plate in a Little League outfit. How had this innocuous-looking kid turned into such a self-centered sleazeball?

"It's weird, seeing his life laid out like this," a voice said from behind me. Ethan stood nearby, dressed in a stylish black suit, a sullen look on his face. "You'd never know what an ass he was from those photos."

"This probably isn't the best time to—"

"He was a careless human being. An arrogant scumbag. Liv's better off without him."

I pulled him into a corner. "You might want to keep your voice down. You never know who might be listening."

"You mean like you? Our *friend* in the DA's office?" Ethan stared at me. "How about it, counselor?" He held out his hands like I was going to slap cuffs on him. "You gonna turn me in?" When he stumbled against a nearby table, I realized he was well on his way to being drunk. I didn't know why Ethan was attacking me like this. What had I done?

"You should sit down." I looked around for Liv or one of his sisters. "Or maybe eat some food. You don't look all that steady on your feet."

"Ah, precisely what I need. Another woman ordering me around." He tipped an imaginary top hat my way. "Thanks but I can take care of myself, princess. Now if you'll excuse me." He stumbled out of the room and disappeared around the corner.

My head began to throb. Everywhere I turned, Zach's face stared up at me. And suddenly I was replaying that last image in my mind—Zach with his hand out, the bullet holes, his collapse on the sand. Blood. So much blood. The room started to spin.

I saw Max standing at the front door with Liv and raced over to him. "I need to go," I whispered. As we walked to the car, I gulped down mouthfuls of air and held tight to Max and it wasn't long before my equilibrium returned to normal.

As we drove away, I asked him what he thought of Liv. After all, this was the first time he'd met her and I was interested in his impressions.

"She's paranoid, although I'm not sure she has reason to be. I can't see anybody coming after her, what with all the press around."

"What were the two of you chatting about there at the end?"

He took a good minute to answer, as though his mind was elsewhere. "What? Oh, that. She asked me how long we'd been dating."

I gave a throaty laugh. "Good. That means she's clueless about who you really are. What did you tell her?"

"That we were just friends. Although I might have winked when I said it."

Most men would have mentioned Liv's looks by now. "She's stunning, isn't she?"

"I suppose. But she's not really my type. Way too needy. My guess is whoever gets involved with her has their hands full."

I hadn't thought of it that way but he could be right. All that beauty might carry a price tag. One that involved a lot of caretaking, a lot of emotional support, and a lot of undivided attention.

We pulled up at my house. "Anyway, not sure that yielded us much," he said as he parked in the driveway. "But it was worth a shot."

I wasn't so sure. Some time during the hour in that house, I had felt a twinge of unease, a sense that something wasn't quite right but I couldn't put my finger on it. It wasn't Ethan, although I had to wonder what was up with him. No, there'd been something else. A glimpse of something askew. A tidbit of conversation. An interaction that seemed false.

It was the same feeling I got in a deposition when I knew a witness was lying but I didn't know about what.

A sudden chill traveled from the base of my spine upward as I unlocked the back door.

34

Detectives Farina and Washington rang the bell at my house early Saturday morning and asked if I had time for a few questions. I'd planned to drive Charley to Naperville to visit Paul's grave today but she was still sleeping and when police show up at your front door on the weekend, you don't say no. Besides, I didn't want them to think I had anything to hide.

It had been a week since they'd searched Zach's house. Forensics must have discovered something on either his computer or that videocam that pointed squarely at me and from there, they must have figured out Zach had been harassing me. My guess is they were here today to find out if I knew and if so, whether I'd put the pieces together before or after the murder.

Washington wasted no time. "We talked to Davante Whitaker, Ms. Matthews, and he told us about the USB stick you had him analyze. According to him, you have a stalker."

I frowned, an expression I'd practiced ahead of time. "I'm confused. I thought you were here to ask me about Zach's murder."

"Humor us. About this stalker of yours? Davante said you seemed desperate to figure out who it was."

"I'm not sure I'd use the word *desperate* but I was definitely concerned. My daughter was frightened and I wasn't getting much sleep. I assumed it was someone I'd prosecuted who held a grudge and that's not something to ignore. So to answer your question yes, I wanted to get to the bottom of it."

She didn't let up. "In fact, you were sufficiently worried to install a new security system in your home and to retain the services of a private detective."

Farina had kids. Maybe Washington did, too. "Any mother would have done the same in my place." I had to keep reminding myself that if I hadn't been on that beach, I would have no idea Zach had been my stalker. That piece of information had to come from them. Just answer their questions. Don't elaborate.

Washington continued. "Sounds like when the police couldn't help, you decided to go off on your own and track down whoever was behind the threats."

I wanted to rant about what an ineffectual response I'd gotten from the police but what purpose would that serve? Instead I stuck to the facts. "I could handle the phone calls but when I got the video … it made my skin crawl. So yes, I hired a PI, someone I knew from high school, to investigate a few leads I turned up. His name is Max Wisniewski. He'll confirm what I've told you." I crossed my legs and tried to appear nonchalant. "Is that why you're here? The police have finally tracked down who's behind this?"

"Not necessarily," Washington said, as though she'd anticipated the question.

"I'm not following. Either you have or you haven't. Which is it?"

Washington glanced at Farina and he gave a slight nod. As I'd suspected, he was the one running the show. "Let's turn to Zach Reid, shall we?" She flipped back a couple of pages in her notepad as though reviewing our previous interview. "The last time we talked, you said you barely knew Mr. Reid. But we've examined his phone records and turned up several calls he made to your cell over the last month."

Play the part. You knew this was coming. I shook my head. "That's strange. I don't remember him ever calling me."

"We also found videos on his computer that feature you. And then there's this." She handed me a print-out of a Word document. It was a series of dated computer entries Zach made after the harassment started. I stopped when I got to the phrase *her birthday's soon so I bet peonies will spook her out.* I should have realized, with all the databases around, anyone with enough time and enough incentive could figure out when I was born.

It was obvious these two had connected the dots. But I needed to pretend the idea had never occurred to me until the last few seconds. You don't succeed as a prosecutor without a fair bit of acting talent so I knew how to control my facial muscles. I raised the pitch of my voice and pasted on a look of astonishment. "Are you saying Zach Reid was the person harassing me?" I scrunched up my face. "That can't be true. My only connection with him was through his wife."

"The physical evidence is all there. The tape, the voice changer, the notebook."

"But why would he come after me? I barely knew him."

"We were hoping you could tell us." Washington's voice was low and ingratiating. "You're sure you never met Mr. Reid until that night at the banquet?"

"Yes. I mean no, I'd never laid eyes on the man. And he's someone I'd remember."

Farina finally jumped in. "What do you mean?"

Careful. Don't give them cause to suspect you know more than you're letting on. Or that you had anything against Zach. "He had a distinct look and manner about him and I'm trained to recognize faces. I'm sure if I'd met him before, I'd remember."

"What about Mrs. Reid? Did you know *her* from before?"

"Both of them were complete strangers to me. Ethan, too." When Farina looked confused, I added. "Liv's cousin. I met him at that same banquet."

"Oh, right. So for the record, no contact with any of these three before that night?"

That sounded like a trick question but it was the truth. I laced my fingers together in my lap. "That's right."

"Let's switch things up a bit," Farina said. "Two weeks ago you closed out your daughter's savings account and took out a second mortgage on your home. Why the sudden need for cash?"

That was a punch to my gut. The hairs on the back of my neck stood up. They must suspect Zach had been blackmailing me which gave me motive. "It's personal. Nothing to do with Zach Reid."

They exchanged looks, then Washington picked up the ball. "Just a few more questions and we'll be on our way. We understand you had a heated argument with Reid at a party at Potawatomi a month ago. Can you tell us about that?"

I hesitated. I needed to downplay that encounter. "It was no big deal. He mistook me for someone else and made an inappropriate remark."

Washington flipped through her notes. "And according to witnesses, you lashed out and told him to keep his hands to himself."

"Like I said, it was a misunderstanding. Nothing more. I'd forgotten all about it."

Out of nowhere, Farina piped up. "Do you own a gun?"

They hadn't come with a search warrant and they hadn't recited my Miranda rights so they were fishing. At the same time, I felt sure they hadn't believed a word I'd said. They believed I was somehow involved in Zach's murder, but they just didn't know how. I was balancing on a knife edge and all it would take was one false move, one wrong word, and I'd be looking at a murder charge.

I glanced at my watch and stood. "I'm sorry to have to cut this short but I lost track of time. I promised my daughter a short road trip today and we're leaving soon. If you have more questions, I'd be glad to drop by the station early next week."

"I thought you wanted to help us find Zach's killer," Farina said, turning his hands palm upward. "We're on the same side here."

My left hand had turned numb. When I wiggled my fingers, there was a tingling sensation that sent a shiver through my arm. Was I having a heart attack? I needed to shut this down right away before I made a slip. "You've caught me at a busy time, that's all," I managed. "Can we table this until Monday?"

They got up. Thank God. Washington tucked her notebook inside her pocket and I stayed still as they walked to the front door.

"We'll take you up on that offer," Farina said. "See ya then."

Washington came back to where I stood and handed me her card. "Oh, and counselor? When we meet, we'll want to take you step by step through your movements on the night of the murder.

And if you do have a gun registered in your name, you might want to bring it along. Help us clear up some lingering questions."

The minute their car disappeared around the corner, I phoned Max but got his voice mail.

"Call me back as soon as you get this. It's urgent." I hung up the phone, my hand still tingling.

35

I couldn't sit still. Why didn't Max call? I'd just pulled out my phone to leave another voice mail when the doorbell rang and there he stood on my stoop. "You sounded upset so I thought I'd come in person," he said. I poured us both some coffee, then we sat side-by-side on the couch, and I replayed what the police had asked and the evidence they'd found.

"They've bumped me up on their list of suspects now that they know Zach was my stalker. So I've been wracking my brain again, trying to figure out any connection to him. Is it possible I prosecuted someone he was close to? I buy he was a sadistic fuck who got off on scaring me half to death, but where's the initial connection? And since he arranged to meet me, why did he look so surprised when he saw me on the beach?"

Max looked thoughtful. "The reason Zach was stalking you isn't important at this point. You're right, it had to be him. For one thing, you haven't heard anything from the stalker since Zach was killed. I think we should concentrate on who wanted Zach dead."

"Maybe someone was following him, looking to take him out, and when they saw him head to a secluded area, they took advantage of the situation, shot him, and left me to take the fall."

"Could be. All it would take then was an anonymous call, you'd be arrested, and the police wouldn't investigate any further. The fact you got out of there before the authorities arrived was lucky. Otherwise, you'd be sitting in a jail cell."

I wrapped my hands around my coffee mug, partly to warm them but also to give me something stable to hold on to. "What do we do now?"

"Money's a good place to start. What have you learned about Zach's finances?"

"Apparently Liv inherits everything—the house, the company, and the savings accounts. But she's got a rock-solid alibi. Plus the killer had to be agile, a hell of a marksman, and have nerves of steel. That hardly describes Olivia."

"What about Apollo specifically? You mentioned they just won a major contract."

"Which is worth millions. So their competitors aren't happy. But if that's the motive, they'd have killed him before the contract got awarded, not after."

"Unless the investors didn't want Zach running the expanded company. Maybe there's something fishy going on behind the scenes."

"Liv doesn't seem to have much of a handle on how the company operates. Now that she's the owner, she'll probably take her direction from the more experienced board members and senior staff, at least in the beginning."

"And if something happens to Liv, who inherits?"

I stared hard at him. "You think the person who killed Zach will come after her?"

"Not necessarily. But I'd like to know who stands to benefit if she's out of the picture."

I thought for a moment. "My guess is Ethan, or maybe her brother Jasper. Or the female cousins I met at the wake, although I can't see either of them being involved."

"What do we know about this brother? His name keeps popping up."

"He could have had a run-in with the law. The family's lost track of him for years now and they don't have particularly warm feelings about him. According to Ethan, he called Liv not too long ago and said he might come for a visit but he never showed. What if he did come into town but with a different agenda in mind?"

"I'll look into this Jasper. You take Ethan. That scene at the wake when he was staggering around was certainly odd. Even if he didn't kill Zach, he might know something that's got him upset. It's worth looking into."

I had a hard time believing Ethan was involved in any of this. Still, we shouldn't ignore him. There was certainly no love lost between him and Zach and he saw himself as Liv's protector.

"Apparently he arrived at the gallery later than expected which means he could have been at the beach and doubled back," I offered. Had it been Ethan behind me, firing those shots? He'd mentioned he'd been in the service which meant he was comfortable around firearms. "What about Liv's suspicions that Zach was gambling again? Could he owe money to some shady characters and they killed him?"

"From my experience, criminals like that would write him off as a bad investment and move on. But we can look more closely at Apollo. Cash businesses like fast food franchises are great fronts for money laundering. Maybe Zach got caught up in something bigger than the restaurant business."

Why hadn't I thought of that before? "The FBI's been sniffing around the Great Lakes Region, investigating a ring that's involved in large-scale money-laundering. Maybe that's why Zach wanted to spook me, so he could blackmail me into mucking around with that case. Let me check if Apollo is one of the places under investigation."

"What about that other redhead you mentioned, the temp you thought Zach might be seeing behind Liv's back? If that's who he thought he was meeting at the beach, the look he gave you might make sense. Zach's murderer could be a spurned husband out to eliminate his rival."

"That theory fits with the blanket and the Champagne. It's worth exploring."

"I'll take that assignment. Cheating lovers are my specialty. Can you get me her full name and the staffing agency she works for?"

"Ethan would know. I'll figure out a way to ask him without setting off any alarms."

"Then we're set. You'll see if Apollo is on the radar in the money laundering case and if so, was Zach involved or did he find out something he shouldn't have? You'll also look into Ethan, what he was up to that night, his background in the military, and his relationship with Olivia. I'll track down Jasper, see where he was the week Zach was killed. And I'll research this Heather once you get me her info. Today's Saturday. Let's give ourselves until Thursday and then get back together again and compare notes. If anything comes up in the meantime, I'm only a phone call away. Did I leave anything out?"

I drummed my fingers on the table as I replayed the conversation with the detectives. "The police think I killed Zach. I saw it in their eyes. So all this strategizing is well and good, but what if it's too late?"

He leaned forward and gently squeezed my hand. "We both know the only way we can prove your innocence is to find the real killer. And you're right to worry. The police have two of the three key components they need to charge you." He ticked them off with his fingers. "One, motive. He was stalking you, threatening you and your daughter. They can't prove he was blackmailing you but you were amassing cash so it's not a big leap. Two, opportunity. You don't have an alibi for the time of the murder. My guess is they've requested the GPS tracking records from your cell provider, which will put you at the scene." He wriggled his third finger. "There's no murder weapon yet. But either they'll get an anonymous tip soon about where to find it or it's long gone and they'll charge you without it."

"That's a cheery scenario you paint. What can I do?"

"Focus. Take the steps we talked about and report back what you find. The rest of the time? Knowing you like I do, this part will be hell, but you wait." He stared into my eyes and reiterated. "You wait, okay?"

It was like watching a tornado far off in the distance, gaining steam, coming my way. Right now I was safe. There was only one problem.

I couldn't move. My feet were glued to the ground

And that tornado was coming closer.

36

I'D MADE A PROMISE to Charley to show her the place Paul was buried so the next day we took off early for Naperville. I know people who regularly visit their loved one's grave but I'd never felt that need. For me, Paul lived in my heart, not in that patch of ground. But Charley needed this, so I put my own feelings in a box, locked the lid, and concentrated on helping my daughter.

I circled the property twice, but I couldn't remember the exact location of his plot. Not only had the grounds grown exponentially but it had been eighteen years since I'd been there. I finally gave up and drove back to a small structure marked "Office" near the entrance where I left Charley in the car and went inside. The reception area had a desk, two chairs and a side table with brochures of the facility and a Bible. I called out, waited, then wandered down the hall to discover an older man with a thick shock of snow-white hair and a lined face sitting in a small office, peering at a computer monitor. He had a hearing aid lodged in one ear and red suspenders held up his khaki trousers. A nameplate reading *Leonard Durst* rested on the cluttered desk.

I gave a slight wave. "Hi, I'm wondering if you can help me? I'm looking for Paul Ostoff. O-S-T-O-F-F. He died in 2005."

The man gave a low whistle. "Holy Moly. Joanie's gonna flip when I tell her. She thinks I made you up." He ambled over to a gray metal file cabinet with gouge marks and a missing handle. He rifled through the third drawer, pulled out a manila folder, and flipped to the second page. "Here we go. Northeast corner of Section 15." He tore off a printed map from a thick pad on the desk and circled the location with a red magic marker, then walked me to the door. "Anything else you need? Receipts? The name of the shop?"

I had no idea what he was talking about but I had what I needed, so I thanked him and returned to the car. Then, using the map as reference, I followed the narrow road to the far end of the cemetery. Both Charley and I got out and searched the stones, and it wasn't long before my daughter shouted, "I found him. Over here." She was standing under a flowering eastern redbud tree, its deep blossoms shading a pink marble marker mounted on a granite base. There was a fresh bouquet of daffodils in a clear vase leaning against the headstone.

I read the inscription. "Joined Forever in Love" was scrolled across the top, then "Ostoff." Seeing the two names engraved underneath—Paul on the left and Natalie on the right—took me aback. I hadn't realized his estranged wife had also died, nor that they'd been buried in the same spot. The last time I'd seen Natalie, in fact the *only* time I'd seen her, was the day of his funeral when she'd stood over the grave in a black shapeless dress, her complexion waxy, her arm around a young girl with tears streaming down her face. A gawky, pudgy teenage boy, dressed in an ill-fitting black suit and wearing a grim expression, shuffled his feet nearby. Penny and Benny, Paul's children. Now here Natalie was, lying right next to Paul.

It was like he'd always said—she'd never let him go.

My gaze moved to the birth and death dates and goosebumps hit my arms. Natalie had died the same year as Paul, only three months later. That was odd. She'd been distraught that day at the gravesite but, as far as I knew, she hadn't been ill. In fact, Paul would never have asked her for a divorce if that had been the case. Natalie must have been in some kind of accident as well.

"Can you leave us alone?" Charley asked, then plopped down cross-legged right next to the grave, as though she'd settled in for a good, long talk. I nodded and returned to the car, my thoughts drifting back to that long-ago summer.

***

THE DAY PAUL DIED, HE'D asked his wife for a divorce. He'd described the scene to me on the phone as he drove back to the city. Natalie had gone berserk, screaming obscenities, pummeling him with her fists, and grabbing objects—a glass paperweight, a hardcover book, a table lamp—and throwing them. A ceramic vase had cut his right temple and blood dribbled onto his collar. The children, hearing the commotion, shot out of their bedrooms upstairs and stood silent in the foyer as Paul tried to calm Natalie down. Her response was to pull back her leg and kick him squarely in the groin, yelling at him to *fuck the hell off,* before threatening to take every penny he had and sue for sole custody.

On his drive back, the accident happened and he was killed. I'd tried to separate the two events in my mind but a part of me had always felt we'd been punished for what we'd done.

After two weeks of staying in my apartment, alternately sobbing, throwing up, and medicating myself to sleep, I'd made an appointment at the campus counseling center. The therapist had likened the experience to survivor's guilt, the same emotion soldiers felt when their comrades died in battle while they lived. The wound felt as deep, as painful, as a stabbing. And even after all these years it had never gone away. Faded, yes, but at certain times in my life, it would ache again. I'd hear "Ain't No Mountain High Enough" on the radio or eat an Italian Beef sandwich or someone would recite Yeat's poem "When You Are Old" and it would all come flooding back.

The therapist had said if I ignored the grief, it would get my attention some other way, through physical symptoms like headaches, stomach pains, even memory lapses. Or my emotions might shut down altogether, making it impossible to get close to other people. She'd told me I'd have to learn to live with the wound, even press up against it sometimes like a bruise, make it hurt and experience that without flinching.

Learning how to do that had taken years. What the therapist forgot to mention was how wounding someone else, like I had my daughter last Sunday on the hike, would send waves of guilt to engulf me, make me feel the loss all over again.

My daughter was chatting a mile a minute, as though telling her entire life story to her long-lost father. I would give anything to know what she was talking about and whether any of it had to do with me. Was she still angry? Had I irreparably destroyed any trust between us? Was she ever going to forgive me for lying to her?

I got out of the car and walked over. "I'm going to swing back to that caretaker. I'll only be a few minutes."

The old man was outside, watering a clump of shrubs, when I pulled up. "Mind if I interrupt your day again?" When he nodded, I went on. "I noticed Mrs. Ostoff died not long after her husband. Is there any information in the file as to what happened?"

"Don't even need to look. Her boy was in the same grade as mine. Word gets around, you know? Suicide. She cut her wrists. The daughter found her in the bathtub when she got home from school."

My throat tightened as another wave of guilt hit. "I didn't know."

"Pretty damn rough on those kids. Life ain't fair, right? I mean, there's Mrs. Ostoff, a boatload of money from her father, but what good was it? Couldn't protect her from heartache."

"There are fresh flowers on the grave. Do you know who brought them?"

"Assumed that was your doing."

Which explained his earlier comments. "No. I've never been here before."

"Still a mystery then," he said in a spooky voice and waved his hands. "Every Christmas I get a cashier's check with enough money to pay for a year's worth of weekly bouquets." He tugged his ear. "The local florist brings them over and tidies up the spot."

"Have you ever seen anyone visiting the grave? One of the children or another relative?"

"You two are the first ones I've seen. 'Course I'm not watching every minute of the day but I think I'd have noticed if someone was coming by regularly." He seemed puzzled. "What's your interest anyway? You a friend of theirs?"

"In a way." That niggling feeling from the wake was back. I knew something was wrong even though I couldn't put my finger on what. It was the same feeling I got every once in a while on a tricky case, usually in the discovery phase when I had all the evidence in front of me and was piecing it together. I'd walk away, take a phone call, go to a meeting, and when I got back to my office, all the pieces would fit together in perfect symmetry and the pattern would be clear. It was like a superpower. If only it would help me now.

My cell phone chirped. A text from Charley saying she was ready to go. I turned back to the caretaker. "Thanks for your help. And if you do remember anything else that might be relevant, will you call me?" I took out my business card and wrote down my office phone number on the back.

I retraced my steps and found my daughter still kneeling by Paul's grave. When she saw the car, she quickly scrambled up, put her fingertips to her lips, then transferred the kiss to her father's headstone before she climbed into the passenger's seat. I looked at her, a question in my eyes.

"I'm good," she said. When I didn't make a move to leave, she added, "We can go."

I drove a few yards, then threw the car into park and got out, feeling Charley's eyes on me the whole way as I walked back to Paul's grave and bent down. "Some kid, huh? I named her Charlotte after your mother. I thought you'd like that." I glanced at my daughter, staring at me through the back window. "You'd like her, Paul. She's kind and smart and creative. But headstrong. You should see her when things don't go her way. Reminds me of you sometimes. Remember that camping trip?"

I smiled at the memory. Paul refused to put on bug spray, saying he hated the smell and it made him feel sticky. But that evening, after hours hiking in the woods, the itching got so bad he had to slather himself with toothpaste, the only astringent in our backpacks. I wish I'd taken a picture—Charley would get such a kick out of that.

Would that stubborn streak of his have grated on me as time went on? What about his chronic lateness? The questions caught me off-guard. I'd never thought about what our lives would have been like if Paul had lived. Would we have clashed over how to parent Charley? Would he have supported my career? Hell, would I even *have* a career if we'd moved to London? The passion I'd felt for Paul had consumed me during those early days but now I wondered about our relationship once the initial glow had worn off. What would we be like now? Would we even still be together?

I shook my head. All these *what ifs* were a waste of time. The important thing now was Charley. "I'll bring her back to visit again, as often as she wants. I shouldn't have kept the two of you apart so long." I straightened up and wiped the tears from my eyes. Another small step in the right direction.

37

Charley popped her earbuds in the minute we drove away and I didn't press her, unsure what to say. She had a lot to process. For now, I'd give her space, wait for her to make the first move, and take my cues accordingly.

But I had planned a surprise and a few miles down the road, it seemed like the perfect time to share it. I reached beneath my seat and pulled out a small package I'd wrapped in plain brown paper. "I thought you might like these." Charley turned off her music but didn't move. "Go ahead. Open it," I said, keeping one eye on the road.

She tentatively peeled back one flap, then tore open the rest and shoved the wrapping to the floor. There sat two books, one with a navy-blue cover, the other burgundy, the pages yellowed and worn. She flipped open the first to the cover page, then glanced over. "He wrote these?"

Tears welled at the back of my throat but I swallowed them down. "Yep." I nodded. "He'd want you to have them."

She hugged the books to her chest and squeezed her eyes shut. It wasn't long before her shoulders shook as big gulping sobs filled the space and her face turned to mush.

"Oh, honey. I'm sorry." I pulled over to the side of the road and parked. "I didn't mean to make you sad. Come here." I leaned toward her and she fell into my arms, burying her head, the books wedged between us. I stroked her hair and whispered words of comfort, until finally she pulled back and said, "I'm not sad, Mom. I'm happy. I feel like he's right here with us. You know, like we're a real family."

A real family. Yes, I know what you mean, my beautiful daughter. I was wrong to keep us apart.

***

WE GOT TO MILWAUKEE MID-afternoon and I decided to swing by the grocery store before we headed home. I pulled into Sendik's parking lot. "Want to come in with me?" I said to Charley.

"I'm fine here." She didn't even look up, too busy reading her father's book. "Maybe pick up some bananas? I ate the last one."

I was juggling a jar of crunchy peanut butter, two tubes of toothpaste, and a bunch of bananas (why hadn't I grabbed a cart?) when a voice called out behind me. "Rachel Matthews. Where have you been hiding?" It was Sondra Nugent whose daughter Lucy was in Charley's grade. The last time I'd seen her was at that infamous awards dinner. In fact, she'd been one of the organizers of the event.

"Busy making the city safe from the bad guys." I tucked the peanut butter in my purse to free up space in my right hand. "Crime always goes up in hot weather."

"Like that shooting down at the beach that everyone's talking about. Any suspects?"

Numero Uno, standing right in front of you. "Not that I know of."

"It's so crazy to think of Zach Reid being murdered. I mean, he was one of our honorees this year and now he's dead," Sondra said. "Well, you of all people would know. I had to do all that rearranging, but I'm glad the seating worked out. At least you two got to spend time together that evening."

My right eye twitched. "I'm sorry, you lost me."

"The request he made. You know—to sit at your table. It was tricky, what with his wife and their other guest and then your five people but I shuffled folks around and made it happen. And then he gets himself killed. I mean, what are the odds? One month he's dining with an ADA and the next he's murdered. Life's so weird, right?"

My pulse sped up. "Zach Reid asked to sit at my table?"

"Well, someone from his office did. Said you and he were old friends and asked if it would be a problem. Some kind of surprise, I think they said. Anyway, that's what I told the police when they called on Thursday. Hey, I'm sorry I brought it up. I mean, him being your friend and all. Is something wrong?"

I'd attended the banquet before I'd received the bouquet. Before the note. Before the video. To me, it had been a social obligation to support my friend from book club. But for Zach, that night must have been the first shot across the bow. The night he'd decided to make me his target. It didn't so much answer my questions as bring up new ones. But the fact he'd requested—no, orchestrated—his presence at my table was a blow. I'd told the police I'd never met Zach or Olivia before that night. But they'd already interviewed Sondra at that point. In their mind, they'd caught me in a lie. Once again, I felt the noose tightening.

As Charley and I headed for home, my thoughts leap-frogged. Motive, opportunity. And now the police believed there was a connection between me and Zach. Something I had kept from them. What more did they need? What were they waiting for?

We turned into our subdivision and there was a split second of eerie quiet before the world exploded.

Parked opposite our house were two police cars, one from Whitefish Bay, one from the city of Milwaukee. As soon as I pulled into the garage, Farina and a uniformed officer got out.

I turned to Charley. "Can you grab the groceries from the trunk, and then go inside and call your uncle Luke? Tell him to meet me at the police station downtown."

"Mom, what's going on?" She looked from me to the approaching men and back again.

"Please do as I say, okay?" I kept my voice as still as possible, not wanting to upset her if I could help it. "Don't worry. Everything's under control." Another lie. My life wasn't under control. The tornado had finally touched down. I could hear its roar.

38

THEY MUST HAVE FOUND the gun.

Farina, his face stoic, read aloud the charges against me, recited my Miranda rights, and snapped on the handcuffs. They had a warrant and he advised me to have a neighbor or a relative take my daughter away, rather than leave her at the house during the search. Then he lightly brushed my elbow and nudged me toward the police car.

I'd never been arrested, never even had a speeding ticket. I imagined tomorrow's headline: *TABLES TURNED FOR NO NONSENSE DA*. Charley burst from the front door. Tears had caught in her lashes and her body trembled when we hugged. "What's happening, Mom? Uncle Luke didn't pick up but I left him a voice mail."

I held her at arm's length and told her to contact her grandfather if Luke didn't call back within the next ten minutes. "You are *not* to spend the night here, do you hear me? The police are going to search the house plus reporters are going to get wind of this and if they find you …" Then I told her not to call or text anyone else for now, not even Spencer, and to take the dog with her, to drive to either Luke's or my father's and stay there. "I love you. Remember that," I whispered, kissing the top of her head. "Now pack your things for an overnight and get out of here. I'll be home before you know it."

I watched as she walked away, then crawled in the back seat. A screen separated me from the two men in the front. No door handles. I sat silent as they drove me downtown to the city jail, parsing out what my next steps should be. It was three in the afternoon on Sunday which meant no bail hearing until tomorrow morning.

I'd be spending the night in jail.

I thought through what would happen next. On Monday I'd be brought before a judge where I'd enter a plea, then … Oh, God, what if Huntley insisted I was a flight risk and the judge refused bail? What if I was incarcerated for months? What if I lost my license to practice law, what if Charley—

Stop it. Why drive myself crazy with these imaginary scenarios? Between my father's courtroom skills and my own pristine reputation, I should be released on bail by tomorrow. Then, aside from restrictions—God, they wouldn't make me wear an ankle bracelet, would they?—I'd be right back where I was before, except I'd be on administrative leave and my cases handed off to others in the office. Of course, I could kiss that promotion goodbye and I wouldn't have access to any case files, computers, or any other resources. But the good news was I'd be able to search for Zach's killer full time without worrying about neglecting my job.

***

WHEN WE ARRIVED AT THE city jail, Farina gave the officers on duty the paperwork. They searched me for weapons, bagged all my personal effects in a clear envelope, and inventoried them. I tried my best to keep stoic and aloof, although a few tears leaked out. The pitying looks I got from everyone at the facility were hard to swallow. I wondered if all suspects felt this helpless. This hopeless. This alone.

Next came mug shots, fingerprinting, and a DNA swab, then a routine physical with a nurse asking detailed questions about my physical and mental health. I'd known the litany of procedures that followed an arrest but I hadn't realized how exhausting, repetitive, and intrusive they were. I wasn't an actual person anymore, but a number.

I'd just about reached my breaking point when Farina finally escorted me to a small, windowless room with a single metal table, four molded chairs, and a closed-circuit camera mounted near the ceiling in one corner. We faced each other and he turned on a tape recorder, then shuffled through the case file in front of him.

Before he could say a word, I reached deep down and found my anger. This wasn't a friend sitting across from me. Quite the opposite. "I won't be answering any questions until my lawyer gets here."

"Look, Rachel, I don't like this any more than you do. If we've got it wrong, we're as anxious as you are to correct our mistake."

"You couldn't possibly be."

There was a knock on the door and Luke stuck his head inside. "Hey, kiddo. I hear your life of crime has caught up with you." He approached Farina and nodded a greeting. "Officer." They shook hands, then Luke continued. "You know the drill, Bob. We'll need the room. And you can turn off that recording." When Farina flipped off the switch, Luke added, "CCTV, too."

Once we were alone, Luke's smile dropped, replaced by a look of concern. He took hold of my hands and squeezed. "How are you holding up?"

"Not great. Listen, Charley was there when they arrested me. Can you get to her before she reads about it in the media? Make sure she knows I had nothing to do with Zach's murder."

"I'm sure she realizes that, but I'll talk to her. Now, let's get down to it. I won't lie. It doesn't look good." Luke had obviously reviewed the charges against me before he'd barged into the interview room. "You have no alibi for the time of the murder, they know about the stalking, and he was killed with your gun."

"I thought that had to be the final shoe that dropped." I gave a weak laugh. "They can't really think I'd be that dumb."

"That's our defense? Your honor, my client can't possibly be guilty. She's not that stupid."

"My defense is someone set me up and the police fell for it. Our only hope is to figure out who's behind this and expose them." I outlined the theory Max and I had been working on—that the person behind this was either Jasper or Ethan or someone we hadn't yet identified and the motive was—no surprise— money. Zach dies, Liv inherits his assets, and either her brother or her cousin step in to help her manage not only her personal fortune but a company worth millions. If Liv failed to cooperate? Well, maybe Liv meets with some kind of accident down the way. I found it hard to imagine either of these men harming Liv, but then how much did I really know? I'd only been around Ethan a few times, and never even met Jasper. Frankly, he was the wild card: estranged from the family and off the grid for long periods of time. I kept coming back to Jasper.

I also told Luke the other possibilities Max and I had considered—Heather's possible involvement, a suspected embezzlement, even a potential link to a money-laundering scheme.

Luke listened but gradually a scowl played over his face. "You're all over the board with these theories. Let's narrow it down a bit. Why would any of these people frame you?"

"Don't you see? I'm the red herring. A suspect to throw to the police. They knew Zach was stalking me and when he arranged to meet me Friday night—"

"Hold on a minute. You're saying you were there on the beach when he got shot?"

If Luke was going to help me out of this mess, he'd have to know everything. I took a deep breath and walked him step-by-step through that night and everything that had happened since. So many stories to keep straight. So many secrets I'd kept hidden. As I talked, a look settled on Luke's face I couldn't quite read. Was it doubt? Was there a trace of incredulity in his eyes as he slowly comprehended what we were up against?

When I'd finished, Luke jotted down a few notes on a pad, then stared up at me. "That's it? You've told me everything? You're not holding anything back?"

"I didn't kill him. I swear."

"Of course not. But honestly, Sis? As it stands now, you are round and royally screwed."

***

Luke left a half hour later, promising he'd pull strings and get my arraignment moved up on the docket. If all went well, I'd be free and back home by early tomorrow afternoon. He'd chase down my father, fill him in, meet with the bail bondsman, and watch over Charley for the night. He'd also let Farina know I'd be pleading the fifth to all further questions.

They sequestered me from the general population in a holding tank and within the hour, transferred me across the street to the County Jail. I zoned out during the second intake as the process began all over again—fingerprints, mug shots, the search for weapons. The only difference was this time I was shown to a changing room where a female guard watched as I slipped out of my street clothes and into a shapeless orange jumpsuit and slippers. A good five hours after my initial arrest, they finally led me down a short hallway to a cell.

Sounds bounced around the walls as I shuffled by the other inmates, from soft crying to angry curses to one woman singing Amazing Grace in a lilting soprano voice. The air reeked of sweat, urine, and bleach. Once we reached the end of the hall, the guard stepped to one side and, squeezing my lips into a tight line, I entered. The heavy, metal door clanged shut behind me and a key turned in the lock.

The space was the size of a small freight elevator, with dingy cinderblock walls and a concrete floor. The stifling air smelled both rank and antiseptic. A twin bed with a blue plastic mattress and threadbare blanket hung off one wall and a metal toilet with a push-button flush sat behind a low screen. The CCTV camera in the corner swiveled as I moved, always keeping me in view. I eased onto the bed, drew my knees to my chest, and made myself as small as I could, like one of those roly-poly bugs I played with as a child. I fixated on a water stain on the ceiling. It looked exactly like a mushroom cloud, like those photos from Los Alamos.

The walls closed in around me and everything hit at once—the exhaustion, the stress, the fear I'd carried around ever since that night at the beach. All I wanted was to close my eyes, numb my senses, and shut out the world. I lay down, pulled the itchy blanket up to my chin, turned my face to the wall, and after only a few minutes, fell into a deep sleep. This time there weren't any nightmares. Only an empty void inside my head where my perfect life used to be.

39

"Rachel Elizabeth Matthews. You stand accused of first-degree intentional homicide. How do you plead?"

Max was right. I might have wanted to kill Zach, but I didn't. Three beats of silence, then I broke it, my voice ringing with defiance. "Not guilty, Your Honor."

My father stood and addressed the judge, his imposing height and booming baritone lending extra weight to his words. He'd even worn his famous tie, navy-blue stallions galloping across a red backdrop—his version of calling in the cavalry. I knew he only wore it for his toughest cases.

"Your Honor. We request that the defendant be released on her own recognizance. She's a respected member of the Bar, a long-serving public servant, and has strong ties to the community as well as family here. She poses no threat to others and can hardly be considered a flight risk."

Huntley rose from his chair, obviously determined not to give me preferential treatment. "While the prosecution acknowledges the defendant's record, she's accused of the most serious crime imaginable, that of killing another human being with premeditation. If convicted, the sentence will be severe, giving her ample motive to flee the country. It's important that bail be set high enough to guarantee her appearance at trial."

The judge's voice was no-nonsense. "While the bench is aware this is Ms. Matthews' first offense, no one is above the law. The court can't show favoritism to her solely because she's one of our own. And given the seriousness of the crime, I agree with the prosecution that there is a real incentive for her to flee the jurisdiction. Therefore bail is set at five hundred thousand dollars, cash or bond." He banged his gavel, signaling the end of this morning's proceedings, and exited the courtroom. I tuned in to the buzz of whispers as people in the gallery gathered their belongings and made for the door. The show was over for today and I let go the breath I'd been holding.

My father grabbed my elbow. "Hang in there, sweetheart. I've already arranged the money for bail so you'll be released within an hour. I've reserved Room 256 down the hall to go over our next steps."

A weight lifted from my shoulders. At least I wouldn't have to spend another night in that cell, plus I could be with my daughter and reassure her. I managed a smile. "Could we hold off on the meeting until tomorrow? I want to be there when Charley gets home from school. Make sure she's not in panic mode."

My father stared hard at me. "You believe that, too, right? That you don't need to panic? Because we'll find a way out of this."

"The only way out of this is to expose the person who really killed Zach and it's looking like that's going to be harder than I thought."

"The police are good at their job."

"And they're convinced I'm the murderer." I glanced over my shoulder as the guard led me away and added, "that's why we've got to prove them wrong."

***

MY FATHER HELD THE REPORTERS at bay with one hand and steered me with his other as we made our way through the crowd waiting outside the courthouse. "Rachel, was Zach Reid your lover?" someone shouted. "Did you and Olivia Reid plan this together?" added another. "Was it self-defense? Did Reid attack you?" asked a third. One determined on-air personality wedged his way around the crowd and managed to stick a microphone in my face but all he got for his trouble was my well-rehearsed *no comment*. I couldn't blame them. After all, here I was, the veritable poster child for law and order, caught in a web of my own making. Now I knew what it felt like to be center stage in the media hoopla. Lightbulbs flashed as my father and I zigzagged through the phalanx to Luke's waiting car, my heart drumming in my ears.

"Thanks for looking after Charley last night," I said when I'd settled in the passenger seat and caught my breath. "I had enough to deal with without worrying about her being home alone." I snapped my seat belt in place.

Luke kept his eyes forward. "Yeah, about that. I didn't want to upset you before the hearing but when I drove over to pick Charley up, the house was empty. At first I thought she might have gone to Spencer's, but she didn't respond to any of my texts.

I finally heard from her around six. She was at Liv's, said she was spending the night there and skipping school today." He glanced at me. "I know it wasn't ideal, but I figured you wouldn't mind, as long as she was safe." He turned onto the freeway and eased the car into the middle lane. "I texted her once the judge made his ruling and told her you were out on bail so my guess is she's back home by now."

I seethed inside but tried not to take it out on my brother. He hadn't done anything wrong and he wouldn't understand why the growing closeness between Charley and Liv bothered me so much. Truthfully, I wasn't sure myself. Partly it was Liv encouraging my daughter's crazy ideas about jettisoning college. But also Liv might be in the crosshairs of a killer, which meant anyone around her might be in danger as well.

As Luke predicted, Charley had driven back home and she jack-rabbited out the door the moment we pulled into the driveway. It was an eerie repeat of the day before, only this time I was free to follow her back into the house. I thanked Luke again, assuring him I'd show up tomorrow in their law offices to go over strategy. Tonight all I wanted was a home-cooked meal, a hot shower, and my own pillow.

Once he was gone, I cornered my daughter. "I asked you to spend the night at Luke's, but you went to Liv's instead and didn't tell anyone. I wish for once you'd just done what I asked and not run off on your own. I've got enough on my plate right now without worrying about whether you're safe."

"I didn't *run off on my own*, Mom. Liv called and invited me over and I knew I'd have a better time with her than at Luke's. I took Ginger with me and we let her run around in Liv's yard and we streamed this old movie, *Chinatown*, and ordered Chinese food. And I *did* let you know. I texted a couple of pictures telling you where I was."

"News flash. They don't give you access to your cell when you're *in* a cell."

Charley frowned. "I didn't think of that. Sorry." She dropped her head, her blond hair falling like a curtain over her face. "It's just being over at Liv's helped keep my mind off you being arrested." She tilted her head up and gave me a tentative smile. "And while I was there, Liv told me straight out she doesn't think you're guilty. That's good, right? I mean, it was her husband who got killed so, you know, it's a plus if she's on your side. In fact, she called the police a bunch of idiots who couldn't find their way out of an empty box." She offered me a half smile.

I should cut Charley some slack. It didn't really matter where she'd spent the night as long as she was safe. As for me, I was tired, dirty, and starving. I hadn't been able to tolerate anything they fed me in jail and though I'd fallen asleep quickly, it hadn't lasted. My eyes popped open in the middle of the night and I'd stayed awake until they summoned me the next morning.

Charley had been through a lot, too, what with learning about her father, visiting his grave, and seeing her mother hauled off by the police. This was no time for an argument. My throat choked up as I whispered, "I just worry about you. Mother's prerogative. Come here, you." I opened my arms and Charley melted into me, the two of us rocking back and forth, holding each other tight. It was so good to be home.

After a minute, she pulled back, worry lines wrinkling her forehead. "I'm scared for you, Mom. Why do the police think you killed Mr. Reid? I mean, you barely knew him."

I stroked her hair. "It's a long story, honey. You know that person who was sending me creepy messages? Apparently, that was Zach. I have no idea why but the police found evidence that pretty much proves it. Plus someone broke into the house before we got the security system, stole my gun, and it looks like that was the murder weapon."

"Whoa. That sounds pretty bad. But Grandpa will get you off, right?"

"He's the best there is, so yes, I hope so. We'll take it one step at a time." I held my daughter at arm's length. "Now run upstairs and do your homework. I'm going to take a nap for a bit and then I'll fix dinner. I'll call you."

I cleaned up the kitchen, then retreated to my bathroom, where I indulged in a long, calming bubble bath. Then I crawled into bed and, before long, drifted off to sleep. At six o'clock I dressed and went downstairs, pulling out salmon, salad fixings, and baby potatoes from the fridge. As the meal cooked, I retrieved my phone from my purse and scrolled through my messages. Sure enough, there was one from my daughter last night around seven, with several photos attached. Liv with chop sticks in her nose, noodles dribbling from her mouth. Another of Charley, dipping an eggroll in duck sauce, a closeup of Faye Dunaway and Jack Nicholson on the widescreen TV in the background. The last was a selfie of Liv and Charley standing in front of the baby grand, each making a goofy face.

Something in that last shot brought me up short. I touched the screen and enlarged the photo. Over Charley's left shoulder was the digital picture frame I remembered seeing on the piano before, the kind that shuffled through different snapshots, changing every ten seconds or so. At the wake, I'd glanced at a few of the photos as they scrolled by, but then Ethan had distracted me when he slurred his words and stumbled into the furniture. Now the frame showed a new photograph I hadn't seen before—a mother and father and their two children, a girl around seven, a boy maybe three years older. My first thought was the girl in the picture looked an awful lot like Charley at that age. I glanced between the Charley in the foreground and the girl in the background picture. It wasn't my imagination. The resemblance was striking.

I studied the photo again. The son, with pudgy cheeks and a gap-toothed grin, must be Jasper. The mother, a brunette with her hair styled in a sleek pageboy, seemed a bit stern with cold eyes and a pursed mouth. The father sported a full beard and wire-rimmed glasses, and was glancing at someone off camera, an enigmatic expression on his face. When I peered closer, I broke out in a sweat. If only I could see the snapshot more clearly. Every time I zoomed in, the faces got more and more blurry. Why hadn't I paid more attention to this frame, examined it in greater detail at the wake when I'd had the chance? Because that prickly sense was back. If what I suspected was true, this picture held the clue to everything that had happened these last two months.

I had to get inside Liv's house and take a closer look and I had to do it tonight. There was no time to lose.

40

It was hard to choke down dinner and once Charley had finished eating, I piled the plates in the sink, then dropped her at Spencer's house, saying I'd be back to pick her up in a couple of hours. If she wondered where I was going, she kept it to herself. Just as well, because I had no logical explanation. I phoned Olivia once I got home.

"Got time for a drink at Swig?" I asked. "It's important."

"Of course. But we don't need to drive all the way downtown. Come over here—I've got loads of food left from the wake and we'll have more privacy."

I thought fast. "Actually, I'm calling from my office and I need to head back here after we meet, so let's stick with the bar, okay? Say in half an hour. Does that give you enough time?" The way I figured it, the trip downtown would take thirty minutes, then that same amount of time to get back, plus she'd wait around a while for me to show up. That gave me close to ninety minutes to break into the Reid house and get a closer look at that photograph. It would be tight.

When Liv agreed, I changed clothes, once again dressing in black—leggings, a long-sleeved T-shirt, gray hoodie, dark sneakers, and gloves. I swept my hair into a thick ponytail and tucked it under a watch cap. The last thing I needed was some nosy neighbor spotting me on the property and calling the police.

I arrived at Liv's house just as the sun was setting, turning the night sky inky blue. The house appeared deserted. I parked around the side, then peeked in the garage to make sure Liv's car was gone.

I knew the front door would be locked so I crept around back. With the encroaching darkness, it was difficult to see and I stumbled over a length of hose laying in the middle of the walkway and went down on all fours. When I stood, pain shot out from my ankle but I couldn't worry about that right now. Every minute counted. Liv could be half-way there.

I hobbled my way to the patio doors. On the off-chance Liv might not have thought to lock up the back, I pulled on the handle.

No luck. The door didn't budge. I pulled out the flat-head screwdriver I'd brought along, wedged the blade under the lip of the bottom facing like I'd seen the security guy do to my own back door, and simultaneously lifted and pulled. The screwdriver caught on the metal handle, flipped in mid-air, and clattered to the concrete. Cursing under my breath, I tried again. This time the door popped open.

I paused. Once I stepped over the threshold, I could add breaking and entering to my rap sheet. But if the answer to everything that had happened to me these last two months lay inside this house, did I really have a choice?

As soon as I entered the kitchen, the security alarm screeched. Moving as fast as I could, I punched in the alarm code Ethan had taught me. Two short beeps sounded in rapid succession, then the noise stopped. I waited, listening for a knock on the door or a shout from outside. But silence still surrounded me like a shroud.

It was pitch black but I didn't dare turn on the lights. After my eyes adjusted to the darkness, I inched my way into the living room and over to the grand piano. At first, I was confused. The pictures were in a different arrangement than in the snapshot I'd seen. Finally, I found the album-like frame with the rotating photos wedged toward the back. I frantically swiped the screen until the family portrait I'd seen on Charley's phone came into view. The glow of the moon shone through the front window, the light falling squarely on the photo.

Icy fingers crawled up my spine. The young daughter in the picture was the spitting image of Charley—same white-blond hair, same blue-flame eyes, same cupid's bow lips. Even the slight tilt of the head was a mannerism my daughter had adopted these last few weeks.

Blood rushed to my ears. Erase the beard, add five years, and the father in the photo was the man I knew, the man I loved, the man I lost. Paul Ostoff.

There it was, the answer to everything. Charley was Paul's daughter. So was Olivia.

As that reality hit, my knees buckled and I grabbed the edge of the piano for support. That's when I saw them, sitting a few inches from my hand.

A set of keys with a marble cube attached.

41

THAT SAME SENSATION OF someone watching me, waiting to make their move. I scanned the room but all I heard was the hum of the refrigerator and the beating of my own heart. Then my ears picked up another noise. A slight click, like a switch flipped on. I froze and strained to listen. There it was again. More like a creak this time. Someone moving around on the second floor, treading softly so no one would know they were there. I turned toward the stairs and watched, as a figure slowly descended, one step at a time, dressed in a white terry cloth robe.

"What are you doing here?"

The bottom dropped out of my stomach, as though I'd plunged down an empty elevator shaft. "I guess we won't be meeting at Swig, after all," I said as a stab of fear twisted inside me.

Liv narrowed her eyes. "Afraid not," she answered. "But don't worry, Zach made it a point to only stock the best." She walked to the bar cart in the corner. "What's your pleasure?" she said, sending a questioning look my way. There was a hardness to Liv's voice I'd never heard before. "We've got Macallan Single Malt. Tanqueray Gin. Or would you prefer to share a bottle of red?"

I stood still, my mind slotting piece after piece of the puzzle together. "It never was Zach. You were the one stalking me. That's why the police found all the equipment here. It belonged to you."

A pleased grin crossed Liv's face. "A mystery's so easy to solve once someone shows you the clues."

I glanced at the picture frame I still clutched in my hands. "This all leads back to him, doesn't it? This elaborate scheme was your way of getting back at me for loving your father."

Liv's face twisted into a scowl. "Not for loving him. For *stealing* him. He never would have left us if it hadn't been for you." She spat out her words, her hands curled into fists. "Know what he called me? His special girl, his fairy princess. Every night he'd tuck me into bed, kiss my cheek, and say he loved me the very best." Her voice rose. "But he didn't. He loved *you*. You're the reason he was driving back into the city that night. You're responsible for his death. It starts and ends with you."

When did she … why did Zach … what about … My mind couldn't light on a single question, so many swirled through my brain.

Liv's mask settled back into place. "So that's a no to the alcohol? Too bad. I hate to drink alone." She picked up a pair of tongs from the cart, dropped two cubes from the ice bucket into a tumbler, and poured a shot of whiskey.

I stared, transfixed, as Liv sauntered over and sat on the white leather couch. She turned on a side lamp, crossed her legs, and leaned back against the cushions, the very picture of nonchalance. The fragile wife dominated by her controlling spouse—the role she'd played perfectly these last two months—had disappeared, replaced by a confident woman in control of the situation. How could she stay so calm? She'd as good as confessed to being my stalker. I could have her arrested.

Was she behind Zach's murder as well? She had to be. It had to tie together. "Go ahead," Liv said. "Ask me anything you want. Now that we're at the end of our little adventure, I'd relish the chance to gloat."

What was Liv's grand plan? She was acting like she held all the cards but the truth was I could walk out the door anytime I wanted, drive to the police station, and lay out the truth. But would they believe me? No, I needed to understand more if I was going to convince the authorities of my innocence. After all, Liv still had that iron-clad alibi. She'd been at the gallery when her husband was shot.

"Zach never physically abused you, did he? That was all playacting on your part." Now that I had the one crucial clue, I hungered to understand the whole scheme.

Liv threw back her head and laughed. "I have to admit, that was one of my favorite parts. That time I came for lunch at your home? I really *had* tripped on the stairs, but I could see you thought Zach hurt me so I didn't outright deny it. After that, all it took was a few innuendos and some frightened looks and you filled in the blanks."

I ran through the sequence in my mind. "You jotted down the number of the kitchen phone when I left to take that call in my office. You bought the flowers, dressed up like a man, and bribed a kid to deliver them."

Liv's sardonic smile turned her face ugly. "Keep going. Let's see how much you get right."

"Your schedule's flexible—you followed me to work, saw where I parked, then snuck back to the garage sometime during the day and left that note." As I talked, I inched closer to the kitchen. At the same time I searched the pocket of the hoodie for my phone. I needed to record this conversation as evidence. Otherwise, it was my word against Liv, the grieving widow. I had to keep her talking and play to her ego.

"I have to hand it to you. All you had to do was hide the videos, the burner phone, and the voice changer in obscure places around the house and wait for the police to discover them. Once they did, they connected the dots and decided Zach was my stalker. The only person who could contradict your story was your husband and he was dead." I had to admit, it had been the perfect plan.

Liv smirked. "It almost seemed too easy."

The pounding in my chest threatened to derail me but I kept on. "That conversation in the car after book club. You acted so concerned for me, then steered the conversation to find out if I owned a gun. And like a fool, I told you not only that I *had* a firearm, but where I kept it." I spooled back. "When I told you I was installing a top-drawer security system the next day, you must have panicked. Broke in once I left for work, spooked me by moving things around, stole the gun, and sprayed perfume in the entry way."

"It's so gratifying to have someone admire my talents. I'll take that phone in your pocket, by the way." Liv stood and reached out her hand.

"I don't think so." I took another step backwards.

"Let's see if I can persuade you.

She reached into the pocket of her robe and pulled out what looked like Ethan's handgun. The police must have returned it once they'd realized it wasn't the murder weapon.

Tilting her head to one side, Liv widened her eyes, and changed the tone of her voice to a high-pitched, breathy sing-song. "I was so frightened, officer! The woman who murdered my husband broke into my house and when I confronted her, she threatened to kill me, too." Liv paused and gave a theatrical sigh. "Luckily I remembered where my cousin kept his pistol. It's a tragedy but what was my choice? I mean, I had to defend myself." Liv batted her eyelashes, the very picture of feminine helplessness. Then her face changed. "Too over the top?" She grinned.

My breath caught in my throat and my hands turned ice cold. Liv had set me up. If she shot me now, after I'd broken in through the patio door and set off the alarm, the police would buy her story and let her off. Everyone would say how tragic it was—Liv shot her best friend, thinking it was Zach's killer come back to murder her, too.

She walked over to me, wrenched my phone away, and threw it against the wall, where it broke apart, the pieces falling to the carpet. Adrenaline coursed through my veins, followed by a prickling under my skin. I needed to buy more time. Figure out a way to get out of this house and away from danger. "That first day ..." My voice broke. Finally, I pushed the words out. "When you saw the picture of Charley ..."

Liv's mouth twisted. "Yes, that *was* a surprise. You never posted anything about your daughter on social media. Guess you're one of those conscientious moms who tries to keep her child safe. Good for you."

"It must have been a shock, learning you had a half-sister."

"I did worry you might make the connection. I mean, you only have to look at her. It's uncanny how much she resembles me at that age."

"I know you want to punish me, but don't do this to her." My voice cracked. "You know what it's like to lose a mother. Don't make her go through that."

"You make my mother sound like someone who got mislaid along the way. I didn't *lose* her. She killed herself. Because of what you did." Tears pooled beneath her lashes. Liv wiped her nose on her sleeve, panting, pacing the floor.

She faced me. "So an eye for an eye. You took my mom, I'm taking Charley." Her tone turned soft. "She already thinks of me like a big sister. Or maybe a cool aunt. And once you're not around, I'm sure we'll get closer. I'll treat her to a trip to New York. Help her get over the loss."

My temper flared. No way was this monster getting her claws into my daughter. "She'll never forgive you if you kill her mother. That'll poison any relationship you might have with her."

"You forget. Charley's going to have an entirely different view of you after this. I mean, you murdered a man in cold blood. And you were ready to do the same to me. Not exactly Mother-Of-The-Year material."

If Liv's fantasy included telling Charley they were sisters, it meant she'd never planned on the courts convicting me. No, she'd intended to kill me all along. After all, she couldn't have me informing the authorities of our connection through Paul. The coincidence would be too glaring, it would send the police digging. Which meant Liv had planted that picture in the snapshot Charley texted on purpose, hoping to lure me to the house tonight. She'd set a trap and I'd walked right into it.

After all, why struggle through a long, protracted trial when you could shoot your father's lover in your own living room and get away with it?

I had to keep Liv talking. Buy time to find a way out of this mess. "Why now? It was eighteen years ago."

Liv plopped back down on the sofa again. "That's an easy one. I was a kid. No power. Both my parents gone. And actually, after my aunt's family took me in, life was okay. I had fun with my sisters, and Ethan and I—well, let's just say we got close. But then he enlisted and got shipped overseas, Alana and Robin moved away, my aunt and uncle took early retirement and started to travel. And there I was, alone again. Abandoned." Her tone turned bitter, acerbic. "And the more I thought about it, the more I realized my life had turned to shit because of one person. Guess who?"

Liv rested the gun at her side and her gaze darted to the front windows. "I moved to New York, took art classes, lived off my inheritance. I was aimless, broke, filled with anger but no way to channel it." She glared at me. "Then I met Zach. Rich. Charming. Devious. Not above breaking the law if it got him what he wanted. He was the perfect accomplice."

I stayed silent. It was a skill I'd worked hard to develop through the years. If you waited ten seconds or so before you jumped in with a comment, the other person got so uncomfortable with the silence, they leaped to fill it. It took discipline to learn to wait. But this time it served me well. Liv was so anxious to gloat and the longer I kept her talking, the more time I had to figure out a way to escape.

"Zach was on the rebound from a trust-fund baby who'd treated him like her pet poodle. I stroked his ego, hung on his every word, and put up with his occasional night out with the boys. But I hated New York—always someone richer, prettier, or younger— and besides, you were here in Wisconsin. I convinced Zach to relocate where he could be a big fish in a little pond. Burger Boy was starting their roll-out and this territory was available for a song. It wasn't a hard sell."

"But you moved two years ago. Why wait until now to come after me?"

Her half-mad laugh shot a bolt of electricity through my body. "You think a plan this elaborate falls into place overnight? I spent *months* planning. Strategizing. Making sure every detail was accounted for. It needed to be foolproof." She smiled. "Besides, I didn't want to kill you outright. That would have been too easy. No, I wanted you to *suffer* and at first, I couldn't think of a punishment big enough. And then something happened I hadn't planned on."

I waited, one part of me listening to the story, the other looking around the room for a possible weapon.

Liv sucked in her breath. "Zach changed. He'd always been tiresome but suddenly he turned mean. Cheated on me and lied to me about it. Hired a housekeeper to spy on me. Stole money from our joint account and lost it gambling. All the love I'd felt for him morphed into hate. It got so I couldn't stand for him to touch me. I knew I'd have to divorce him but that meant a hit financially. And then it came to me. Why not kill two birds with one stone? Get rid of my philandering spouse, inherit the business, get control of all the money, and frame my father's whore for murder. I researched you, found out you'd be at that awards dinner and arranged for us to meet. I pretended to cower under my oaf of a husband and you played your part, rescuing the damsel in distress."

But she couldn't have done it alone. There was still that alibi.

"You've conveniently left out your partner in all this," I said. "Someone followed us that night after book club. Plus you were at the gallery show at the time of the murder. It's one thing to pay a kid to deliver flowers, it's quite a different story to hire a professional assassin to commit murder. Where would you go about finding one? Plus so much exposure. My guess is you paired up with someone you either trust explicitly or have some hold over." Liv's beauty meant she could have any man she wanted, at least until the guy dug deeper and discovered her true nature.

This time my silence didn't have the intended effect. She didn't take the bait.

I tried again. "Since you're not going to let me walk out of here, satisfy my curiosity," I said. "Who is it?"

"Mind if I turn on a few more lights? It's so dark in here, I can't see where I'm aiming." Liv walked to a light switch near the front door and adjusted the rheostat to brighten the room. In that split second when she turned her back, I saw my chance and sprang toward the kitchen.

A gunshot echoed through the space and I felt a searing pain in my left side. When I looked down, my black T-shirt had turned dark and wet with blood.

"Stay right where you are, bitch." Liv's shrill command bounced off the walls. "Turn around so I can see your sniveling face." When I didn't move, she raised her voice. "Do it now or I'll shoot you where you stand. And next time, it won't be in the side."

I slowly did an about-face. Suddenly, my vision blurred and I fell to my knees. The photo of Paul and his not-so-happy family lay two feet away on the carpet, splattered with my blood. Liv approached, the gun clasped firmly in her hand.

"You've wasted eighteen years hating me," I gasped. "Was it worth it?"

"Who are you to tell me how to live my life? What have you ever done that's so grand?" Liv spat out.

I raised a daughter. A loving, thoughtful, caring human being who doesn't deserve to have her heart broken this way. I had to find a way out of this. Charley still needed me. I struggled to stay conscious, the pain in my side growing sharper with each breath.

Liv went on. "Tell me. When you first met my father, did he tell you he had a family?"

"He said he had two teenagers, Penelope and Benjamin."

"Ah, yes. Penny and Benny, like some insipid nursery rhyme. The kids in grade school bullied us constantly. As soon as our mother died, we both changed to our middle names."

I'd have caught on sooner if they hadn't. Olivia and Jasper hadn't rung any bells. "I'm sorry." My vision blurred with tears. "I was young, I was in love." I knew that didn't excuse me. It was wrong of me to get involved with Paul while he was still married. I squeezed my eyes shut, picturing my daughter in that last text she'd sent me, arm-and-arm with this sadist.

Then earlier memories of Charley flooded in. That first morning when the nurse placed her in my arms. The day she took her first steps. Charley delivering a eulogy at her grandmother's funeral. The best times of my life had been with my daughter.

But then I thought of the ballet recital I'd missed because I was out of town for a case, the state swim tournament I'd skipped because a trial ran long, a trip to Disney World I'd cancelled because we were short-staffed. All those times I'd chosen my job instead of Charley. The weight of what I'd missed slammed into me and I doubled over. And now it was too late. *Please be okay. Don't let this woman take over your life. I'm so sorry. I love you so much.*

I opened my eyes.

Liv was pointing the gun straight at my forehead.

42

Liv had her back to the windows so she didn't see the headlights as a car pulled into the driveway. Someone was approaching the front door. If I could stop Liv from pulling the trigger, whoever had showed up might distract her long enough to give me a chance to get away.

"Wait," I screamed. "There's something you need to know about your father. Something he told me on the phone right before he died."

Liv raised the barrel of the gun up. "What are you talking about? Think fast, before I change my mind."

It had been a bluff but Liv didn't know that and I'd bought some time. Any minute now I expected to hear a knock or the doorbell but instead of that, a key turned in the lock and the front door swung open. Liv turned at the sound, a look of confusion crossing her features as Ethan walked into the room.

His eyes widened as he took in the scene and saw the gun in Liv's hand. A muscle throbbed near his jaw line and his face hardened. "What in the hell is going on here?"

He locked eyes with each of us in turn. I had managed to move a little way away from Liv but I didn't have enough stamina to make a run for it. Besides Liv wasn't thinking rationally. She might very well make good on her threat and shoot me if I tried to escape. And if Ethan was the accomplice in this scheme, my troubles had just doubled.

"Olivia, answer me," Ethan said. His mouth froze in a puzzled frown as he slowly took a step nearer his cousin, his eyes never leaving her face.

"What are you doing here?" Liv cried. "I thought you said you were staying downtown tonight."

Ethan took a step closer. "I was on my way there when I got an alert on my cell that the alarm had been triggered. I tried calling, but when you didn't pick up, I got worried and decided to drive over. And I'm glad I did. Looks like we've got ourselves a situation here."

"She shot me," I shouted, holding up my hand, caked in blood.

Liv had her lie ready. "I heard a noise and when I came downstairs, I saw this figure dressed all in black rummaging around in the dark. How was I supposed to know it was Rachel? I thought she was a burglar."

"But now clearly you know she's not." Ethan was only a foot away from Liv. "Give me the gun and let's take the temperature down a notch, okay? Figure out the best way to handle this."

Liv shook her head violently from side to side. "No, you don't understand. She's out of her mind. She's saying crazy things."

Ethan's voice was a growl, stern and forceful. "What are you talking about? What kind of crazy things?"

"She's accusing me of killing Zach, she says she's going to call the police." Her voice was pleading, desperate. "Please, Ethan. You know what I've been through. I can't go to prison, you know I can't. I'd never survive being locked up. Please. You have to help me."

Was Ethan the accomplice? Was he Liv's lover as well as her protector? Or was he totally in the dark about what was happening? I couldn't read his body language, couldn't make up my mind. And my life depended on the answer.

Ethan held his hands out, palms forward. "Livie, you need to calm down." He closed the gap between them. "Do you trust me?"

When she nodded, he continued. "You're not going to jail, sweetheart. I'll keep you safe like I always have. But first, you need to give me that gun." When Liv didn't move, he lunged cheetah-quick and grabbed her wrist, but Liv pushed him and the two of them tussled back and forth, back and forth, grappling in a frenetic dance while I watched transfixed.

A shot rang out.

All three of us froze for several seconds, then Ethan dropped to the floor and landed spread-eagle on the rug, looking dazed and confused. His stomach exploded in blood.

Liv's face turned deathly white. She dropped the gun, and whispered "Ethan", then knelt beside him and gathered him in her arms. "Ethan," she said again, this time a bit louder. When he still didn't respond, she yelled "ETHAN," and shook him like her life depended on it. By this time, his eyes had turned glassy and unfocused. "Talk to me," she whimpered. "Talk to me." She cradled his head to her chest, rocking and wailing his name over and over. "No, no, no, no," she wailed, sobbing and shaking uncontrollably. "This is all your fault, I hate you!" she yelled at me, then turned back. "Ethan, I need you. Tell me what to do. Don't leave me," she screamed.

Ethan twitched and his hand moved and before I realized what was happening, he'd grabbed the gun which lay beside him on the floor, aimed for Liv's heart, and pulled the trigger. She fell forward onto his chest and he barely had time to wrap his arms around her and kiss her cheek before his head rolled to the side and he stayed motionless.

I grabbed the gun, sticking it in my pant pocket, then rushed to their bodies to feel for a pulse. Ethan's was thready but holding, Liv's weak and erratic. I grabbed Ethan's phone, called for help, then peeled off my hoodie and pressed it to Liv's chest to staunch the blood.

She opened her eyes and whispered something I didn't catch. I leaned closer, putting my ear to her lips. "I don't … forgive you," she managed, and in that brief moment, I pictured that young girl, still reeling from her father's death, finding her mother's lifeless body.

"I know," I whispered as I gently stroked her hair. I stayed there on the bloody carpet, holding Paul's oldest daughter in my arms, until the medics pulled me away.

43

I approached the officer standing guard outside Ethan's room in the ICU. "Any change?" I asked, but he shook his head.

Two days had elapsed since Liv died. And, despite heroic efforts by the cardiac team at Froedtert, Ethan remained in a coma. If he did recover, he would face a charge of first-degree murder in the death of Zach Reid. The authorities had yet to determine if they'd label his killing of Liv as self-defense or charge him with that death as well. If the latter, I would be the key witness. Had he killed Liv to save me or to cover up his role as her accomplice? Or had it been for another reason altogether—had he been in love with Liv and knew she'd never survive a prison term? Perhaps we'd never know.

My own wounds turned out to be minor. The bullet hadn't punctured any vital organs so even though I'd lost a fair amount of blood and had to stay overnight for observation, I'd been released after twenty-four hours. Since then I'd spent most of my time holed up with Charley, helping her deal with everything that had come to light.

I glanced through the observation window at the figure in the hospital bed. The police had focused their attention on Ethan's backstory in the last forty-eight hours and had more than enough evidence to convict him. Not only had he been deployed as a sniper during his two tours of duty in Afghanistan, but he'd continued to hone his skills once he was back. He was a dues-paying member of the Waukesha Gun Club and routinely showed up for target practice on weekends. The theory was he and Liv, despite their blood ties, had been lovers off and on for a while, possibly as far back as their teenage years. The police had found a diary in Liv's handwriting in a hidden safe in her closet that pretty much sealed his fate. It detailed the elaborate steps the two of them had taken to first stalk me, then frame me for murder.

The question of why Ethan had gotten drunk at the wake remained unanswered but I assumed his guilty conscience had played havoc with his emotions. Liv's journal entry only briefly referred to that day, writing "E and I kept our distance from each other. No use drawing unnecessary attention to the two of us."

As she'd confessed to me that night, Liv had hatched the scheme over a year ago, when Zach's behavior became so intolerable she decided to divorce him. The police had discovered she'd met with an attorney to discuss her options, but he'd advised her that, because of the pre-nup she'd signed, she'd walk away with very little. That must have been when she decided not to settle for scraps when, as Zach's widow, she could devour the entire meal.

After I'd been discharged from the hospital the night of the shooting, I'd met with Bob Farina and outlined what Liv had confessed to me about the elaborate scheme. That, plus Liv's diary and the confirmation from birth records that she was in fact Paul's daughter, was enough for the police to dismiss all charges against me. Liv's plan had failed and I was a free woman.

But something still nagged at me, an itch I couldn't scratch. I couldn't help feeling it all seemed too neat, that there was a trip wire still hidden in plain sight, poised to blow my world apart.

Ethan lay immobile in his bed, tubes branching in and out of his body, a breathing tube hooked up to a ventilator nearby. The beeping of the machines echoed into the hallway. His sisters and parents had flown in yesterday and were keeping vigil and conferring with the doctors about the next steps. They'd trooped off to the cafeteria earlier and I'd nodded at them when they passed me, but they didn't speak. For now, I was *persona non grata* in their eyes since they adamantly insisted on Ethan's innocence. Yes, he was protective of Liv, but no way would he have condoned murder, much less been her accomplice. And the idea that the two of them had been lovers? It was out of the question, they maintained, salacious gossip no one could possibly believe. They'd all been there during those teenage years. Ethan and Liv had not been lovers. It was all a lie.

I understood why they felt that way. We all have our blind spots. It's hard for us to see the truth about those we love. It's only when someone shines a light on what's really going on behind the masks that any of us can see clearly.

What was going to happen to Ethan? He might well die from his injuries but if he did survive, he'd likely spend the rest of his life in prison. If he knew what the future held, would he beg them to pull the plug, to let him go peacefully in his sleep? Would he want to save his family the anguish and embarrassment of a public trial?

Just then, a piercing alarm blared from one of the rooms and when the duty nurse ran in that direction, she collided with a metal cart in the middle of the hallway. Meal trays went flying, then clattered to the floor. I looked up, and an electric charge shot down my spine.

It was him. It was Paul.

Tears flooded my eyes. He was exactly the same, only dressed like a lumberjack—faded jeans, a plaid shirt with rolled-up sleeves, a John Deere cap. But it was him—his rangy walk, slow and elegant, his winsome smile. "Rachel," he said when he reached me. "I came as soon as I could." That voice I knew so well, the one that always reminded me of thick warm honey, the one I'd longed to hear all these years, echoed in my ears as my knees buckled and I fell to the floor.

***

WHEN I CAME TO, I found myself stretched across a bank of seats in the visitor's lounge, Paul stroking my hand. "Sorry to ambush you like that. I thought you knew I was in town," he said.

The pieces slotted into place. I hadn't lost my mind. "For a moment there I thought …" My words trailed off and I rubbed my temples. My head felt twice its normal size. "Jasper?"

He reached for a cup of water nearby. "You need to hydrate. Drink this."

In between sips, my gaze traveled over his face. "You look just like him." I closed my eyes and let a sense of loss envelop me. No, not loss so much as longing. Longing for the life I never had. The father Charley would never have. The years I'd spent waiting for a man who was never coming back.

I examined Paul's son more closely. He had the look of someone who worked with his hands, knew how to fix things, and was comfortable in his own skin. "One thing you should know, though. He'd never have been caught dead in that cap," I said and we both laughed.

I went on. "It's good you didn't show up earlier because I had you pegged as Liv's accomplice. You were like this mythical figure no one knew much about, some phantom man who'd disappeared into thin air. I honestly thought the Mansfield family might have made you up."

"You know about my mom?" he asked.

"Yes. I'm sorry for my part in that."

"You don't need to apologize. If anyone deserves sympathy, it's my dad. That man was a saint. Mom was in and out of treatment all her life. And he stayed with her through it all, gave up his writing for years at a time so he could help her. I'm not proud of it but when she accused him of cheating, my first thought was *good for you, Dad. Grab whatever happiness you've found with both hands.*"

When Paul and I had been seeing each other for a month, he shared with me that, after their second child was born, Natalie changed. Some days she'd be almost giddy, pulling the kids out of school and taking them on some impromptu outing. Once she'd driven them across state lines to Michigan to spend the night, not even leaving a note behind. Other times, she'd stay in bed weeping for days. Five years before, she'd been hospitalized when she locked the bathroom door, ran a hot bath, and cut her wrists with a straight razor. Her doctor prescribed pills to stabilize her brain chemistry but she skipped taking them, saying they made her feel like everyone was out to get her.

When Paul said he'd had enough, he was going to get a divorce and wanted me to move with him to London, I thought long and hard about what I wanted going forward. And even though it went against everything I'd been taught, I decided love trumped morality. Because this man was my soulmate. I couldn't imagine life without him.

"Liv blamed me for your parents' problems," I said. "That's why she came after me—to ruin my life, like I'd ruined hers."

"She was a kid. A hurt, angry kid. She didn't understand. I was sixteen, practically an adult. I loved my dad and I thought he deserved more. When you came along, I could tell something had changed. I'd hear him singing in the shower. I remember I caught him once outside in the garden—he was bending down and *smelling the flowers.*" Jasper's booming laugh rang out. "So no, I never blamed you. I felt sorry for you—losing him like you did with no one around to comfort you."

"You never really lived with the Mansfields so Liv lost you, too."

"I just didn't fit in with my aunt and uncle's family. I'm a simple guy. They wanted me to go to college, maybe medical school. All I wanted was to graduate and start working for myself. So I moved back home after that first summer, crashed at my best friend's house senior year and when I got the money from Mom's trust fund, I moved to Iowa. I bought a small farm and met Jenny, who was like me. Our big dream was to raise chickens, throw pots, and have a bunch of kids. I lost touch with the Mansfields, and after a while, we all seemed okay with that. That was, let's see, four horses, three kids, two dogs, one turtle, and a hundred dairy cows ago. That's my ordinary and very lovely life in a nutshell. Plus I write poetry. Two chapbooks published and another on the way. I like to think that's Dad's influence."

"You're so different than I imagined." I reached out and touched his cheek. "God, he'd be so proud of you." I thought of the unpublished manuscript I'd taken from Paul's apartment the night he died and kept hidden all these years. His third book. Once all this was behind us, I'd send it to Jasper. "Liv said you were coming to visit. Did she make that up?"

"Actually she did call me. No idea why she decided to track me down after all these years. That was three months ago. She started talking about how she'd found out about this daughter our dad had fathered years ago, how she'd met you and Charley. Then the conversation got strange. It reminded me of how Mom used to get. She said Charley was going to move in with her, the two of them were going to go to Europe, maybe live in New York. It was like you weren't even in the picture, like Charley was an orphan. It didn't make any sense."

But it did in some bizarre, alternative-universe way. I'd taken Liv's father from her. Charley was payback. I'd been clueless.

"Liv begged me to come visit her but the more we talked, the more toxic she seemed. I just didn't want to get bogged down in her problems. Besides, I knew Ethan was here in Milwaukee, and he'd always been Liv's champion, so I took the easy way out and never showed. Do you think I could have talked some sense into her, maybe even put a stop to this whole mess?"

"Her plans were in place by that point. I doubt there's anything you could have done."

"Maybe so. But I still feel guilty," Jasper said.

"Yeah, there's a lot of that going around. Anyway, one good thing that's come out of all this is my daughter now knows about her father and she wants to research her entire genealogy. When I tell her she's got a half-brother only a car ride away, she'll want to meet you and her nieces, or is it nephews?"

"Two nephews, one niece. And don't forget the turtle." He squeezed my hand. "And of course, we'd love to have her. You, too, if you can find the time. I hear you're a busy prosecutor so I'll understand if you can't make it but you're welcome. I wrote down my info." He handed me a slip of paper. "Get in touch when you feel like it and we'll make a plan." He stood. "Now I'm gonna go look for the Mansfields and see what they know about Ethan. I haven't stayed in touch with them like I should have. I'm gonna remedy that." He gave me a wide grin. "Take care, Rachel. It's great to finally meet the woman who made my dad so happy."

He gave me a hug, then headed off to the elevators. At the last moment, I rushed after him. "I just realized. It's you, isn't it? The flowers on his grave."

Jasper didn't say anything, just tipped his cap, and grinned as the elevator doors closed.

44

I PULLED OUT MY cell, dialed the police station, and had them patch me through to Farina. "Hey there, Counselor. I've been meaning to call," he said once we connected. "Clear the air a bit. Hope there's no hard feelings about—"

"You were only doing your job. But there is something I'd like your help on. Is there any chance I can peek at Liv's journal? Charley knows Liv was her half-sister and she's asking questions. I want to make sure I'm clear on everything that went down when I give her the answers. Would that be a problem?"

"If Ethan lives, it'll be used in his trial so chain of custody and all that, but you're welcome to come down to the station and look through it sometime."

The itch was back. "What about now?"

***

FARINA SET ME UP IN a small conference room off the main area and laid the journal on the table in front of me.

I flipped to the front page. Olivia's handwriting was what I'd expected—graceful, flowing, each letter elegantly formed. Occasionally there were strike-throughs or underlined words but mostly it read like a seamless stream-of-consciousness.

In the spring of 1997, Rachel Matthews destroyed my family.

Of course, back then I didn't even know she existed, much less her name. But I knew something was wrong that Sunday in the park when my mother stopped unpacking the picnic basket and, shielding her eyes from the sun, stared long and hard at a red-haired student coming out of the university library, talking to my father. She and I had driven all the way in from Naperville to surprise him, but instead of flagging him down, she hustled me into the car and we drove back home.

Late that night, when my father came home, I crept to the top of the stairs and heard words that shocked me, words like whore and slut and scumbag spewing from my mother's mouth. My father said very little. Jasper was out with his friends so he never knew.

It wasn't until after mom was dead that I learned the truth, and even then I wasn't sure my aunt told me the whole story. But one thing was sure—that redhead was responsible for ruining my life. If it hadn't been for her, my father would never have been on the freeway that day. And my mother would never have slit her wrists.

Still, Rachel and I were strangers until that night at the banquet. There she was, alive and well. Not the slip of a girl I remembered, but it was her. I smiled, then lowered my head. It was all I could do not to lunge across the table and stab her in the throat.

People might say fate brought us together that evening. But fate had nothing to do with it.

After that, there were lengthy dated entries outlining the steps she and Ethan (who she referred to as "E" in the journal) took to first harass me and then frame me for murder. It was no big trick for Liv to follow me to work one day and see where I parked. Both of them drove by my house at various times during the week to photograph me, even used drones for aerial or tricky shots.

As for the break-in, Liv had phoned Ethan as soon as I dropped her off after book club, telling him about the security system I had ordered and outlining where to find the gun. And the garage door vandalism hadn't been the work of the mean girls after all. Liv had hired a group of teenage boys and paid them each a hundred dollars to do the dirty work.

Flipping ahead, I read the entry for the day of the murder.

Zach's downfall was his horniness. If there was sex involved, he'd fall for practically anything. With my theater background, it was no problem to imitate Heather's southern drawl and send him a provocative voice mail inviting him to play along with a horny pirate/sexy slave girl fantasy. Then I sent her on some errand so they couldn't touch base. All the way to the train station, he was practically jumping out of his skin. I almost felt sorry for him—

It was hard, acting nonchalant at the gallery, when all I could think was whether E would be able to get away with it. Would Rachel call the police instead of running? Should we take the ransom money rather than leave it behind? So many moving parts and each one timed just so. But I trusted E to pull it off. Once I got his all-clear signal, and Rachel arrived at the show, I breathed a lot easier. My meltdown when the police told me about Zach was Oscar worthy, in my humble opinion.

Rachel's sleeping in the guest suite tonight. She'll do

anything to help the grieving widow. And me? I'm like the spider in that old nursery rhyme, toying with the fly. I'm pulling its legs off, one by one. Watching it squirm. Enjoying every minute.

I replayed the events the next morning when the detectives had come to the Reid's house. Now it made perfect sense that Liv had given them permission to search even without a warrant. She *wanted* them to find the evidence she'd planted, couldn't wait for them to put the pieces together. She knew once they realized Zach was my stalker, they'd take a closer look at my alibi at the time of the shooting. I'd already guessed the anonymous tip that led the police to the gun must have come from Liv and the journal confirmed it. After that, all Liv and Ethan had to do was sit back and watch as the dominoes fell.

I closed the flap and sat, hands folded together, resting on the leather-tooled cover. In the eyes of the world, Liv was the villain, the evil person who set out to punish the woman who had stolen her father.

But Liv didn't see herself that way. To her, what she'd done wasn't revenge.

It was justice.

I slowly re-opened the journal, flipped to the last few pages, and mulled over the entries. And then a new thought lodged in my brain, as though a tumbler had dropped into place in a lock. My breath caught.

I'd been wrong. This wasn't over. Not yet.

45

I'd only been there once before but I remembered the way. The setting sun practically blinded me as I drove west on I-94, then took the exit north to Lake Country, turning at the bend at the top of the hill, then left, and finally winding down a gravel road to the house. I glanced back several times, trying to figure out who was following me. I needed to see Max, explain to him what I'd figured out.

When I knocked, he came to the door within seconds as though he'd been watching for me, his two-day old stubble and floppy hair giving off a certain puppy-dog charm. He was haggard, his face splotchy and bloated as though he'd been crying. I flashed to the night we'd danced—the smell of sandalwood, the warmth of his arms around me. "I'm assuming you've seen the news."

"Why didn't you call me?" He grabbed me and we hugged. "God, I've been so worried about you. Are you okay? Is Charley?"

"We're both fine. It was a nightmare, but it's over now. Can I come in?"

A puzzled look crossed his face. "Of course." He stepped aside and closed the door behind me.

"I smell smoke," I said. "Is something burning?"

"Some yard waste out back. Sorry, I wasn't expecting company," he replied.

A duffel bag sat at the foot of the stairs. "Looks like I've caught you at a bad time."

"I'm headed up north to meet with a new client. But I'm not in any hurry."

My ears caught the sound of another car turning into the gravel driveway but Max didn't seem to notice. "That's surprising. I thought you would be."

He frowned. "I'm not sure what that means."

"Since my case is solved, it makes sense you'd be anxious to land a new assignment. After all, you've got to make a living, right? Speaking of which, you haven't sent me an invoice but as soon as you do, I'll mail out a check."

"Rachel, you sound angry. Is this about the two of us? Because we discussed this. I make it a rule not to get involved with clients."

"I'm not your client anymore." I stared hard at him. "But then I never really was."

"That's cryptic. What are you talking about?"

"Do you remember that evening I spent here?"

"Fondly." There was a smile in his voice. "In fact, I've beaten myself up for not throwing my rules out the window and crawling into bed with you." His blue-sky eyes burrowed into mine as he took a step toward me.

"It was too late by then. You were in too deep."

His face hardened and I caught the slight twitch of his neck. "I'm not following."

"Remember that morning when your ex showed up? I hate to admit it but I'm a terrible snoop—I eavesdropped on your conversation with her out on the steps. She said something about the *tall, skinny bitch* you'd been seeing. That was Olivia, wasn't it? She hired you last year to follow her husband. She needed dirt on him to use in her divorce."

"What? No. Why would you think that?"

"Our bumping into each other that day in the diner wasn't accidental. It was all part of the plan. I hire you to help me find my stalker, and Liv gets herself an insider reporting on everything I say and do. What could be more perfect?"

"No way. Rachel, we go way back. Where's this coming from?"

"That night when Zach was murdered and I phoned you from Liv's house, you practically bit my head off when you found out where I was. I couldn't figure out why but now it makes perfect sense. You wanted to celebrate. After all, you'd just committed murder for her. The two of you could finally be together, plus there was all that lovely money. But she blew you off. Chose to invite me over instead of spending the night with you. You must have been livid."

"Stop it. This is crazy." He started to pace. "You know I couldn't have shot Zach. I'd just arrived when you ran up from the beach."

Goose bumps rose on my arms. I didn't think he'd attack me but as a precaution, I backed up a few paces and steered toward the kitchen where Max kept his set of razor-sharp steak knives tucked into a wooden block. "I have to admit you were clever. You planted the tracker on my car earlier so you could say you followed me. But you didn't need a device. You knew where I was going because you're the one who sent me there. First, earlier in the week, when you concocted that ransom demand, then that night when you called me once I'd pulled into the parking lot. Liv lured Zach to the rendezvous, you lured me."

"Rachel, please. You have to listen to me."

"And kudos for that split-second timing. You must have parked down a side street, hot-footed it to the beach and hid in the bushes, and when Zach appeared, you shot him with the gun you'd stolen from my house. Then you raced back to your car and hid the weapon in your glove compartment to plant later. When you saw me, you drove up and pretended you'd only just arrived."

"Because I *had* just arrived." Max took a few steps and closed the gap between us. "I told you. I got stopped by a cop for speeding. Hell, I even showed you the ticket."

"Ah, yes, the famous speeding ticket." I shook my head and shuffled my feet. "You're right, you *did* show me a ticket. The one you got t*he day before*. On purpose. You smudged the date. It was dark, the print was tiny, and you counted on me not examining it all that closely. But here's the thing, Max. With everything going on, you forgot to *pay* that ticket so it's still on file. I called it up in the system a few hours ago and examined it again. And sure enough, it was issued the day *before* the murder."

"You've got this all wrong. The news report said the police have Ethan Mansfield in custody. Something about a journal of Liv's they found indicating *he* was her accomplice."

"That's because her entries kept mentioning "E", the person who helped her execute her scheme. The police assumed it was Ethan, her cousin, and rumor has it, her lover. The theory is when he walked in on her and me that night at her house, he shot her so she wouldn't reveal his part in the scheme. But then I remembered our conversation at the diner and how everyone in high school called you Elvis. It wasn't a stretch to realize *you* were the "E" in that journal. Did you tell Liv your old nickname? Did the two of you have a laugh about it? Did you serenade her with your guitar, maybe even write her a love song?" The energy in the room had ratcheted up. I could feel it in my bones.

Max lowered his head and let out a long sigh. "It seemed so unfair, you know? There was Zach with all that money, chasing everything in a skirt, making Liv miserable. And there I was, so tired of working hard and never getting ahead." He shrugged. "I guess there's no way you'd let me walk out of here? For old time's sake?" Our eyes met and I saw the boy I'd known all those years ago—the outsider, the poet.

"Afraid not."

"Then I've got no choice but to …" He raised his head and lunged for me, thinking I'd been headed for the knives, but instead I ran the other way, and flipped the switch on the backsplash. The opaque blinds came to life, the same way they had that night I'd stayed over, only this time they went up instead of down, exposing four heavily-armed police officers with semi-automatic weapons pointed directly at Max. One of them raised the bullhorn at his side and bellowed out, "Max Wisniewski. Come out with your hands up or we're coming in."

While Max was distracted, I grabbed a steak knife as insurance, holding it in front of me while Max whirled around and around, desperately looking for an escape route. When he realized he was surrounded, his arms dropped to his side and he gave me a sheepish grin. "You have to admit, it was one hell of a plan."

Heavy boots thudded up the porch steps and a burly man, shaped like a refrigerator, burst inside. He grabbed Max, clapped handcuffs on his wrists, and pushed him toward the front door. Before they disappeared from view, Max turned and caught my eye.

"My timing's always been off with you." He paused, then added, "In my defense, it wasn't only about the money. I did love her."

And I loved her father. But look at the cost. "Love makes us do crazy things sometimes. Things we know we shouldn't. Things that go against every principle we believe in, everything we know is honest and true." I lowered my head. "Liv was right about that. I destroyed her family and never thought twice. I'll have to learn to live with that."

The police officer tugged at Max's sleeve but he didn't move, giving me one last look. "Who'd have thought we'd turn out like this?"

I thought back to that night we'd danced and how I'd imagined there might be more. It was a good dream. Just not with Max.

The words caught in my throat. "Not every story has a happy ending."

Epilogue

SHULA KAR POKED HER head around the door of my office and gave a knock. "Got a minute?"

I motioned for her to join me. "I was just heading out. What's up?"

She dropped into the guest chair. "I wanted to make sure you're set for Monday. I know it won't be easy reliving the whole experience but your testimony is the major plank in our case."

"I realize that, and no, it won't be easy. Max let his heart lead him instead of his head, which all of us, me included, have done at one time or another. Only in his case, a man lost his life. An insensitive, boorish man, I admit, but murder's still wrong, no matter what." I sighed. "Although I can't help thinking the wrong person is paying the price."

"He shot him in cold blood, Rachel. Even if she was the one pulling the strings, he was the one who pulled the trigger."

"You're preaching to the choir. And I still believe if you break the law, you pay the consequences. Only when it hits this close to home, it doesn't seem so cut and dried."

"Promise me you won't say that on the stand."

"Don't worry. I'll leave my opinions at the door and stick to the facts. The perfect witness." I sat up straighter and leaned toward Shula. I could be a gracious loser if nothing else. "Listen, I'm sorry I haven't stopped by to congratulate you. Deputy District Attorney. Quite an achievement and it couldn't go to a more deserving person. I look forward to working for you."

"Not *for* me, I hope. *With* me. Huntley told me you put in a good word when you took yourself off the list. That means a lot to me."

Even though I had been cleared of all charges related to Zach's murder, I'd still fled the scene, withheld crucial evidence when the police questioned me, and ran my own undercover investigation, which led to another death. That had been my choice but I knew I'd effectively killed any chance of moving up in the ranks anytime soon. Huntley had said he'd keep me on the short list but I knew it would cost him and I'd said no.

Shula stood. "A few of us are heading over to Murphy's for an informal celebration." She glanced at the three towering stacks of case files on my desk. "If you're not too bogged down with work, care to join us?"

"I'll take a rain check. I've got tickets for *Les Miserables* at the high school." I glanced down at my cell. An incoming call. "Speaking of, I need to take this. It's my daughter."

"I'm off, then. See you Monday."

Shula left and I picked up the phone. "Hi, sweetheart. Everything set for tonight?"

"It's a nightmare, Mom. First I couldn't find my costume, then Spencer's car had a flat, and now I'm at school, and the girl playing Fantine has laryngitis and can't sing."

"Take a breath. I'm sure Mrs. Shepard has a contingency plan. That's why you have understudies. Everything will be fine."

"You're still coming, right? I mean, you're not going to make up an excuse about having to work late or a last-minute case that's come up, or anything? Because I'm super nervous and I really, really need you to be here."

"We'll all be there—Grandpa, Luke, Ed. Oh, and I hope it's all right but I'm also bringing Ethan with me. He called to chat and when I told him about the play, he asked if he could come."

"Yeah, sure. I'd like that." She paused. "Can I ask you something weird, Mom? If you and Ethan get married, would that make him my cousin but also my stepdad?"

I laughed. Charley still didn't quite understand the whole DNA thing. "You're not related to him by blood, honey, because it was Liv's mom, not your dad who … anyway, why are we even talking about this? Ethan and I are just friends. We like hanging out together."

I pictured my daughter's eyeroll. "Whatever you say. Only hurry, okay?"

I tossed my jacket over my shoulder, tucked my cell in my pocket, grabbed my purse from the drawer, then stuffed three folders inside my briefcase to review tonight after the play.

And paused.

Old habits die hard. Yes, my career was important and the next time I got a chance to move up the ladder, I'd go for it. And yes, I still believed in the sanctity of the law, that we break the rules at our peril, that I had a duty to protect the innocent and the powerless. But I also knew I was no good to anyone without the safety net of my father, my brother, and my daughter. I dug out the folders and put them on top of the pile with the other briefs.

Then I turned off the lights, closed my office door, and left the work behind to join my family.

ACKNOWLEDGEMENTS

It was my great good fortune to pick up Agatha Christie's "The Murder of Roger Ackroyd" when I was a teenager and that idea, that a murderer can be hiding in plain sight, has stayed with me ever since. I have always wanted to write a suspense novel and the result is the story you've just read. I hope you enjoyed reading it half as much as I enjoyed writing it.

And now some thank-you's to people who helped shepherd this book from the initial idea to the final publication.

To my best writer pals, Jennifer and Barbara, who keep me focused, keep me learning, and keep me laughing in equal measure.

To the members of the Women's Fiction Writers Association, who are always there to answer my questions, steer me in the right direction, and bolster my ego with their support and best wishes. A special shoutout to the subgroup of WFWA who are indie writers and in particular Paulette Stout and Lainey Cameron. When I made the move to take control of my writing career and go out on my own, I did so knowing you had my back as well as most of the answers.

To Patrick O'Donnell, alias Sarge, of copsandwriters.com who answered my endless hypothetical questions about police procedure, and Sharon Riek, ADA, for providing insight into how the life of a county prosecutor actually works (tons of hours, tons of paperwork, and an endless number of balls to juggle).

To Samantha Skal, developmental editor extraordinaire, for her wise and thoughtful feedback and encouragement for this book. Sam knows suspense so when she gave me her seal of approval for my first attempt at the genre, it gave me the confidence I needed to plow ahead.

To all the debut authors I have interviewed on my podcast Hear Us Roar. Talking to each of you about your writing process and your path to publication has been like earning an MFA over these last five years and I'm eternally grateful to you for sharing your story not only with me but with our listenership as well.

To the bloggers, reviewers, bookstagrammers, bookstore owners, librarians, and fellow writers who helped make my debut novel, *Truth and Other Lies*, such a success. It launched my career in ways I could only imagine. I can't begin to thank each one of your personally because I'd leave someone out and kick myself in the morning.

To my husband Scott, for the endless lunches he's brought me so I could keep writing, the knotty plot twists he's helped me unravel, and the love and support he's shown me from day one.

To all those fighting to end violence against women in all its insidious forms. May you never lose faith, always find funding, and keep up this important work, even in the face of raging indifference and bureaucratic obstacles.

And finally, to you, the reader. You are the reason I wrote my last book, this book, and all the ones to come. I know how precious the act of reading has been to me over the years and I'm proud to be part of that culture in my own small way. May you continue to seek out and read good fiction and find in it a measure of solace and community to brighten and enhance your daily life.

Book Club Questions

1. We know from the outset that somebody has been killed. Were you surprised to learn who it was? What clues led you to that conclusion?

2. The author keeps the reader guessing about who was behind the scheme to frame Rachel. Did you figure out who it was? Why or why not? When did you know?

3. Blindspot is about the choices we make and the possible consequences, about avenging the past. Are there things that have happened to you that you can't forgive? Are people more than the worst thing they've done? How do you feel about people taking the law into their own hands to achieve justice?

4. Rachel's father lectures her about work/life balance. Do you feel like your own life is balanced? Does this depend on your age and which stage of your career you are in?

5. Have you ever been forced to reveal a secret you'd kept hidden from your family? If so, what were the consequences?

6. Rachel suspects her stalker may be someone she works with. Discuss professional rivalries you've experienced and what you see as the ideal work environment.

7. After their informal luncheon, Liv asks Rachel to be her friend. Discuss your own adult friendships and how they came about. What goes into meaningful relationships once we're "grown-ups?"

8. Have you ever been betrayed by someone you trusted? What happened afterwards?

9. Rachel and her daughter are often at odds. Did this relationship ring true? Did it reflect interactions you've had with your own children or your parents?

10. What's the most extreme thing you've done to protect someone you love?

Maggie would love to join your book club discussion
Go to https://maggiesmithwriter.com/book-clubs/
or email her at ms@maggiesmithwriter.com

Can I ask a favor?

But first, a huge *thank you*. With three million books published each year, you chose to read mine and I'm so very grateful. I worked hard on this one and hope you enjoyed it. Which brings us to the favor.

Surveys have shown most people choose books based on the recommendations of family or friends – the famous "word of mouth". So if you liked BlindSpot, would you please consider posting a review?

It doesn't have to be full of fancy words or complicated analysis, it doesn't have to be witty or wise, it doesn't even have to be all that long. In fact, I think the best reviews are short, succinct, and most importantly, sincere.

And if you need help getting started, here's a simple formula I've used:

1. One sentence describing what the book was about.

Ex: Ambitious district attorney hunts down the person stalking her but winds up arrested for murder when he turns up dead.

2. One sentence describing what you liked most about the book.

Ex: I enjoyed the fast-paced plot—it kept me turning pages long into the night.

3. One sentence saying who will like the book.

Ex: Fans of suspense thrillers with meaty character development will likely devour this one.

4. End with one last tag to encourage people to buy the book.

Ex: Put this one on your TBR. You won't regret it.

Of course, you can always write more, but here's an interesting fact: A short review counts just as much as a long one in the eyes of Amazon, GoodReads, BookBub, Barnes & Noble, and IndieBound and will help bring this novel to the attention of people like critics, agents, and event sponsors who can boost my career.

And best of all, you'll help other readers discover a book they might enjoy.

Take Back The Night
Organization

If you or someone you love are a survivor of sexual harassment, sexual assault, rape or other sexual violence, learn your legal options from victim-focused attorneys.

Call 567-SHATTER (567-742-8837) for free legal assistance or go to https://takebackthenight.org/legal-assistance/ and complete the form.

No one should have to suffer alone. There is help. Reach out for it.

Take a stand against sexual violence today.

Born in Oklahoma, Maggie graduated from college with a Ph.D. in Psychology and promptly relocated to Wisconsin to start a national art consulting company. She added novelist to her resume with the publication of her debut novel, *Truth and Other Lies*, released in March 2022 with Ten16 Press.

In addition to her fiction writing, Maggie hosts a weekly podcast *Hear Us Roar* (25,000+ downloads) where she interviews debut women's fiction writers, and she is Managing Editor for the Chicago Writer's Association literary E-zine. She lives with her husband Scott and her aging but adorable sheltie and keeps tabs on her three young adult children when they let her.

For more information, please visit her website or follow her on social media:

https://www.maggiesmithwriter.com
Instagram: @maggiesmithwrites
Threads: @maggiesmithwrites